# PRAISE FOR *TURBULENCE*

"A thoughtful exploration of the blurry difference between heroes and villains. Ethical questions are deftly scrutinised in a depth that a comic book or film would struggle to match." *The Sun*

"Basu knows his stuff... he conjures up a vast array of imaginative powers [and] unflinchingly depicts the costly consequences."
*SFX Magazine*

"...inventive and very clever. But most of all, it is fun. If you have ever picked up a comic book and enjoyed it, then this is a must-buy."
*Starburst Magazine*

"It is, unabashedly, a new style modern superhero novel with a distinctive twist. It is also current, smart, energetic and a sparkling read. Most of all, the frenetic pace is great and the dialogue fizzes with whip-sharp quips and comments. It's funny, it's intelligently witty, it's great. Loved, loved, LOVED it." SFF World

"An excellent book, a thoughtful read that throws out questions without any easy answers, that opens up the superhero genre to deeper analysis, and yet is also an incredibly enjoyable superhero story itself." Fantasy Faction

"As unpretentious as it is entertaining, as compelling as it is thought-provoking, it establishes once and for all that the novel is as much a home for the superhero tale as film, tv and comics... it's not just an astute and captivating read, but an important one too."
Too Busy Thinking About My Comics

# RESISTANCE

# RESISTANCE SAMIT BASU

**TITAN** BOOKS

**RESISTANCE**
Print edition ISBN: 9781781162491
E-book ISBN: 9781781161203

Published by Titan Books
A division of Titan Publishing Group Ltd
144 Southwark Street, London SE1 0UP

First edition: July 2014
1 3 5 7 9 10 8 6 4 2

Names, places and incidents are either products of the author's imagination or are used fictitiously. Any resemblance to actual persons, living or dead (except for satirical purposes), is entirely coincidental.

Samit Basu asserts the moral right to be identified as the author of this work.

A CIP catalogue record for this title is available from the British Library.

Printed and bound in the United States.

**What did you think of this book?**
We love to hear from our readers. Please email us at:
readerfeedback@titanemail.com, or write to us at the above address.

To receive advance information, news, competitions, and exclusive offers online, please sign up for the Titan newsletter on our website.

www.**titan**books.com

# CHAPTER ONE

A giant lobster rises slowly out of Tokyo Bay. It is an old-school kaiju, three hundred feet long, and stands upright, its hind limbs still under water, in defiance of biology, physics and all codes of lobster etiquette.

It totters slightly, taking in the scenery, and waves its massive claws in the general direction of Tokyo. It screams, an angry, unearthly sound that scatters a passing flock of seagulls. It turns, creaking, to left and right, looks at Chiba, and at Kanagawa, but then does what every kaiju must.

The giant lobster strides towards Tokyo.

Norio is sparring with a trainer robot in his 124th-floor penthouse on the island of Odaiba, when the call comes. He performs the standby mode kata, and the robot powers down, humming softly. He waves an arm and a holographic talkscreen appears, floating in front of him as he paces around the dojo. It's Azusa.

"Monster," she says.

"Type?"

"Lobster."

"Navy?"

"Waiting."

"Air Force?"

"Two jets. Four missiles."

"Impact?"

"None. Should I send out the signal?"

"Do it."

Norio disconnects, issues a command, and a giant screen on a nearby wall flickers to life. He mutes the excited chatter of the news anchor with a gesture, and stares at the kaiju onscreen as it lumbers towards Odaiba. At its current pace, it will take at least twenty minutes before it starts the usual property damage. More than enough time.

The Kaiju King's creations usually surface in time to feature on the primetime evening news, but this one is clearly in a hurry, and wants to catch sunset over the Tokyo skyline as it tears up the city.

At least the giant lobster looks suitably monstrous – the last one, three weeks ago, had been a seriously oversized seaweed chips packet with arms. But this one could have had its own Toho franchise. It could have held Godzilla to at least a few draws. The lobster's maroon exoskeleton shows no signs of missile damage apart from a few burnt spots. Before the Kaiju King's powers transformed it into its current behemoth form, it had been an ise-ebi, a spiny lobster. Norio looks it up, and is annoyed to find that normal spiny lobsters don't have claws – the Kaiju King has added those, and his research process is clearly flawed. Clawed or not, Norio has met this lobster's kind before, in expensive restaurants. Usually as sashimi, though he is quite fond of eating ise-ebi roasted alive. An option that is possibly available today.

Norio fights the memory, but fails. Dinner with his father and brother at some ridiculously exclusive restaurant in Asakusa. September 2012. They'd talked about lobster that night as well – an American lobster, a normal-sized one, had been found in Tokyo Bay, and his father had been very annoyed. Norio remembered how spectacularly bored he'd felt. He'd wanted to talk about superheroes.

The tattoo on Norio's wrist throbs, and he shakes his head, clearing eight-year-old cobwebs. He looks ruefully at the tattoo. It's a goryo, a vengeful aristocratic spirit. It had been the right choice for him, no question, but he wished he could have picked a creature that didn't rhyme with his name.

He strides to the wall, presses the secret panel, and after it slides open, pushes a button. Another section of the wall clicks, and the secret elevator opens. Norio walks in.

In Tokyo's Akihabara Electric Town district, a woman in her mid-twenties shuffles out of a second-hand electronics store. She's short and slightly unkempt; her akiba-kei T-shirt has seen better days. She snakes through crowded lanes overflowing with comics and electronic stores, ignoring the hypnotic strobing neon signs everywhere around her. She pauses for a second outside a costume cafe to exchange scornful glances with the French-maid-costumed servers and their spellbound otaku customers. Hoverpad operators offer her free rides; she ignores them.

Her tattoo, a wolf made of lightning, glows again, red and

urgent, and she picks up the pace. She dodges into a mangakissa and runs up a narrow flight of stairs to a floor full of private cubicles. She runs down a corridor full of purikura photo booths, sliding past groups of giggling cosplaying teenagers mirror dancing with holographic anime versions of themselves. At the end of the corridor is a closed cubicle, its door streaked with stains, an "Out of Order" notice stuck to it with frayed tape. She taps the door and it slides open to reveal a shining metal elevator. She looks up at the camera, draws a sign in mid-air. A robotic voice asks her to identify herself.

"Raiju online," she says, and the door slides shut.

In Shibuya, a sushi chef, hat askew, runs down Spain Slope, causing much merriment among a group of German students ambling by a trendy bistro. They film him on their phones as he rushes into his restaurant, barks orders at his trembling assistants, scolds an American couple for pouring too much soya sauce on their salmon rolls, and rushes into the toilet.

Once in, he leans against a toilet cubicle and looks at his arm, where a tattoo of a nightmare-devouring baku glows green. The cubicle wall spins around, pitching him into a dark room behind it, and the words "Baku online" can be heard before the wall closes with a loud click.

And in a love hotel in the Kabukicho red light district, a stunningly beautiful man in a ballerina outfit apologises to his wailing client. He watches the scruffy businessman stomp out of his boudoir, pops a pill, and hums a popular soap opera theme as he pulls up his stockings, covering a glittering purple tattoo of a horned oni.

* * *

In the preparation chamber, a gigantic hall in an abandoned Hisatomi toy factory on the southern edge of Odaiba, Norio stands in his harness as robotic arms swing around him, attaching his battle-suit components to his body. Azusa's harness is opposite his, and he watches with the usual mixture of amusement and furtive desire as her slender body disappears like a reversed egg-hatching video, as the round, genderless components snap into place, leaving them both looking like action figures. He'd have preferred an American-style body armour, more sleek and muscly, less rounded, chunky and asexual. But he hadn't had a say in the equipment design.

Norio's augmented-reality visor slides down, and through the video feed he watches the giant crustacean's progress towards Odaiba. Why did they always come to Odaiba? Why not take a right turn and head for the amusement park across the bay? The beast floats steadily towards the man-made island, its entirely wrong body causing only the smallest of ripples in the bay. Most of the mammal and reptile kaiju make a huge mess, wading, splashing, falling down, sending massive waves in every direction. This incredibly ugly Tokyocidal behemoth is one of the most graceful Norio has seen.

Far above the lobster, TV and livestream crews hover, shouting excitedly, each claiming exclusive footage – they used to come in lower, but some of the kaiju had flame breath or hidden wings, and helicopters are expensive. The lobster finds them as annoying as Norio does; it screams at them, and snaps its claws upwards in a futile attempt to pluck them out of the sky.

About five minutes to combat.

Lights go on in quick succession above three tunnel openings on the eastern wall of the preparation chamber. The rest of the team is here. Battle-suited, Norio and Azusa leave their harnesses and head towards the delivery pod. Behind them, come the other three mecha-pilots, all armoured in transit, all moving slightly unsteadily: the maglev transportation gondolas from central Tokyo to Odaiba have been built for speed and efficiency, not comfort. But the five do make an impressive spectacle as they walk towards the battle; in the anime based on their adventures, they usually show this walk in slow motion. Each battle-suit is both white and the mecha-pilot's specific colour and has their chosen demon emblazoned on its chest. The multi-coloured AR visors obscure their faces: by mutual pact, they have chosen not to know one another's real-life identities. They'd decided this would make it easier if any team member were captured, or killed. So far neither has happened.

The delivery pod hurtles underground, playing an annoying catchy tune, and then launches into Tokyo Bay, heading for ARMOR station, their command centre. The pilots stand in silence: in their TV show, this is usually the point where they exchange friendly banter and their leader, the mermaid princess Amabie, tells them what the mission is. There is no need for Azusa to do this: the giant lobster on their AR visors is a fairly substantial hint.

Not too far away, the kaiju makes its first kill: a TV helicopter hovers too low, its crew either reckless or new at this game, and the lobster powers out of the water and snaps it in half. The team freezes the image of the beast entirely out of the water on their visors; it is always better to see the whole kaiju as early as one can, since some of them have wholly unexpected body parts hidden underwater. In this case, it's a hundred feet of additional lobster tail. The other helicopters hover on, cameramen shooting excitedly; the kaiju, framed in a fireball, surrounded by falling chunks of helicopter and human, is a photographer's dream come true.

"Are you leading this one, Amabie?" asks Raiju.

Azusa shakes her head. "Goryo," she says.

The others nod.

The pod docks into ARMOR station and its doors slide open. The underwater hangar lights up. They've all done this before, several times, but the pilots cannot help their breath catching for a moment as they see their battle-mechas.

Five giant mecha-demons, each thirty feet tall, stand in the hangar, ominous, powerful, silent. As Goryo steps off the delivery pod onto the hangar floor, the creatures' eyes light up, and their chests open, revealing hollow metal spheres, nine feet in diameter, inlaid with complex circuitry and AR screens. The pilots race to their demons and as they clamber in, the mechas draw them into their bodies. At Norio's signal, they power up, and float up to the hangar roof, towards the release chamber.

A minute later, Team ARMOR shoots upwards through the dark, muddy waters of Tokyo Bay.

They surround the kaiju underwater. Azusa's golden mermaid-mecha's tail undulates as it circles the beast's tail. The first strike is Norio's, and his black skull-faced ghost-mecha speeds ahead of the monster and turns, waiting for the others to take their positions. Raiju's red wolf-mecha poises, waiting to run up the kaiju's back. Oni and Baku's hideous metal faces lurk near its lowest pair of limbs.

"ARMOR engage," whispers Norio.

His black spirit mecha streaks out of the water, shooting pulses of shimmering white plasma at the lobster.

Amabie's arms extend into sixty-foot-long spikes; she spears its tail.

Oni and Baku's mecha limbs transform into giant hammers, and they pound at the kaiju's legs.

Raiju leaps out of the bay behind the monster, landing with a crunch on its shell.

Rings of white light trace the ridges and crags left on the beast's body from Goryo's assault, burning its shell as they go, and Raiju's weight thundering onto its back at full power decides the issue. The kaiju tilts forward, lurching, claws snapping furiously, but its shell does not crack. Screaming, it topples forward, a crustacean skyscraper crumbling in slow motion. What is left of its lobster brain forgets for a moment whatever made it this unnatural size, made it stand upright.

The splash from the fall hurts the creature more than the mechas did. A wall of water rises in every direction, knocking Raiju off its back, sending Oni and Baku scrambling, leaving only Amabie hanging on grimly to its tail. Goryo plummets into the depths at full speed to avoid getting crushed by the falling lobster above him.

The beast streaks forward underwater, and the mechas race after it. The incredible design of their control spheres has left all the members of the team upright and unharmed, even as their mechas twist and topple around them. Now they brace into attack position and charge at full speed.

Stuck to the kaiju's thrashing tail, Amabie retracts a spike, shuffles forward and impales the beast again, and it shudders and writhes, its mad northward dash halted. Amabie's mermaid-mecha drags itself further up the tail, and looks for more imaginative ways to hurt the lobster. But the kaiju is in shallower waters now, and it thrusts forwards and upwards, leaping out of the bay by the shipyard just to the south of the Odaiba Telecom Tower. As the beast swings its tail about, Amabie lets go just in time to avoid being crushed to a pulp against a huge cargo ship.

By the time the rest of Team ARMOR catches up, the giant lobster is waiting for them. Perched on a massive tanker, its tail crushing containers on the shore, its six claws poised to strike, its insanely heavy body somehow held up by its four skinny hind limbs, water flowing off its shell and glittering in the light of the setting sun, the Kaiju King's finest creation yet is ready for battle.

And battle is just what it gets.

A horn-missile from Oni's mecha, bobbing squat and ugly behind the tanker, fizzes up from the water and scores a direct hit on the monster's right eye.

Amabie's metal-scaled mermaid tail launches a ball of adhesive goo that disables one of its lower claws.

Raiju's wolf-mecha emerges roaring from the water and gets smacked squarely on the side for her pains. The lightning wolf goes flying across the shipyard, scattering massive shipping containers like dominoes.

Baku taunts the kaiju with machine-gun fire, skimming away just out of the creature's reach, keeping it distracted.

As Goryo's mecha-demon breaks the surface to the north, Norio looks at his teammates in wonder. He knows why *he's* doing this, but he's never understood why four other human beings, all mostly normal and hopefully sane adults, have agreed to help him. He doesn't know about the others, but

Azusa seems to be in this fight out of sheer nobility. To protect and serve the citizens of Tokyo? That seemed illogical. Unless she has a secret burning need for revenge as well. But who is she avenging? His father?

The lobster dives off the tanker, thousands of tons of angry beast hurtling straight at Oni. The demon-mecha skids away, but not fast enough. The edge of an outstretched claw catches the mecha's right foot, and for a moment it looks as if Oni is captured, but a foray by Baku along the beast's underbelly distracts it long enough for Oni to slip away.

"Please explain why I gave up two hours of sweaty sex for this," says Oni on the communicator.

"We pay more," says Norio.

"My mecha's badly damaged, in case anyone cares."

"No one cares."

"Another inspiring speech from our glorious leader," says Oni, and returns to the fray.

The lobster thrashes for a gut-churning two seconds in the water, shudders violently, and is still. The mechas rise above the surface and hover in the air, circling, waiting. Norio has seen this before; there's no conclusive way to prove his theory yet, but he knows the lobster part of this kaiju is now dead, simply unable to cope with its new behemoth body, with the sheer impossibility of pretending to have any control over its massive limbs and nerves and sloshing liquid insides. No one knows what the Kaiju King's power involves – magic? Induced metamorphosis from some dystopic future? Freak natural organic nuclear reactions? Whatever it is, the beast has now surrendered to it. It is all monster now, and has only one thing on its mind.

The waters swirl, eddy and foam as endless antennae and the first pair of claws emerge. The kaiju rises.

"Form up?" asks Baku.

"Hold position," says Norio.

"The public wants us to form up."

"What?"

"Seventy-seven per cent of viewers say we should form up right now."

"Get off the internet. We have to crack its shell."

The monster emerges from Tokyo Bay, rising eerily, silently, turning on some magical mid-water suspended hinge like the world's largest and ugliest drawbridge.

"A hashtag about how you suck as a leader is trending, Goryo," says Raiju.

"Shut up, Raiju. I need a lightning strike. Aim for the plectrum at the base of the antennae. Take your time, don't miss."

"Aim for the who?"

"Look it up, since you're online. Why are you online? You want some netvillain to hack us all?"

"I'm not an idiot. I'm surfing from my phone."

"Stop."

The kaiju stands up again in the water between them, a towering nightmare made flesh. It screams, and the mechas rattle and shake.

"Raiju?"

"Yes, sorry. Just sending a message asking how everyone would feel if we just went home, since we're so terrible. Bloody whiners."

Norio understands Raiju's anger, but the truth is there is no one left to help ARMOR fight the kaiju any more. Every time one of the Kaiju King's overgrown children attacks the city, superpowered criminals run amok, and civilian defence squads, both human and powered, have more than enough to do. At least the real supervillains stay hidden – they don't like coming out while the media is occupied elsewhere.

The kaiju turns around, facing Odaiba again.

Team ARMOR springs into action.

Goryo, stung by complaints about his leadership, heads the charge, zooming up in front of the kaiju and hitting it with dual sonic blasts – ineffective – and showering its carapace with plasma. The beast swings its claws, but Goryo is out of range.

Oni, Baku and Amabie plunge into the bay again, hacking at the creature's legs.

"At least this one isn't breathing fire," says Baku.

No doubt stung by this criticism, the kaiju charges at Goryo. Twin flaps on either side of its head open, and jets of smoking liquid gush out, arcing through the air. Goryo swings aside, but is caught in the stream. His mecha's controls fail, and the machine shudders and lurches in the corrosive onslaught. Goryo cuts his engine, and the mecha-demon falls stone-like into the water.

"Acid spit," says Norio. "Oni, Baku, rise and engage."

"Actually, Goryo," says Raiju. "That's not spit."

"What?"

"I just looked it up," says Raiju. "It peed on you."

"What?"

"Well, you asked me to look it up. I know where the plectrum thing is now, if that's any help. The lobster's bladder, though, is located…"

"Focus," Azusa says coldly, silencing the team's laughter. "Kill it!" screams Norio.

The red lightning wolf rises high in the air and turns. Its jaws open, a cannon emerges. The other mechas fall back. The kaiju swerves, looking for its next victim. Then Raiju bathes it in lightning. The kaiju's carapace cracks down the middle; shards of shell fly out in fractal patterns. Sizzling, hissing, screaming, it convulses, but somehow manages to stand. Smoke billows from the crack in its shell, and huge quantities of thick black kaiju blood ooze out, dropping into the sea in smoking globs.

"ARMOR form," says Norio. "Let's give the people what they want."

The mechas shoot away from the monster, and a ragged cheer rises from the news helicopters hovering far above them. A hundred feet above sea level, the mechas transform and unite. In an impossible dance of mid-air toy building, plates emerge and slide, limbs interlock, blades swing into place. Bursts of multi-coloured light streak across the sky, keeping the kaiju distracted. Five spirits merge, a single giant figure towers over Tokyo Bay. ARMOR is formed.

Norio hadn't come up with the name – Advanced Robot for Monster Onslaught Resistance is a term that was cooked up by their anime producers. But ARMOR itself is Norio's creation, Norio's child. The giant mecha-warrior hovers, arms folded across its chest, warrior's helmet and crest sliding into place on its bullet-shaped head. Its blank, eerily beautiful diamond eyes light up. Its wristbands click as rockets slide into place in their launch tunnels. The last ray of the setting sun gleams on its elongated, razor-sharp shoulder pads. Three hundred feet tall, impossibly strong, Tokyo's greatest defender stands ready, and cries of jubilation ring out across the watching world.

The kaiju charges.

With impossible agility, ARMOR leaps back to avoid its acid jets, then kneels, splashing, in the water. Its right arm straightens, and rings of blue light shoot out, knocking the kaiju back, halting its mad rush towards the mecha gladiator.

The kaiju wavers.

ARMOR runs at the monster. Giant waves merge into a wall of sound as it speeds towards its enemy, and a sickening crunch echoes across the bay as it slams into the beast's thorax, folding it in half, sending it flying backwards. The cracks in the kaiju's carapace widen; its mysterious power source groans and somehow holds it together.

ARMOR launches seven missiles from its left wrist. They swerve and converge, and fireballs blossom on the kaiju's chest. Chunks of monstrous flesh hurtle in every direction, and rivers of black ooze sizzle into the bay. The beast screams in pain.

"Sashimi time," says Norio.

ARMOR launches into a series of quick charge-up katas. Parts rearrange themselves, humming and clicking, plates rising, folding, turning, a hundred aeroplane wings sewn together.

A seventy-foot-long sword emerges from ARMOR's right arm. The kaiju sees its death approaching, swinging, gleaming, glittering in helicopter spotlight beams. It cries out one final time, bellowing its defiance to the emerging stars.

The first stroke pierces its heart. ARMOR draws the sword out, covering itself in a mist of kaiju blood. Five more precise slashes, and it's over. All that remains of the Kaiju King's monster is a mountain of steaming shell and flesh trickling into the all-forgiving bay. ARMOR performs its customary celebratory air-punch, turns and strides into deeper waters, unfolding, transforming, reshaping itself into its five-part mecha-army.

"Do you mind if I stick around for a bit?" asks Baku. "I've actually ordered industrial amounts of seaweed and rice. My lobster volcano roll is a big hit nowadays, but *kaiju* lobster roll..."

"No, but could you please stop telling us exactly who you are and what you do?" asks Norio.

"Of course, Goryo. Apologies. I just want to see if kaiju meat works while fresh."

"I don't want to know. Good work, team."

Baku hovers near the kaiju's corpse as the other four victorious warriors disappear into the murky waters, projecting holograms to confuse the following news crews as they wind their way back to ARMOR base. Oni and Raiju chatter excitedly, reliving the fight. Azusa is silent, as always, and so is Norio. His day is far from over, and the ordeal he has to face now is potentially more dangerous than a kaiju battle.

Norio Hisatomi has a celebrity auction to attend.

At four a.m., a tuxedo-clad Norio lounges poolside at Tokyo's most glamorous new hotel, the Ginza Mikado, trying not to let his extreme tiredness and irritation bubble to the surface.

An ambitious society matron spots him from across the pool, and tries the time-tested technique of wading into the fluorescent-lit warm water, approaching Norio in a straight line, with the single-minded precision of a hungry shark. In a few seconds, her piercing giggles and admirably toned figure have captured the attention of everyone at the gathering, with the single exception of her quarry. Norio looks away deliberately, desperately wishing she were just another kaiju. And in doing so, he spots something far above him, silhouetted against the neon-hued night sky, something that actually makes his jaw drop. He sits up sharply. He blinks, shakes his head, and looks again.

It's real. It's still there.

With his left arm, he gently dislodges a Brazilian supermodel's death-grip on his right, rises, and excuses himself. Ignoring numerous parting witticisms, he strides out of the pool area, through the lobby, away from lurking paparazzi, and into an elevator.

A few minutes and several bribes later, Norio is on the Ginza Mikado's roof. He runs, swiftly passing vents, chimneys, and a couple of intertwined off-duty cleaners. He finds the corner where he had seen it, standing on the roof.

Where he had seen *him*.

It doesn't look like a statue. It looks like... him. Black cape, fluttering in the gentle breeze. That unmistakeable twin-pointed silhouette, perfectly framed in the cityscape around them, so many skyscrapers, so many people, so many stories.

Norio clears his throat nervously, reminds himself he's a billionaire, an action hero, and nobody's fanboy. He struggles to say the word, feels ridiculous, but there's nothing else to say.

"Batman?" asks Norio.

No response.

Norio asks again, louder, and is met with silence once more. Rage wells up within him, and embarrassment, and more rage. Of course it's not him. It couldn't be him. He isn't real. It's so easy to forget that, in a world where nothing seems real.

"Do you have any idea how much trouble you could get

into, standing around in that costume?" he asks. "Not just with the bloody super-copyright lawyers, but with every passing supervillain who decides you'd make the perfect trophy?"

"It's just a mannequin," says a voice behind him. Norio spins around just as the dart sticks into his neck. The night blurs, and Norio falls, heavily, staring through the all-enveloping haze at his assailant. She's short, curvy, mid-forties. Very pretty.

"Hello, Norio," she says. "Sorry to do it this way, but I need to talk to you, and it's so difficult to catch you alone. I'm—"

"Tia," slurs Norio, and passes out.

# CHAPTER **TWO**

Before waking up wholly, Norio makes the mistake of leaping up, ready for a fight – and hits his head. He is lying, he finds, on the lower portion of a bunk bed in a small cabin full of wooden furniture and ornate maroon drapes. He climbs out of bed, rubbing his head. There's a lump on the top of his skull threatening to grow to epic proportions, and a dull pain on his neck, where Tia's dart hit him. He doesn't know whether the throbbing sound that fills his head is inside it, or all around him. The cabin is windowless, and in a few moments Norio realises that the slightly queasiness he feels isn't because of unknown drugs in his body, but because the whole room is moving. He cannot tell from the shape of the cabin whether he is in a private train or jet. Or maybe a caravan? He notices that his clothes have been changed: he is now wearing a terribly loud Hawaiian shirt and a kilt. He wonders if this is a violation of his human rights. The shirt alone…

The door opens, and Norio tenses, ready to attack.

"Oh good, you're up," says Tia brightly.

Norio waves a pained hand at his clothes. "Was this really necessary?"

"Oh, you should have seen some of the other outfits we tried. We just didn't have too many options in your size, sorry."

"What's wrong with the clothes I was wearing?"

"Nothing." Tia smirks.

"Well?"

"Please don't run berserk or anything – I hate sweeping up after myself."

Norio has seen news footage of Tias in action, taking on a militant base in Zimbabwe: a platoon of beautiful rifle-toting women in combat fatigues storming a base under heavy fire. He has seen, in shaky handheld footage, clusters of Tias turned to dust by RPG fire, replicating and reforming from survivors without falling out of step. He knows what she is capable of, and spares himself the effort of trying to overpower her. He sits down on his bunk instead.

"Where are you taking me?" he asks.

"I've kidnapped you, darling. I'm new at this, but I do know I'm not supposed to tell you where I'm going to hold you." Tia giggles. "That said, I don't plan on holding you anywhere, but there are other Tias nearby who are much more liberal than I am. And you're wearing a kilt, too."

Norio suppresses a smile. "I'm hungry," he says.

"You poor thing." Another Tia emerges from the first, and walks out of the cabin.

Norio blinks in astonishment. Watching Tia replicate on a screen was easy, like watching any other piece of technical wizardry, but in real life there is something disturbing about the ease with which she steps out of her own body without a break in conversation. He wants her to do it again, to see her new body flow out of the old. He can't take his eyes off her.

She sits next to him on the bunk, uncomfortably close, and looks keenly at him.

"First of all, apologies. Tried to get through to you in less, you know, dramatic ways, but your secretary... Bodyguard? Butler?"

"Associate."

"Very cute, by the way."

"And an excellent detective." Norio yawns and stretches. "She will be with us soon. I've been kidnapped before. It only ever ends one way."

"She has no idea where you are, love," chuckles Tia.

"Wait and see," says Norio.

"You don't have any tracers on you either. I checked while you were asleep." Tia grins lecherously. "I checked very thoroughly."

Norio shrugs.

Tia rises. "I'm not a kidnapper, Norio," she says. "I just have a few questions for you."

"First, I have a request," says Norio. "If we are flying at this moment, I want you to promise me we're not going through any known charged zones. I have a lot invested in not turning superhuman."

Tia looks surprised, then amused. "This is a submarine," she says.

Another Tia enters and sets a tray of food on a table near Norio.

"Indian," she says.

Norio grimaces.

"I feel like I should give you a feedback form," says Tia-on-the-bed. "How has the experience of this kidnapping been so far, compared with your other kidnappings?"

Tia-by-the-table grins, and walks over to the bunk bed. "Above average? Good? Excellent?"

The Tias merge. It's the strangest thing Norio has ever seen, all sea monsters included, but he looks on as if two gorgeous women blending together is something he sees every day. He crosses over to the table and starts wolfing down the food. Rice, lentils and fish curry, very simply prepared. He would die before admitting it, but it's very tasty.

"To business, then," says Tia.

"Are you planning to kill me?"

"No."

"What do you want to know?"

Tia wrinkles her nose in distaste at the question she is about to ask, but goes for it.

"Are you a supervillain, Norio Hisatomi?"

Norio laughs out loud. "No," he says. "Anything else?"

Tia gets up, and paces about the cabin.

"Now I think you're a good guy, Norio," she says. "And I'm a big fan of team ARMOR."

"I have nothing to do with team ARMOR," says Norio on autopilot.

Tia smirks. "You've certainly done a lot of good work, both as Goryo and as Norio."

"See previous answer."

"Sure. Anyway, this isn't about ARMOR. This is about your other life, the celebrity billionaire playboy Norio bit. Even there, as far as I can see, you look good. Saved people from supervillain attacks, lots of charity work, lots of funding to superhuman research. No involvement with Utopic's dirty bits. But I get the feeling that there's a lot that's missing."

"This is our first meeting," says Norio. "You really can't accuse me of hiding things from you."

Tia laughs. "Fair enough," she says. "And here we are, somewhere in the Pacific Ocean on a nuclear class submarine. The perfect place for a boy and girl to get to know each other."

"Why do you have a submarine?"

"It's an American Navy sub. They lost it to zombies during the Trinidad infestation, 2016. I found it. Cleaned it. And then, well, I forgot to return it."

"Never been in one before."

"Finish your meal, and then we'll go for a walk. You'll find me in the control room. Ask for the captain."

The submarine is full of Tias. Norio meets several on his way to the control room, which turns out to be quite far from his cabin – engineer Tias in stained overalls, soldier Tias watching over missile chambers, and surplus-to-requirements Tias running around the submarine in various stages of undress for no apparent reason. The control room, when he finds it, isn't what Norio expected either – not that he knows anything about submarines, or that the rest of the sub had led him to expect something out of a World War II film, but he'd expected at least one periscope in the middle of the room. Instead, the brain of the submarine is cool and spacious, full of computer screens, a haphazard grid of monitors of different sizes, each showing a complex pattern of falling green symbols. Norio is reminded of those old *Matrix* films his brothers had been so fond of – he'd enjoyed them too, despite the clunky special effects.

"I like to wear sunglasses and a trench coat when I sit here sometimes," says Captain Tia, swinging around in her chair in front of the monitors. "I pretend it's just me, saving the world from evil machines. It could happen."

"You look remarkably young for your age," says Norio.

Tia laughs, and presses a button. All around her screens flicker and change, and Norio finds himself facing hundreds of pictures and news videos of himself. Tia rolls a sleek black chair towards him, and he sits, turning, taking in the room. Tia faces the screens again, and operates a complicated system of dials and touchpads laid out in front of her. Norio has seen displays far more complicated than this, of course, but those were never about him.

"Let's see now. Norio Hisatomi, age twenty-five, born 1995, third son of Ryuga, head and sole architect of the resurgence of the Hisatomi Zaibatsu, and only child of Ryuga's mistress Megumi, pop singer and occasional actress," says Captain Tia, as dozens of screens throw up family photos Norio hasn't seen in years. "Born in Tokyo, raised in London and Los Angeles, officially adopted by Ryuga after his mother's death in a car accident in 2003. Poor baby."

"I know what my story is," says Norio.

"I'm not telling *you*, love," says Captain Tia. "I'm telling her."

Norio sees, in the shadows to the far right of the monitor, a Tia in glasses and a severe black dress. She nods sharply in his direction, and gestures to Captain Tia to continue.

"Who are you?" asks Norio.

"Tia Prime," she says.

"What is that, the oldest Tia?"

"Yes."

"Aren't you all the same person?"

"Yes."

"So how can you be older than the others?"

"Every split is a new birth."

"How do you all keep track of who and where you are?"

"Private social network. Pretend you've been kidnapped and feel less free to ask personal questions. Captain?"

"Yes. Ryuga keeps Norio in the UK because his other two sons are scared of him."

"They were not scared of me," says Norio.

"Scared because the father was fond, and the mother was hot. Norio does exceptionally well in school but gets a bit of a rep for a violent temper. Very good at drama and photography. Visits Tokyo about once a year."

"Twice," says Norio. He seems perfectly relaxed, except for his left foot, which is tapping on the metal floor with increasing frequency.

"In 2009, when the First Wave of superheroes goes public, Norio is thrilled. He writes his father a long letter about embracing the future, loving change, humans and superhumans working together."

"Like a letter? On paper?" asks Tia Prime. "Who does that?"

"Him. Pay attention. His father doesn't reply, but he has the letter scanned and saved, and sends a copy to his friends in America. Business moguls who will later form part of the board of what's now known as Utopic Industries. So it's possible that Utopic Industries' earliest aims and goals were built around a lot of very hopeful, sentimental, things our teenaged Norio wrote in his letter."

Norio whistles. "Are you serious?" he exclaims, swinging

his legs up on a table. "I had no idea."

"It can't have been a good letter, given what Utopic became. Anyway. In 2012, the Kaiju King—"

"Who?" asks Tia Prime.

"That lobster we saw? His daddy. Tries to destroy Tokyo at least once a year. Doesn't seem to want anything else, or any kind of limelight. Arrives as part of the Second Wave in 2012. His first attempt at monster building, a chunky dragon, takes out the Statue of Liberty replica in Odaiba. The Unit destroys the monster, but in the process the Hisatomi skyscraper is damaged. Ryuga Hisatomi and his two older sons are killed. Norio, seventeen years old at the time, finds he has become the head of a small but powerful zaibatsu. He disappears."

"Drugs," says Norio, smiling. "These idle rich, you know. Irresponsible."

"Norio spends the next six years in the darkest, most dangerous corners of the world," Tia continues. "He is involved with crime syndicates, supervillains, secret martial arts trainers and weapons experts. Norio is an early example of the urban phenomenon known as 'Brucing'."

"I don't know Brucing," says Tia Prime.

"You've been away. Brucing is where well-off human teenagers decide, after personal setbacks like missing trust funds or, you know, dead parents, to go off to dangerous parts of the world and get the training they need to become martial arts champions and detectives. To stay in the game even if the world is full of superhumans. It's the new 'going to India to find yourself', but with a lot less marijuana."

"So you wanted to destroy the Kaiju King? He was your nemesis?" Tia Prime asks Norio.

"You're still trying to pin me to ARMOR? No. The Kaiju King didn't kill my family," says Norio. "The Unit killed my family. You should know that."

"I had left the Unit by then," says Tia Prime. "What's this, Captain?"

"Well, the Unit didn't kill Norio's father, the fight did. The Kaiju King's dragon died when The Faceless impaled it on Norio's father's tower."

"And killed most of the people inside it," says Norio, his voice perfectly calm. "It doesn't matter whose fault it is, of course. But since you have taken so much interest in the matter, you should know that the villain and his monster didn't kill my father. The world's greatest superhero team did."

Captain Tia leans forward. "So suddenly 'Are you a supervillain?' doesn't seem that stupid a question, does it, Norio?"

Norio shrugs. "I just wanted to show you that this connection you're trying to draw between me and ARMOR is false. I have nothing against the Kaiju King. And I have nothing against the Unit. I spent a couple of years wanting to kill The Faceless – why am I calling him The Faceless? I spent a lot of time wondering how to kill the mass murderer Jai Mathur, your friend and ally."

"Never," says Tia. "I tried to kill him the first three times we met, and left the Unit because he was in it."

"Well, good for you. Anyway, so thoughts about avenging my father sort of died when Mathur showed many times over the years that he couldn't be killed. So there's really nothing I can do about him. Life is unfair. Superpowers are unfair. But my life has been known to arouse envy too. Try not to pity me."

The Tias study him closely for a few seconds.

"Tell me the rest of the story," says Tia Prime.

"I don't want to give out spoilers," says Norio. "Do you mind if I walk around this submarine for a while?"

"There's not much else to see except torpedo cradles, server rooms and so on," says Captain Tia. "You drive mechas, I don't think the sub's fibre-optic networks are likely to get you breathing heavily."

"I don't—" Norio begins, but Tia Prime cuts him off.

"We know about ARMOR, Norio," she snaps. "And your denial is, well, silly at this point. Let's say this master detective lover of yours finds our sub like you say she will, what will you say when she shows up in her ridiculous little mermaid-mecha?"

"We are not lovers," says Norio.

"That's true. Why not?" Tia Prime enquires, all traces of annoyance vanishing. "You seem so perfect for each other. And she's kind of sexy in that intense horror-movie heroine way."

"I said, we're not—"

"Why don't you sit down, Norio," says Captain Tia gently. "We're going to work together after this, and it's important that we get to know each other better."

Norio smiles. He sits, putting his feet up on the control table again, and surveys the screens on which his life has been laid out. Norio is not particularly vain, but as he looks at an array of screens all featuring him, sharply dressed, stepping out of hybrid cars, inaugurating vertical farms, demonstrating a braingate neural interface to a group of thrilled disabled people, announcing the invention of a nanoparticle-embedded resin that will make Hisatomi cars and maglev trains six times lighter... he decides he looks good. He looks very good.

"So, Norio's father dies in 2012 and he disappears for six years," says Tia Prime.

"Then he returns, spectacularly, at a zaibatsu meeting and takes charge of the company," says Captain Tia. "Is it true there was a ninja costume involved, Norio?"

"Yes. No. Well, it was store-bought. But it got the job done."

"Big win. He'd been doing all kinds of financial whiz-kiddery for a year or so before this, of course, so when he finally comes back to Tokyo in 2018 all the pieces in his master plan fall together, and it's as if Norio has been on top of the eligible bachelor lists right through."

"Something about a pig?" says Tia Prime.

"Yes. The only flaw in Norio's plan is that his green genetically modified two-headed pig, Capitalist, isn't a society hit. At around the same time the ARMOR giant mecha-warrior makes its first appearance. Norio and his – associate – Azusa gather a group of people from Tokyo that they've known online for a while – they played RPGs together, and were even reigning champions at some game or other before that group of fused Korean supergamers took over all online gaming – and boom, they formed a super mecha pilot team."

"Well played," says Tia Prime.

"I deny everything," says Norio.

Captain Tia hushes them both. "Almost done, now, control yourselves. ARMOR protects Tokyo from sea monsters so well that the government stops hiring international mercenary teams to do the job, leaving Tokyo Bay's defence more or less in ARMOR's very capable hands. At the same time, Norio becomes a major player in the business world. But something's changed."

"The pig?" Tia Prime asks.

"No. The pig is dead. Focus. Instead of looking at human-super cooperation, like Utopic, which by this point has grown to become the world's fattest mega-super-whatever-corporation, the Hisatomi zaibatsu focuses on humans – there's even an informal don't-hire-supers policy. Norio becomes one of the most alpha network people on the Tokyo social scene, and is kind of responsible for the social trend where superheroes, while appreciated for their work, aren't really seen as acceptable in high society. It's the opposite of the US, with its superpowered President. Okay. The end."

Norio applauds politely. "Very good," he says. "And now?"

"And now you take questions, Norio," says Captain Tia.

"What if I refuse to answer?"

"You want us to threaten you? Why?"

"It just doesn't feel like a kidnapping otherwise."

"Let's see. First we could tell the world that you're in Team ARMOR. Make your teammates targets. Then we could take all your money. Then we could... I don't know, tell the world about your secret connections with Utopic? Never friend you back anywhere on the internet? Write bad reviews on all your hero ratings profiles? Storm your base and steal ARMOR?"

"I'll take questions," says Norio, wincing.

"First. You're secretly on the board of directors of Utopic, despite being all no-supers for your own company. I get why you don't like supers, no one who has had anything to do with Jai ever does. But Utopic is the big daddy of the whole scene where... well, you know what they do. Why do you work for them? It seems like cheating. Utopic seems a little... shady, no?"

"You don't have to be polite about Utopic," says Norio. "The company's a hideous beast that embraces human-super cooperation in public and performs experiments on supers in secret zoos. Also, it's taking over the world."

"Then why do you work there?"

"I don't. I wouldn't mind being part of something that turned supers into juice and then gave that juice to everyone, but when Utopic finally manages to bottle powers, they'll sell them for huge profits. Part of which will come to me. I own part of Utopic because my father did. From when it began, before it went the way of all big companies. Utopic keeps me very rich."

"So after your whole dark knight rises to the top of the skyscraper story, you end up working for this – hideous beast?"

"It's a loving expression. Look, are you trying to sleep with me? Or hire me?"

"Neither."

"Shame. But in that case, my morals are really no concern of yours, are they?"

"He's right," says Tia Prime. "Next question, Norio. How much do you hate the superpowered?"

"I don't."

"Do wish none of this had happened? That superhumans had never existed?"

"As in, strongly enough to smuggle myself on a series of illegal plane trips and dream of a world without superhumans, and turn myself into some kind of ultimate anti-super weapon? No."

"But you don't like superhumans."

"Of course I don't. You only like the new world elite if you're a part of it."

"What about the reforesters, the photosynthetics, the

landscapers, the cleaners, the healers, the clean energy gang?"

"No. I recognise they're doing a good job. Still won't work with them. Sorry, how does it matter whether I like them or not? Where is this headed?"

Captain Tia clears her throat nervously and looks at Tia Prime.

"The thing is, Norio," says Tia Prime, "someone's killing off supers."

"Someone's always killing supers," says Norio with a shrug. "Usually bigger and meaner supers."

"Someone very smart, and someone with a plan. These aren't random incidents. Huge fights, disasters, explosions. Public places. There's a pattern to it."

Norio smiles. "And you thought that was me? I'm… quite flattered, but I lack both the desire and the resources."

"No, we didn't think it was you," says Captain Tia. "But we could use your help."

"I'd love to help you," says Norio. "Look, there's Stockholm syndrome kicking in."

"But before we work together, we have to be clear about a few things. The whole man of mystery thing you're doing must work well with most ladies, but we don't like it. We know you're up to something," says Tia Prime. "We know you have a larger plan."

"Of course I do," says Norio. "The further expansion of my business empire, and hopefully the downfall of my rivals. And the lamentation of their women. What is your point?"

"Where did you get the technology for ARMOR from?" asks Captain Tia.

"Designed it," says Norio.

"No you didn't," says Tia Prime. "It's too advanced."

"I'm very smart."

"You would have built more."

"I will, later," says Norio. "Any more questions?"

"You've found Sundar," says Tia Prime.

"Who?"

"My friend. A superinventor. You have him."

"Three things. One, there's more than one person with every really useful power now. I've met another body-doubler, Russian. Do you know him? You're prettier, before you ask. Two, I don't work with supers. Three, no."

"You're lying," says Captain Tia. "I like you, and we could make the world better together. Just the two of us. But you're lying."

Norio smiles.

"I like you too, Tia," he says. "I'm sure you hear this all the time. And I'd love to work with you, or even for you, but I can't. Not until I meet the man you're working for."

Tia frowns. "What makes you think I work for any man?"

"Work with, then. My English was never perfect. But there's only one way we can come to any kind of agreement."

Norio leans forward and smiles wider.

"I want to meet Aman Sen," he says.

Tia sighs and looks away. "Aman has been dead for four years now," she says quietly. "You can't have missed that news, Norio. Everyone knows. He died saving the world. He became a symbol. His T-shirt is more popular than Che's, for god's sake."

"And he passed on his hacker powers to you before he died?" asks Norio.

"He made software that ran itself."

"Lies. Of course he'd want to pretend he was dead. Everyone in the world was hunting him."

"I don't want to talk about Aman's death," says Tia. "He meant the world to me. But you know he's gone, Norio. It was pretty much a world-changing event. Everyone reported it."

"Of course the rumours of his death would be everywhere – he controls all networks!"

"They found a body."

"They found several bodies. This is sillier than me pretending I'm not in ARMOR, Tia. Of course Aman is alive. And when he's serious about working with me, he'll meet me."

"I wish Aman was alive, Norio," says Tia, and there are tears in her eyes. "But he's gone, and the world's out of control again."

"Did you ever really think you had a chance of controlling the world?"

An alarm rings out. The images of Norio on the control screens vanish to reveal on the long-ignored sonar controls the pixelated images of what look like four floating demons in the water, growing larger every second.

Team ARMOR is here. Team ARMOR looks angry.

Captain Tia leaps up and slams her fist on the controls.

"How the hell did they track us?" she yells.

"Azusa's really very good," says Norio, leaning back in his chair.

"Get rid of them!" yells Tia Prime.

"We have missiles on board," says Tia. "Tell them to back off, Norio, or we'll use them."

She hails the approaching mechas. They do not answer. Azusa's mermaid-mecha leads them in ominous silence, blank eyes glowing.

"Tell them, Norio!" shouts Captain Tia.

"No," says Norio. "You're not going to harm them, or me. You're going to shut down your sub, and let them board."

"Why would I want to do that?" Tia roars.

"Time for me to ask you a question, Tia," says Norio.

Tia glares at him. On a screen behind her, the infra-red camera shows long metal sucker-arms extending from Amabie and docking on to the sub.

Norio's eyes glitter as he moves in close.

"Are you a supervillain, Tia?" he asks.

"Of course not."

"Well," says Norio, as a screeching noise announces the arrival of Team ARMOR's excellent submarine-cutting equipment, "would you like to become one?"

# CHAPTER **THREE**

It had taken their agent about four minutes to come up with the United Nations Interception Team's name, but the search for the perfect headquarters has taken a decade. And as Uzma Abidi walks up the broad steps to the Unit's new base on Liberty Island, she has to admit they might have finally got it right.

The world's first and greatest superhero team had moved out of London in 2012: their marketing people had insisted the Unit needed a skyscraper by the Thames and the British government had quietly refused to give them one.

Parliament had wanted the Unit gone for a while by that point, anyway. The prestige that came with hosting the Unit brought far too much trouble with it, especially with the protests and riots that had followed the superathletes scandal that had closed down the London Olympics. Brief disastrous stints in Dubai, Shanghai and Rio had followed – the buildings that had survived their stay had been sold to local superhero teams. And in 2014, when Sher and Vir, the only two Unit members who had flatly refused to live in America, had left, there had really been no reason not to give in to collective pressure and move to New York.

Uzma had always wanted to live in Manhattan, to walk wearing insanely long boots through bustling streets with a styrofoam coffee cup in one hand and a phone in the other. They'd rented a whole skyscraper: Ellis, their agent, had found an aging building on 42nd and Broadway which he'd said was perfect. Uzma hadn't understood why, but they'd moved there. And then everything had gone to hell.

It wasn't just the paparazzi and the hordes of tourists and accompanying pickpockets and muggers who had surrounded the building all day, every day: the core Unit members had all had Stealth Cloaks since 2013. The real problem was, predictably, supervillains.

When the Unit's heroes were in the building, they had media-hungry villains roaring challenges from the streets, threatening civilians until the heroes showed up to fight them, and even Jai got tired of pulverising villains, many of whom turned out to be cosplaying litigation-happy humans, after a few months. The NYPD was sick of providing protective cordons for their fans, and even sicker of officers dying under supervillain onslaughts.

It had been even more annoying when they were out on missions: they would come back to find their tower in ruins. The best way for villains to get their App-o-calypse notoriety ratings (and mercenary payscales, and reality show advance offers) shooting upwards was to inflict property damage on anything Unit-related, especially after 2016. By then, pretty much every iconic monument anywhere in the world had already been destroyed: blown up, punched in or otherwise defaced by young ambitious supervillains with stars and cameras in their eyes. And while there were plenty of superarchitects eager to reconstruct the Pyramids and the Eiffel Tower, you couldn't speed-build a skyscraper in the heart of Manhattan without drawing huge crowds and seriously disrupting traffic. Not on a weekly basis.

Three years of living in anonymous government buildings and army bases around the world had followed. Uzma had hated it. Not just because of the inconvenience, but because every official she'd met since the Unit's founding had tried to control her, make her rearrange the world according to their beliefs in exchange for free food and lodging. And she had snapped sometimes, many more times than any government in the world was comfortable with. Many of the assassins sent after Uzma in the last few years had been hired by people who share space with her in official photographs, smiling nervously at some international summit or other. And the invitations to official international gatherings had stopped since she'd last addressed the UN General Assembly, yelling loudly enough to be heard across the gigantic hall. She had ended the Middle East crisis, ended the America–China proxy war in central Africa and freed Tibet in one fiery speech. It had been covert operations since then.

But things have been better for Uzma and the Unit since SuperPrez Sara Rhodes' ascension to the US Presidency. When Rhodes announced a year ago that the new Statue of Liberty (the sixth version) would be built on top of a thousand-foot high tower that would also serve as the Unit's new headquarters, and that Liberty Island was now closed to the public, there hadn't been much opposition to the plan at all. Of course, everyone had given up on the Statue of Liberty by then; it had been broken four times and brought hideously to life once, by the Shadow Puppeteer a year ago. The new statue stands on top of the octagonal tower as if it had always been there. Uzma is determined to make it a symbol of hope once again.

Jason and Anima await Uzma in the lobby. She enters, sweeping off her Stealth Cloak. Jason greets her with his usual warm smile. Anima doesn't acknowledge her presence at all, and keeps swiping away at the holo-screen floating in front of her. It's some new game, Uzma sees, featuring a bright orange blob bouncing through a dungeon. Jason nudges Anima, and then she looks up, sees Uzma, sighs, and makes the holo-screen disappear with an exasperated gesture. Behind Uzma, Jai strides up and stops. Uzma can hear his armour whine slightly as he scans the foyer for potential assassins. There aren't any: the building isn't even supposed to be complete for another two months. There will be a grand opening, with many visiting heads of state. There will be assassins aplenty for Jai to butcher then.

It's been more than a year since Uzma last saw Jason and Anima, but there doesn't seem to be much to say: Uzma has to watch the news, and knows what they've been doing. Life has moved so fast over the last decade that Uzma often forgets that she's hardly ever spent any time talking to Jason: whenever she sees him, her brain goes bald, new guy, Anima's boyfriend, moves stuff around with his head, polite, cute, too young. Jason. But his face, like those of her other teammates, is such a familiar sight on screens anywhere she goes that, like the rest of the world, she's tricked herself into believing she knows him well.

Anima will be eighteen soon, and Jason's life will become

much more complicated: he'll have to start dating the real-life woman along with the anime warrior princess. Uzma watches Jason size Jai up as they step into the spacious elevator. The young telekinetic has held his own against Jai in sparring sessions in the past; Uzma can tell he's itching to have another go.

The rest of the Unit is already assembled in the central chamber on the top floor. They rise as the four enter. Ellis, who had been sitting in Uzma's place at the head of the seven-sided table, greets them with handshakes and hugs and sends an intern off to get coffee. A man in a black suit with a very forgettable face is also present: the new UN liaison. He introduces himself, knowing no one but Ellis will remember his name. His name is Johns.

Uzma sits, accepts her coffee gratefully, and looks at the three remaining members of the Unit; faces so familiar from screens all over the world that it's difficult to remember she's not seen them for a while, and doesn't really know them well.

Wingman looks as he has since she first met him ten years ago, when the marketing team had informed her, in so many words, that the Unit was too South Asian and they needed to get an all-American type in there quickly, preferably as leader. And you couldn't get more all-American than Wingman – craggily handsome, greying at the temples, shining white teeth now on full display as he exchanges pleasantries with Jason. Uzma hadn't allowed him in until Vir left, and has disliked him for years, a dislike that she has always known is irrational. Perhaps it is Wingman's all-encompassing positivity that grates against her nerves like nails on a blackboard; perhaps it is his perfect body language, his charm, his immense popularity (he has spent the last two years starring in his own biopic in between hero missions). Perhaps it is because he has slowly been replacing her as the Unit's spokesperson, as the networks trust him more than they do a woman with a Muslim name. Or perhaps it is because Mr "New Clooney" has ranked above her in the 100 Sexiest People list for two years running now.

To Wingman's right sits Wu, staring into space as always. At the moment it doesn't look like there's some ancient spirit in residence in her frail body: they tend to be much more alert and curious than Wu is herself. Uzma had resented her inclusion in the Unit as well, after Tia left, but the Chinese government had threatened to declare the Unit hostile unless they had a Chinese hero for every American. Not that Wu was in any way a Chinese government posterchild – she had been a performance artist following in Ai Weiwei's dissident footsteps, but they hadn't banned her yet when her transformation occurred. She clearly didn't fit into any of the Chinese government's Harmony Warrior squadrons either, so they were quite relieved when the Unit took her in. There just wasn't any space for a sorceress/oneiromancer in the Chinese military superteams. Especially one as young and volatile as Wu. No one knows the full extent of Wu's powers; Wu herself definitely doesn't. But Uzma has seen her hovering in the air with an ancient spirit glaring out of her eyes, seen her bring rain down on parched lands, seen her annihilate a horde of song-raised zombies with a whispered secret word, and is grateful to have the sorceress on her team. The UN hasn't officially recognised the existence of magic yet, but it is clear that it is very real, and very dangerous. Whether it had existed all along, or the powers of the Second Wavers who turned into magicians created it, is still not known.

Next to Wu sits That Guy, and Uzma suppresses the urge to throw her coffee mug at him. At least That Guy has learnt not to speak at Unit meetings; the last time he tried to argue with Uzma, Wingman had tossed him across the table, and for one shining moment Uzma had felt real love for Wingman, and the Unit had been united in real joy.

That Guy had spent twenty-eight years on Earth doing absolutely nothing of value, but had taken one of the First Wave flights. He'd acquired the power to be in any photograph, any list, any meeting he wanted to be in. No one had invited That Guy to the Unit – no one, as far as he remembered, had ever invited him anywhere – but over the years, they had come to accept his presence, his irritating little cough, his inevitably mistimed laughter. They'd tried to use him to infiltrate super-terrorist gatherings, but he had failed at that. He only really wanted to be in the Unit, when he wasn't attending lingerie parties and film premieres. Uzma had assumed he'd be killed in combat soon enough – four heroes had already died in the Unit's service – but That Guy had stubbornly survived.

That Guy sees Uzma looking at him, and stares shiftily at his lap. Uzma's grip on her coffee mug tightens. She even used her Voice on him once, telling him he didn't want to be a part of the Unit, that he should be anywhere else. He had almost died then, screaming, half his body teleported away, and Uzma had relented.

Everyone has their drinks now, and Ellis takes charge, striding around the room with a large holo-screen, making one of his excellent state-of-the-world presentations – how on earth did he find the time? Uzma has perfected the art of nodding and looking interested as the words roll over her; she focuses, instead, on her teammates. Anima's not even pretending to listen; Jason plays footsie with her under the table for a few minutes until something makes him sit up; Wingman, too, Uzma notices, is suddenly all ears. This is the signal Uzma uses to know when to start paying attention: Ellis is talking about superhero ratings. Another of the new cybervillains has started posting millions of fake reviews on all the hero-for-hire sites: the Unit's marketing team is talking to banks about installing their multi-step offline security systems. And it's not just the villains: large groups of indie heroes are offering their services for ridiculously low rates, and writing glowing recommendations for each other. Hero guilds all over the world are in uproar. Uzma does not see what this has to do with the Unit, whose members don't officially get paid, but then Ellis says something that makes even her sit up.

"With your permission, I'd like to find the best hacker of the lot and add him or her to our roster of hopefuls," says Ellis. "There's no reason That Guy has to be one of the official seven – we could even have eight members. If we could find another Aman Sen, one not affiliated to a villain team, it would help us greatly."

"That's assuming the original Aman Sen is not in hiding somewhere, and behind all this," says Wingman.

Jai shifts in his chair, and Uzma doesn't need to look at him to know how much hatred that name stirs within him, under the layers of serenity instilled by her commands. She can feel it radiating from him.

"Aman Sen is dead," says Uzma, so subtly that no one in the room even realises she's using her Voice. "I don't want him brought up again."

The others nod obediently, in exact synchrony. Uzma stifles a pang of guilt.

"Why are we here, Ellis?" she asks, tapping her coffee mug gently. "Does the world need saving again?"

"Um, yes, like always," says Ellis. "But before we get to that, Johns needs to brief you all on several fascinating developments from the world of science and technology. No, really, guys, he does. It's all very important."

There's a collective groan, and Anima opens her game holo-screen again, but Johns has been waiting for months to give the Unit his update, and he will not be denied. Ignoring the yawns and hostile stares, he taps his wrist, and speaks as a series of holograms unfold and dissolve on the table.

Uzma does her best to stay focused as Johns speaks eloquently about braingate neural interface systems, new 3D printing techniques involving biobricks, genetically engineered plants that grow water bottles, new foldable flying cars, ultracapacitors, photovoltaic paints, and significant developments in wave, wind and space-harvested solar energy. Uzma knows it is vital that they all stay abreast of all this cutting-edge information, and she tries very hard to actually listen, but she cannot blame Wu for falling asleep when she does, and notes that even Wingman's enthusiasm seems to be running low. She turns her thoughts, instead, to Aman. They'd fought the last time they'd met, when she had finally confessed that she was thinking of getting married to – who was it now? The human rights guy, yes. He'd said she'd never see him again. That had been two years ago. He wasn't dead. He couldn't be. That T-shirt that the whole world seemed to be wearing now – that wasn't even his face. She'd done her part, she'd Told everyone she knew who had seen him that it really was Aman on those shirts, that he was gone. And she'd waited for him to call her. And she was still waiting.

She looks at Ellis again. He doesn't seem particularly concerned – what new crisis is this, that can wait until the UN guy whose name she's already forgotten finishes droning on about, what is it now, nanofilaments embedded in resins? Will it at least be an impending apocalypse, some super-threatening mega-adventure for which Uzma will be able to summon up the slightest bit of energy, motivation, interest even?

Developments in science that would make everyone's life better are a good thing, of course, but how do you deal with a world full of superhumans? What do you teach in schools when the laws of physics are violated in public on the news every day? How do you prevent young people from joining any of the seventeen major superhero-worshipping cults that have sprung up in America alone? How do you prevent ordinary humans from just giving up when they can no longer dream of emulating the people they admire, when their lives' work can be undone casually by any passing superhuman? Uzma clenches her fists; she wants to beat up the UN guy now. She pushes the coffee mug away; it's dangerous. She realises again that she has no interest in defeating another villain, preventing another nuclear explosion or fiction-portal-crossing alien invasion. The real crisis, she knows, is that humans have become the second species. The real problem is that supers, even the Unit, have started treating humans as lower than themselves: as people who can be classified, who have a function. Fans, threats, cattle, workers, farmers, assistants, employees, agents, audiences. Backstagers. Extras who have to come up with the new stuff:

the new economics, history, laws, the new journalism. Not for themselves, but to build a world sane enough to cope with supers. A world they'll never own, and will spend their lives trying to catch up with. Aman had droned on about this for years. She hadn't listened then. But she knows now.

Uzma stands up.

"Get out," she Tells Johns.

"So we're launching three hundred squadrons of unmanned drones to identify unauthorised superpower-seeking flights and shoot them down— Excuse me?" says Johns as his body walks from the table to the door. He hasn't even begun to register shock or surprise when the door slides shut behind him.

Uzma has the Unit's undivided attention, though. Anima shuts her game down and gives Uzma a big grin.

"I wish you hadn't done that," says Ellis quietly. "They've been asking for your removal for a while now. I've had to deal with a lot of pressure."

"What's the mission?" Uzma asks him.

"The Unit needs to be seen together," says Ellis. "It's been a long time. There are rumours of rifts, and—"

"What's the mission?" Uzma repeats.

Ellis sighs. "Rowena Okocha," he says. He moves a finger, and a photograph of a young woman floats in the centre of the room. Mid-twenties, pretty, dark, dreadlocks, huge eyes, white coat. "AIDS researcher. Took a Second Wave flight. She was observed for several months, no change."

"What happened then?" asks Jason.

"Utopic hired her," says Ellis.

"Captured her for their private zoo, you mean," says Uzma. "Did they cut her up?"

"I don't know," says Ellis. "But they lost her two months ago, and they want her back."

"What's her power?"

"Her blood removes powers." Ellis looks even graver than usual.

Wingman shakes his head. "Not another Mutant Cure treasure hunt, please," he says. "Utopic's playing with us."

Ellis swipes the air four times, and with each movement a new picture appears. On the left half of each image is a superbeing turned monstrous by its power: one appears to be made of rock, another covered in spines, the third a screaming mask of living flame, the fourth a green gas trapped in a plastic bag. On the right half of each is a human face. Each face is smiling.

"Still seems like a hoax to me," says Wingman. "Our friends and benefactors at Utopic are probably laughing at us right now."

"No," says Ellis. "They're worried. Of course they didn't tell us when they found Rowena. Or how long they kept her. But since they lost her they've tried everything they could to get her back. And you know what they're capable of. They wouldn't have come to us if they hadn't run out of options. And if this wasn't a Unit-level problem."

"They were trying to mass-produce her blood, no doubt," says Uzma. "Weaponise it. And use it on, let's see… us?"

"Of course they were," says Ellis. "But someone else has her now. And they're worried enough to tell us about it, and they'll let us keep her if we find her."

"How did they lose her?" asks Wingman.

"Someone broke into their zoo and took her."

"Will they let us go to their zoo and look around?"

"They might," says Ellis. "But you know you won't find their other subjects, Wingman."

"Then I don't see why we should help," says Wingman. He remembers to look at Uzma for assent. She nods.

"They should send in the SuperSleuths, or, you know, actual detectives," says Jason.

"They won't put this one on the market," says Ellis. "It's us, or no one. Too much at stake."

"I'm amazed Utopic didn't just kill her when they found her," says Uzma. "Isn't the board mostly supers by now? They've certainly spent enough time flying around and hoping."

"That's probably why they're so worried now. They have as much to lose as—"

The familiar jingle rings in everyone's head, and they all groan. A high-pitched male voice echoes in their heads.

"DON'T FORGET TO WATCH THE INCREDIROTIC SEXPLOITS OF BENDY THE SEXMAN!" it cries. "NEW SEASON STARTS TONIGHT, TWO AM EASTERN, ON VUTOPIX!"

The broadcast ends, and they shake their heads growling.

"Bloody Viral," says Jason. "Why doesn't *he* go missing?"

"I think he has more people hunting him than even you, Uzma," says Ellis.

"Can we kill him?" asks Uzma. "That would solve all our popularity problems."

"Well, if you can find him, you'll find Utopic's zoo," says Ellis. "They've hired him exclusively now. So... is that a definite no on the Rowena mission?"

"We'll think about it. Do you have anything else?"

"Lots of super deaths and disappearances," says Ellis.

"More than usual. Villains and heroes, both."

"Patterns? Common enemies?"

"Fights, mostly. Super-duels in public places. But not all of them – there was one yesterday that broke a dam in Slovenia, another one flattened a pop concert in Guangzhou."

"Lots of civilian casualties, I suppose."

"Yes. More than lots."

Uzma winces. "And you think there's a link somewhere."

"If it isn't a link, it's a very disturbing new trend. We've had super-hunting problems before. It might be some kind of non-guild high-stakes combat tournament. We don't know yet. We've tried to find the root, but got nowhere. We've tried mercenary superteams too, even the SuperSleuths, before you ask. Nothing. But if the Unit went out and knocked a few big heads together, we might get new information."

Uzma looks around the table. "We'll beat up some people and see what they have to say," she says. "What else?"

Jason looks startled. "There's more?"

Uzma smiles at him. "I forget how new you are," she says. "It's not like your comics, Jason. It's not one crisis at a time."

"The comics have multiple plotlines too. Sometimes the whole universe gets—" Jason stops and grins. "You're ragging me."

"New guy," says Wingman, and thumps him on the back.

"I'm newer," says That Guy.

"Shut up," says Uzma.

She turns to Ellis. "Anything on a grander scale?" she asks.

"Utopic-friendly governments have been putting a lot of pressure on us to send you after Kalki," says Ellis. "But I know your views on that."

"I think I need to Speak to them," says Uzma. "Kalki's not a threat. He's only eleven years old. He's been in hiding all his life."

"He's a god," says Ellis. "He's trouble."

"Anyway, you know my answer to that. What else?"

"Bunch of magicians on an island in the Indian Ocean trying to build a portal to another dimension."

"Good for them. Is that it?"

Ellis looks nervous. "Nothing specific, but there is something that has been going on for a while and I think I should mention it."

He has the Unit's attention. Ellis not wanting to bring up a crisis is a first.

"The end of the world," says Ellis. "Every psychic with a decent track record has been predicting it for a while."

Most of the Unit members relax, and smile.

"Nice one," says Wingman.

Ellis shrugs. "I know, it's nonsense. Happens all the time. Just thought I'd mention it, because – they're all quite specific about the date."

"When?"

"Three weeks' time," says Ellis.

"You'd better finish your movie, Wingman," says Jason.

In the middle of the laughter that follows, Wu raises her hand. Uzma looks at her kindly.

"You don't need my permission to speak, Wu," says Uzma. "What is it?"

"The world will not end in three weeks," she says.

"We know," says Uzma.

"But mankind will," says Wu. "The spirits have spoken."

# CHAPTER **FOUR**

The beast can see two lights. Far above it, over the whispering leaves, through the stark black silhouettes of mighty branches, it can see a great white orb in the sky. The beast finds this strangely comforting, and intensely attractive; it wants to rise up and meet the light.

Slowly, it unfurls its leathery wings, stretches them, and the light from above shines through them, lighting up the branches below it with veined shadows. There are claws on the edges of the beast's wings, and it flexes them tentatively, shuffles from left to right, and looks up again, up past its endless, razor-sharp beak to the soft light above. It screeches harshly, crouches low, curves its spine. It is ready.

Another harsh screech. A *whoomp* echoes through the jungle, and then another, as it flaps its wings again. It leaps, struggles, finds its balance, and shoots up over the forest and into the sky, higher and higher, its wingbeats drum-like in the warm, wet night.

\* \* \*

Six hundred feet below in an underground cavern, watching the pterodactyl's flight on a screen, Aman Sen cannot help shouting in delight.

Aman chose Late Island for his secret lair in 2014 mostly because he really liked the name – an uninhabited volcanic hideaway called Late had seemed a good place for the late Aman Sen to skulk around in. He'd been disappointed when he'd found it was actually pronounced *latte* – Aman had never been that obsessed with coffee. But as it turned out, it didn't really matter what the island's name was – he'd made it disappear from the internet. So, in a sense, he'd killed it. Late Island can still be found in offline atlases, of course, and there are plenty of Tongan fishermen and world-travelling yacht-dwellers who can tell interested parties exactly where it is, but fortunately for Aman it isn't a question many people ask.

The island sits like a fresh cowpat in the heart of the Pacific Ocean. It's six kilometres wide, on the Tofua volcanic belt, fifty-five kilometres south-west of Vava'u Island. It's surrounded by steep cliffs, and is mostly jungle, apart from the bit where the volcano, which has gently dissuaded settlers down the ages, pokes its head above the forest canopy. Even with directions, Late Island is extremely difficult to get to – surrounded by rocks and extremely non-Pacific oceanic swells eager to guide passing boats on to those rocks.

Aman's supervillain lair is mostly underground, carved into the basaltic rock on the northern shore of the island. It wasn't built with any kind of discernible plan, but it has room for everything your average supervillain might desire: shark enclosures, submarine bays, gigantic halls full of glittering stalactites and bizarre coral sculptures. The aboriginal earth-shifter who'd sung the lair out of the rock for Aman had disappeared three years ago, muttering something about building maze-playgrounds in deep-sea caverns for whale calves.

Aman stands in his control chamber, staring at the giant holo-screens that hover between complex rock and limestone structures, each flickering and strobing as pulses of raw data streak across them. Right in front of him is the viewscreen following the pterodactyl as it circles the edge of the island, looking for prey.

With Aman stand two Tias, a man and another woman. The woman is thin, dark, dreadlocked; the man holds her close to him as he watches the flying saurian, his face flushed with pride.

"Thank you," he tells Aman. "I can't believe this is actually happening."

"It's your power, Ulrik," Aman says. "I just gave you a place to keep it."

"You mostly sat around and issued orders," says a Tia. "Anyway, now that it's up and about, what do we feed it? And how do we keep it on Late?"

"Ulrik will have to clone more species," says Aman. "We could have a whole dinosaur island thing going on up there."

"I don't like where this conversation is heading," says Tia. "Ulrik, you can't clone… dragons and things, can you?"

"No," says Ulrik. "Only things that actually existed. But the dodo's almost ready."

"Good," says Tia. "One Kaiju King is more than enough."

A small holo-screen pops up in front of them, showing a metal door sliding open. Captain Tia and Tia Prime walk through it, and into the control chamber to join them.

"What's new?" Captain Tia asks.

"Utopic's gone to the Unit to look for Rowena," says Aman.

The woman smiles, and squeezes Ulrik's arm.

"Not for me?" Ulrik asks. "Should I feel insulted?"

"Well, they never really saw what you could do," says Aman. "If you'd sensed a little T-Rex DNA near your prison they'd have made you feel more special."

"They made me feel quite special enough," says Rowena. "Are you sure they have no way of tracing us, Aman?"

"I'm not completely sure," says Aman, looking at Captain Tia, who glares back at him.

"Look," she says. "I have no idea how they found the sub, right? It was probably a lucky guess."

"Or a super," says Aman. "Maybe that Azusa is a tracker of some sort."

"He won't employ supers," says Tia Prime.

"He just tried to employ you."

"He wasn't serious," she says. "He really had no idea what to do with us once he'd won. It was kind of cute."

"He asked us if we wanted to be supervillains," says Captain Tia. "And when we said no and multiplied by a hundred and pulled out guns, he didn't know what to say next."

"So he just let you go?" asks Aman.

"Let's say we let each other go. I mean, we had a nuclear-class sub, an army, and a hostage."

"What did he do then?"

"He tried to hire us. We said no. He wanted to meet you. We said you were dead. Then he made some threats about how he was very dangerous and not a nice guy at all. We were making fun of him, and he snatched a gun and said he wasn't kidding."

Aman raises his eyebrows. "Why are you so fond of this Norio again?"

"Young. Hot," says Tia. "Anyway, I dared him to shoot me and we were getting this good tension going when his girlfriend showed up in a weird white armour thing and he got embarrassed and went away. Very cute."

Aman paces around the control chamber, looking at Rowena and Ulrik.

"I promised you a safe place to carry on your work," he says finally. "But you should know a lot of people are looking for us."

"And have been since the First Wave," says Ulrik. "This hasn't bothered you at all, from what we can see."

"We're pretty good at hiding from the Unit, yes, we've done it for years. But it's really up to you whether you want to stay or not," says Aman. "I don't know if this is a completely safe place for you."

"Do you know of any safer?"

Aman grins. "No," he says.

"You have to stay," says Tia Prime. "Everyone here is nice. And if you want more lovely people, I can make them. Plus, bonus, it's not a Utopic zoo and we don't want to pickle your insides and sell them."

"You broke us out, Tia, and we'll always be grateful for that," says Rowena. "And I've never seen Ulrik happier. But I need more subjects for my tests."

"Your tests can wait for a bit," says Aman. "Let things settle down. You already have the world's biggest corporation and its most powerful superteam hunting you. Hang out with your boyfriend, help him clone mammoths and stuff. We also have many different kinds of fish."

Rowena smiles. "Thank you," she says. "For the first time in years, I feel safe."

"And you can feel that way for years," says Tia Prime. "We're off the map, Rowena. No one will ever find us."

On cue, an alarm rings out, and red lights flash through the base. Several screens pop up, showing, from several angles, the approach of an enemy vessel. And then another. And then more.

And then there are five.

Demon-shaped mechas approach Late Island. Aman waves his hand, and a rotating 3D hologram of the island and the base fills the middle of the chamber. The mechas are spaced out evenly around the island, surrounded in turn by swirling schools of curious fish.

"They'll be here in two minutes," says Aman. He casts a searching glance at Tia. "Another lucky guess, you think?"

"Shit," says Tia.

"Why are we here again?" asks Baku.

"Silence," snaps Amabie. "They could be listening."

"Funny how we never worry about that with the giant monsters we seem to have misplaced during our last two fun outings," says Oni. "It's really far, and I've missed a whole bunch of clients, and I'm thirsty. I'd forget all of this if there was a monster to kill. Is there a monster to kill?"

"Patience, Oni," says Norio.

"I don't do patience," says Oni. "Why are we here?"

"We're on the trail of the Kaiju King," says Norio. "Now all I ask is that you follow my lead. And trust me."

"And *obey* me," mutters Oni.

"This isn't the mission, Goryo," says Raiju. "You need to tell us these things in advance."

"Noted," says Norio.

"Now quiet," says Amabie. "Initiate simultaneous charge on my mark."

"Initiate my sweet brown ass," says Oni. "We rescued Goryo. We chose not to see his face when you brought him in. He sounds ugly anyway. But this is all very sinister, Amabie. This is supervillain ground. Just tell us... are we terrorists now? Are we fighting for the government? What's going on?"

"We're changing the world," says Norio. "Now shut up, and trust me."

He hears muttering on the radio, but Team ARMOR holds its ground.

"We are with you, Goryo," says Raiju after a while. "But we signed up to be heroes. Just remember that."

"I will," says Norio. "Get ready now. Their defences will be strong."


"Okay, so now might not be the best time to bring this up, but we have no real defences," says Tia.

Rowena's eyes widen, and she turns in panic to Aman. But Aman is smiling.

"I know you think he's cute," he says, "but we still have enough of an arsenal to blast Bruce Sokko and his Flying Robot to little cute bits."

"Yes, but face it, Aman, we're not going to kill him," says Tia.

"But we can't let them on the island," says Aman.

"Isn't this the Japanese billionaire you wanted to work with?" asks Rowena.

"Yes," says Aman. "But his response to being kidnapped is really not what we wanted."

"What should we do?" asks Rowena.

"Maybe you and Ulrik should take the sub out for a spin," says Tia.

"No, we're surrounded," says Aman.

"I want to stay," says Rowena. "I'm a part of your team now."

"Sorry about that," says Aman. "Tia. Options."

"Well, they're knocking very hard. We might have to let them in. We'll show them our gardens and science labs and hopefully they'll go back to fighting sea creatures," says Tia. "I don't know why they're pushing it so far, but they know we know who they really are. And that we can tell the world in a second."

Aman looks troubled. "I knew we should have found more fighters."

Tia Prime walks up to him and clasps his shoulders.

"Relax," she says, and kisses him.

"Can you make them go away quickly?" asks Aman. "I've missed you."

"You go and hide behind a curtain or something," says Captain Tia. "I'll deal with this."


Tia hails Norio, and they link. The underwater signal is weak, and Norio's helmet-covered head flickers as it materialises in the control chamber. Norio sees Captain Tia clearly enough, though, with ARMOR's signal amplifier. She looks extremely annoyed.

"Stalker," she says.

"Sorry," says Norio. "But if I'd asked you to bring me here, you'd have said no."

"What do you want?"

"Aren't you going to ask me how I found you?"

"You'll just say Azusa's a really good detective."

Norio smiles, and Tia wonders whether he looked this wolfish when they'd spoken last.

"Let me in," he says.

"No."

"Then I'll huff and I'll puff," says Norio, as his mecha comes up close to the side of the lair.

"We have missiles, you know. Lots of them."

"Pacifists with missiles. Inconvenient. We can threaten each other as long as you like, Tia. But one of my team needs to use a toilet. So let me in."

"Ask him to step outside. It's only the bloody ocean. What do you want, Norio?"

"I want to meet Aman Sen."

Tia sighs and crosses her arms.

"You have more trouble accepting his death than I do, Norio," she says. "And we were really close."

"Let's run a little test," says Norio. "I'm putting you on mute, so you can't tell my teammates my name."

He switches on the mecha's primary communicator.

"Raiju? Your phone is on, isn't it?"

"Yes," comes the abashed reply a few seconds later.

"Could you tell all your followers where you are and what you're doing, please? Let them know who lives here."

"I don't know who lives here."

"Aman Sen."

"Really?"

"Just do it, please?"

Tia gestures angrily on the holo-screen.

"Okay. Done," says Raiju.

"Now check whether you can see your update."

"I can't."

Norio's smile is cold.

"Network, probably. I'll keep trying," says Raiju.

"Don't bother," says Norio. He switches off the com, turns to Tia, and moves her volume up with a gesture.

"Aman's alive," he says. "I want to meet him."

"He left behind online protocols that would—"

"Don't bother. Let me in."

"No."

They glare at each other in silence for a few seconds.

"I have bigger guns than you do," says Tia. "I don't want to use them. I'm sorry, but there are secrets on this island that are important to the world. Please, Norio. You don't know what you're asking. Just trust that I only want good things for you. I'm no danger to you. Go away. Please."

"I wish I could," says Norio. "I hate this conflict. But there's something I have to do, something that will save the world, and I can't do it without Aman."

Tia frowns and studies his face, but cannot read it.

"Tell me," she says.

"You know how all the psychics say the world's ending soon?"

"They always do."

"Well, it's true this time. And only I – we – can stop it."

"I'm bored," says Tia. "And since you're not going away, I'm telling all the world's journalists everything there is to know about ARMOR."

"I honestly don't care any more," says Norio, his voice strangely fervent. "I'm too close now to go back."

"Oh, and I'm taking all your money. I hope you have spare cash."

"None of this matters to me, Tia," says Norio. "I may not even survive this mission. But I have everything I need to finish it, except Aman. There's nothing you can say that will make me turn back. Fire at me if you have to, but I'm coming in. If I die, so be it."

"All right then," says Tia.

An alarm beeps in Norio's control sphere. His mecha's sensors tell him that missiles in the base have locked on.

"You'd really kill me?" he asks.

"I've killed before," says Tia.

"Sundar dies if I die," says Norio.

Tia's gaze wavers. "Sundar built your mechas," she says. "I knew it."

"Well, he designed them," says Norio. "I had them built. But yes, it's his work. His last work, as it turns out. Goodbye."

He waves his hand, and the holo-screen disappears. Goryo's demon-mecha powers up, plasma cannons emerging, ready for a desperate charge at Aman's base.

Overriding Norio's communication systems, a holo-screen pops up in front of his face.

"Let's talk," says Aman.

Goryo, Amabie and Oni dock into the submarine bay. A squadron of grim, rifle-toting Tias escort them out of their mechas. Oni staggers off with a Tia. Norio attempts casual banter, but these Tias do not respond. They wait until Norio and Azusa have taken off their armour-suits, and then frogmarch them through stalactite caverns and metal corridors until they reach Aman's war room. Three Tias stay in the room, guns casually pointed at Norio and Azusa.

* * *

Norio's face lights up when he sees Aman, and all the threatening things Aman had planned to say disappear in a barrage of compliments. Aman had quickly looked up appropriate formal bows, but Norio is almost American in his greetings. Thankfully, he stops short of being European. It is only when a Tia tells Norio firmly to shut it, that this effusiveness stops. Norio sits down at the head of the long conference table, three chairs away from Aman, and grins ruefully. Azusa stands beside him, staring coldly at the security Tias.

"I have behaved terribly so far," Norio says. "From the bottom of my heart, I apologise."

"Well, I suppose we started it," says Aman. "Tell us, then. What's the plan?"

"I want you to come back with me to Tokyo," says Norio. "There's a new armour waiting there that's just your size. It's like the one Jai Mathur wears – he stole it from you, didn't he?"

"That was a long time ago," says Aman. "And I don't know if I want more armour. I'm no fighter."

"The armour is just a gift. So you will be safe in the world outside, and will have no reason to hide any more," says Norio. He stands up, his eyes shining. "I don't expect you to offer your unique services for nothing. As for whatever you're building here, whatever you're planning to do, the Hisatomi zaibatsu has considerable resources that are now at your disposal. Do you build machines here? We specialise in rare metals, you know. Indium, neodymium, gallium, whatever you want. You obviously have all the money you need, but believe me, I have systems. All yours. No obligations."

"That's very generous," says Aman. "But I don't need to run an industrial empire."

"Yes, but you do need an offline presence to match—"

"Secondary," says Aman firmly. "What do you want from me?"

"Many things. But I do not come to you empty-handed. I come to you with hospitals, a fleet, a—"

"Stop," says Aman.

"No, don't," says a voice from the door. Rowena slides in.

"Rowena, go back to your room," says a Tia behind Azusa. "We'll talk later."

"I want to know more about the hospitals," Rowena says. "I'm sorry for butting in, but I need patients."

Norio surveys Rowena with great interest. "What do you do?" he asks.

"She's not a super," says Aman. "She's our base doctor, and she's leaving."

But Rowena stays where she is.

Norio shuffles a chair closer to Aman and a Tia comes up behind them.

"I've noticed bad things happen when you move around," she says.

Norio waves apologetically and leans closer.

"Do you know how my father died?" he asks.

"Yes," says Aman. "And I thought you'd refused to work with supers after that."

"I had," says Norio. "But a man can change. Sometimes a man has to, when the whole world is at stake."

He moves another chair closer, but Tia stops him with a poke of her rifle.

"Sorry, sorry, I'm just overexcited," says Norio, raising his visibly shaking hands and placing them, palms down, on the table. "This is just too big for me. I have this plan. It's all clear in my head, but now that I'm actually here, my tongue is tied in knots. I cannot believe I'm about to embark on this glorious adventure with Aman Sen. *The* Aman Sen."

Aman grins. "Relax. I'm much less impressive in person," he says.

"Not at all," says Norio. "You're exactly what I expected. Azusa?"

"Yes," she says.

And then, in one incredibly swift motion, Norio lunges forward, snake-like, and jabs two fingers into Aman's throat.

As Aman falls, unconscious, Norio rises, turns, and snatches the rifle from the Tia standing open-mouthed nearest him. Behind him, Azusa dives to the floor. Aman drops heavily and stays down.

Rowena screams.

The two other Tias in the room point their rifles, yelling, but Norio already has his gun pointed at Aman's head.

"Stay calm," he says.

"What the hell are you doing?" roars Tia.

"Drop your weapons," says Norio.

The Tias glare at him, but obey.

Azusa springs to her feet and stares at Norio, unable to conceal her complete bafflement.

"Norio. Listen," says Tia. "I know you hate supers, but Aman's the best of them all. He's Jai's greatest enemy too. He's the last person you could have anything against."

"Get the guns, Azusa," says Norio. "Rowena, I'm glad you

stayed. You're coming with us. We're definitely going to need a doctor."

"Stop this. Stop it now," says Tia. "We can make things right. We can work together."

"I don't think that's going to work out," says Norio. "Because, you know, this whole 'your world is ending' thing you've been hearing about? That's me, I'm afraid."

"You're supposed to be one of the good guys."

"I'm really not," says Norio. "Sorry."

He fires, three times. The Tias turn to dust.

Rowena screams again.

"I hope you know what you're doing," says Azusa.

"Are you with me or not?" asks Norio.

"I am with you... Master," says Azusa. "Always."

# CHAPTER **FIVE**

"So tell me again," says Uzma, shouting to be heard above the drone of the hoverjet as it flies speedily over the rotting heart of Prague, "why are we here?"

Ellis makes an expansive gesture. Uzma follows his hand as it moves across the landscape of central Prague; from the smoking ruins of the castle, where ancient gargoyles grimace in the embrace of fast-moving flames, across the sprouting termite hills that used to be the beautiful Mala Strana, over the Charles Bridge, where twin rows of statues stare blankly at petrified tourists and blue-clad guards as they huddle in groups trying to defend themselves against marauding hordes of insect-men, and onwards to the Old Town, where giant bees fly in incredible loops over the shattered Astronomical Clock. The sky is full of buzzing shapes, grotesque amalgamations of human and insect: hands and pincers, antennae and screaming faces, translucent wings and skin overlain with chitin.

"The future. Brought to you by Utopic," says Uzma.

"There's no evidence this is their work," says Ellis.

"Because you're scared to look hard enough."

"If they're involved, we can be sure it was an accident. There is no reason they should do this deliberately."

"There never is, is there?" says Uzma. "What do you want us to do about this?"

"It's the end of the world, right?" Ellis is famous for his composure, but the strain is beginning to show. "Prague was completely normal two hours ago. What do I want you to do? Do what superheroes do, Uzma. What else is there?"

Uzma gives the signal, and the Unit makes its move.

That Guy disappears.

Wingman leads the charge, large black feathers sprouting on his arms and back as he leaps off the hoverjet into the air, shooting in every direction from his plasma wrist-blasters. The hoverjet swivels and heads south, on the eastern bank of the Vltava River, towards the New Town.

Anima and Jason follow Wingman: the Princess of Power's green energy field lets her fly, and she whizzes off, back towards the castle, spears of light streaking out before her, barely visible in the bright sunlight. Jason takes a deep breath, and dives off the hoverjet. He does his usual spectacular thing, drawing a sheet of metal off a roof in mid-fall, shaping it into a surfboard, winding his way through roofs and spires as he assembles a cloud of sharp metal around him.

At Uzma's signal, Wu steps gently off the hoverbird too, her eyes blank and pupil-less, an eerie glow emerging from her skin as she stands in the air above the rooftops of the Old Town, a tiny, ominous figure. Her body convulses into a spirit dance; dark clouds appear swirling in the sky above her, lightning flashing at their edges.

"You should go too, Jai," says Uzma. "I'll be fine with Ellis."

A giant bee-man smashes into the hoverjet's windscreen at this point, and Uzma screams as the man-bug slides off the glass, leaving an ugly green-red smear behind him.

"Maybe he should stay," says Ellis. "We don't want you assassinated in the middle of all this."

Uzma shakes her head and gestures at Jai, and he steps off the hoverjet too, just as it reaches Wenceslas Square. He has no way to fly, but Jai has fallen from great heights innumerable times over the last decade. He breaks his free-fall by grabbing a passing man-locust, and uses the fluttering monster to steer him towards the National Museum's steps, where he lands lightly, rips his steed in two, and calmly surveys the hordes of screaming tourists and their insect-man attackers. He cracks his knuckles and gets to work.

Local hero teams have been battling the insect horde since the first monstrous grubs burst through the courtyard of the Kafka Museum in Mala Strana at dawn. Looking around, Uzma sees a few familiar faces – a lot of Europe's mightiest defenders are here, in very questionable costumes, locked in combat in the air, on the ground, and even in the river. Thanks to them, the insect plague has been contained to a few square kilometres in central Prague; that this is also the most densely populated area in the Czech Republic is unfortunate, but the EU teams have set up a perimeter and are blasting any of the monster hybrids that try to go beyond it to quivering, gooey shreds.

The real danger, Ellis tells her, is underground. Apart from the ancient warrens of tunnels that run under the old city, Prague's metro is excellent, and the insect-men have been going for many rides, laying clusters of eggs along the way. But a team of French underground artist heroes, activists who've evaded both supervillains and the French police effortlessly for years in the catacombs of Paris, are on the job, and there have been no reports of major infestations anywhere in greater Prague. And if they manage to contain the infestation, the huge swathes of rude French graffiti that have blossomed mysteriously all over the Prague metro will be a small price to pay.

Uzma flinches again as an exceptionally robust locust-man tries to enter the hoverjet through its sliding door. But Ellis moves faster: he slides it shut, leaving a foot-long stinger twitching and spilling slime over the hoverjet's interior. Ellis swipes a hand, and the control panel for the hoverjet's guns appears in front of him. He starts pressing holographic buttons, and stabbing white lights emerge from either side of the hoverjet, fending off more flying intruders.

"What do you call these damned things?" asks Uzma.

Ellis speed-reads a few messages on his phone, shaking his head, before turning to her.

"PragueNet's calling them 'Ungeziefers'," says Ellis. "Though given where it started I think they'll be called Gregors eventually. Quite funny, really."

"I have no idea what you're talking about," snaps Uzma.

"It really doesn't matter," says Ellis.

It had all started, Ellis tells Uzma, with Roman Novak, a literature professor, who'd been on one of the First Wave flights a few days after Uzma's own. He'd turned into some kind of giant insect, disappeared into the underground tunnels crisscrossing Prague, and had never been heard of since.

"So Utopic got him," says Uzma.

"They claim they didn't," says Ellis. "But of course they did, at some point over the last eleven years. More importantly, they knew this was coming. All Utopic subsidiary offices in Prague were cleared out last night. Before you ask, yes, this is Utopic's doing. And again, there's no evidence."

"He must have broken out of whatever zoo they were keeping him in," says Uzma. "And now he's come home."

What had Utopic wanted with the insect-man? Had they planned an army of super-insects? What horrors had they subjected the professor to? Why were they trying to destroy a city they owned large parts of?

Another giant bee-man is caught on the hoverjet's windscreen, stabbing in vain at the figures seated behind the unyielding glass. Uzma shudders as she watches its horrible torso twitch as it slides off, human hair fused with striped bands of bee fur, now splattering everywhere as the hoverjet's cannons rip it apart. What other monsters did Utopic have locked away? And what would happen if they all escaped?

Wingman's communicator comes online, and Uzma watches through his feed as he slices his way through a man-termite infestation on the balcony of a boutique hotel in Mala Strana. He's a killing machine when he gets going, but with every plasma burst that takes out the wriggling, squirming, utterly disgusting man-grubs chewing their way through the old building, he's blasting out the walls and woodwork as well: there will be very little left of the beautiful neighbourhood when he's done.

"Are we just on pest control duty here, or is there something I'm supposed to be looking for?" asks Wingman.

"Is there a central nest?" asks Uzma. "You should work your way towards that."

"I'll know when I find it," says Wingman, as an empty-eyed grub rears up in front of him and gets blasted into a fine shower of bug-bits. He shuts down his communicator and gets back to work.

They'd spent the last week knocking super-heads together. A trip to the Ultradome in Las Vegas, where fake superpro-wrestlers (usually down-on-their-luck supervillains looking for a showbiz career) went through the motions for cheering audiences across the world, had proved satisfying in terms of violence, but fruitless in terms of leads. They'd gone to underground super-combat tournaments in Mexico, beaten up super-warlords in North Africa, and broken up an upper-class British secret super-society of human-hunters in Soho. But no one Uzma had Asked knew where this particular apocalypse was coming from, or who was behind it. What was the point of this sabre-rattling from Utopic? Was the insect invasion just a rogue superbug gone crazy, or was it part of some larger, more sinister plan? If this was what one Utopic creature could do, what would happen the day they threw the doors to the whole zoo open?

Jason comes online. "Uzma," he gasps, "there's a problem."

"You think?" asks Uzma.

Through the swirling shield of bricks and metal Jason's built around himself, she can see he's running up the path to Prague Castle, leaping easily over lumps of insect wax that have split the cobbled street. As she watches, a caterpillar that appears to be made of several people sewn together bursts out of an antique shop. Jason leaps and rolls as it charges at him, and his viewscreen tilts and swirls crazily. He's back on his feet in an instant, and a shower of wood and brick torn from the buildings around him sends the caterpillar scuttling back, looking for shelter.

A series of green power-blasts lights up the street through the cloud of dust, and as Jason looks up Uzma sees Anima arrive, her giant anime eyes glowing and sparkling. A volley of green power-shuriken, and the caterpillar writhes, rippling horribly, and then bursts, scattering bone, blood and insect goo all over the Unit's heroes.

"I'm waiting," says Uzma.

"I don't know where we're staying tonight, but I'm calling first shower," says Jason. "Anyway, listen, these creatures – it's not just eggs."

"What do you mean?" asks Ellis.

"Well, they're not just hatching. There's also some kind of undead scene going on – if they eat your brain and spit into it, you turn into one too."

"That's sweet," says Uzma. "Kill them all, please?"

As Jason disconnects and goes back to carving a path uphill towards Prague Castle, Ellis gets another call. Uzma hears the sound of distant thunder over the noise of the insect-men buzzing around the hoverjet. Looking back, she sees Wu in the distance, bathed in a bright white glow, directing bolts of lightning into rooftops.

They fly low over Wenceslas Square, already largely empty: Jai often has that effect on public places. They see him, a tiny dot below them, surrounded by attackers, and Uzma is filled with horror. Hundreds of bodies are piled up in the square, human, monster, and others that are so mangled it is impossible to tell. Jai is on the warpath, notching up an incredible death count with horrible ease and unearthly joy. These are the only times he's absolutely free, and Uzma never wants to look into his eyes when he's done.

"We're going to have to suppress the casualty figures on this one," Ellis says beside her. "But all the powers that be are demanding executions – don't bother capturing the leader alive when you find him."

"Yeah, he might know things we shouldn't," says Uzma. "Killing him is clearly our only option. You know, I find Utopic's hold over the UN even scarier than what they're doing here."

"Do what you think best. We have to bring in the team now – we've found the central hive."

"Where?"

"Under the Kafka Museum. Where we should have started looking, really."

"Why?"

"Never mind. This is going to be a publicity nightmare, by the way."

Uzma glares at him. "You think I care about that?"

Ellis shakes his head. "I know you don't," he says. "That's part of the problem. I shouldn't have brought you here today. You've probably saved many lives, but still."

They send out the signal.

A minute later, the hoverjet shudders as Jai launches himself off the Bata headquarters and lands neatly on the hatch; Ellis slides it open. Everyone in the hoverjet covers their noses as Jai strides in, dripping ooze and blood. He squelches into his seat. There are no words to say.

The hoverjet speeds over the Old Town; the pilot has flown them before, and knows exactly where to turn and swerve. Wu doesn't even look as the jet spins in mid-air behind her.

She releases one final bolt of lightning, shuts her eyes and then lands on the hoverjet's floor quietly as they draw her in.

Jason and Anima streak over broken rooftops towards the Kafka Museum. Wingman is already there, killing time, shooting monsters. Ellis gets a priority call from New York and retreats to a corner of the hoverjet, muttering into his phone.

The red sloping roofs of the museum and the buildings around it have been covered in river mud and an ugly grey-brown resin. Worker insect-men swarm all over the complex, too busy to gape at the hoverjet as it flies in. Uzma is closer than she wants to be; she sees beasts with human heads and large, grubby white insect bodies, and cannot decide whether they're worse than the ones with insect bodies and fleshy hind limbs. She doesn't have to study them too closely, though; the hoverjet revolves, spraying the roofs with bullets, and scores of mutant bodies fall to earth.

In the centre of the museum courtyard, where the first gregors had broken out, is a large crack in the pavement that's been coated with wax. Maggot-men crawl out of it in large numbers, ignoring their impending doom, slime trailing out of their hindquarters.

Jason, Anima and Wingman fly into the hoverjet.

"Someone has to go in there and grab the main bug guy and destroy all the hive eggs," says Uzma. "Any volunteers?"

There are no volunteers.

"Well then," says Uzma, "Jai?"

Jai nods. "The rest of you should stay safe," he says. "None of you are invincible."

"Hang on there, friend," says Jason. "We've killed as many of these bugs as you have."

"Which brings us to an interesting question," says Ellis. "UN HQ is saying that this mass murder of Prague's citizens needs to stop right now. We need to find a way to negotiate."

"These are the same people who tried to give zombies the vote," says Uzma.

"Well, it might sound ridiculous to you, Uzma, but they are people," says Wingman. "If baseline humans have accepted us in their social and legal frameworks, other altered humans must—"

"You were the one out there shooting them, Wingman," says Uzma. "Now suddenly you're Mr Peaceful Resolution?"

"The situation's changed," says Wingman, his voice exuding compassion.

Uzma wishes she had the strength to beat the condescending smile off his face.

"All right," says Uzma. "I didn't want to come here in the first place."

"You couldn't have told us this before?" Jason squares up to Ellis.

"I'm sorry I brought you here," says Ellis. "But now they're talking standing commissions, years in court. Look, we didn't know what the body count was when we brought you in. A few dozen insect monsters is one thing. They're ugly, too, and it looks good on camera when you squash them. But now we're talking about thousands of people in one of the world's major cities."

"I say we leave," says Wingman. "These people have rights. Let the EU teams take the blame for their murder. I say they deserve to live in peace."

"Well, if it's time for negotiations," says Uzma, standing

up, "then I guess we're lucky the world's best negotiator is right here."

"It's really not safe for you," says Wingman. "Let the situation stabilise, and then local teams—"

"Take the jet down," Says Uzma.

As the hoverjet's pilot tries to find a landing spot amidst the squelching filth and swarming human-insect monsters in the Kafka Museum's courtyard, Uzma subjects her teammates to a quivering, incandescent gaze.

"Ellis and Wingman have managed to steer me into a position where anything I do is wrong," she says, ignoring all attempts at protest. "Now I didn't spend a lot of time in the film industry, which is really where I wanted to be in the first place, eleven years ago – but I never made the mistake of trusting anyone again. I don't know who you're loyal to. I don't know if any of you are on Utopic's payroll. And I honestly don't care. But I do know one thing – I'm not anyone's pawn. And if we're going to go ahead – with this monster hive, or the next – I need to know, very clearly, how many of you are in my team. My team. I'm going to do what I think is right, with or without the UN. With or without you. Not because I want to fix the world, but just because I'm here and I'm mad as hell. I know Jai is with me. He doesn't have a choice. Who else?"

"I am," says Anima, smiling for the first time in days.

"Me too," says Jason.

"We're all on the same team, Uzma," says Wingman.

Wu blinks in an encouraging sort of way, her mind clearly elsewhere.

"I'll take that as a yes all around," says Uzma. "I don't like using my Voice on any of you. Now we're going to go and have a chat with this literature professor and see what he has to say for himself. Any questions?"

There are no questions. The loudest sound that can be heard is the ominous buzzing of a swarm of bee-men flying out of the crack in the ground, ready for battle.

The Unit goes to work.

They storm their way through the bee-monster attack, Anima, Jason and Wu doing most of the damage. Jai stands at Uzma's side, chopping down any attacker with silent, deadly precision. They enter the gregor hive and make their way deep underground. Wingman carries Uzma.

Danger waits at every turn: centipede-men, bright and deadly wasp creatures, strange and slimy larval beings that fit no known description. But there is no room for doubt now, and the Unit acquits itself magnificently. Jason's protective cloud of whirling shields is now made entirely out of insect body parts. Anima shows no fatigue whatsoever, her laugh growing more cheerful with each burst of glowing green energy, the patterns on her flying daggers turning more intricate as her dying enemies' bodies build bridges across gaps in the hive for her teammates. Wu floats above them, a strange hum emanating from deep within her body, her eyes wide open and unseeing. The shadow-spirit that rides her now is slow and delights in death; Wu curls her fingers, and attacking insect-men choke and fall dead, a macabre puppet-show like no other.

The gregors have found an old city that lies buried deep under the foundations of Prague, and turned it into their hive. Ancient statues poke their heads out of tapestries of wax and slime, there are rows of broken pillars, walls that show their aged bones in between earthen mounts and nests full of cracked eggs and moulted gregor skins. Cocoons dot forgotten arches like stalactites. But the Unit has no time to solve the mysteries of this buried city: they are only here to hunt, and kill.

After what seems like hours, they find Roman Novak. He sits, a monstrous cockroach-wasp-termite creature, bloated and grotesque, covered in filth, in what must have been a throne-room in some forgotten age. The once magnificent hall is lined with warrior termite creatures, lined up and ready for battle. But they stand no chance against the invaders. There is one tricky moment when a termite-man lunges straight at Uzma, but Jai is faster; he catches the beast's pincers in his hands and rips it apart in one smooth motion.

In a few minutes, Roman is the only insect-man left alive. He makes no attempt to attack, it is not clear if he even knows they are there. His insect face has grown out of the middle of his human one; his human eyes and ears hang in useless bits of skin at the base of his antennae.

"Tell us how this happened," Uzma Tells him. "Tell us what Utopic did to you."

Roman's body flops to one side, and dozens of little feet emerge from under a wing. They wiggle uselessly, too weak to take his bulk anywhere.

Uzma asks him more questions, but the gregor has no answers. Finally, Anima cannot take it any more, she leaps into the air with a shriek, a katana of light blossoming from her hands, and cuts off the beast's head with a single stroke.

The heroes stand, heads bowed, in a room full of corpses. On the ceiling, a few white grubs enter the hall and skitter about.

"I thought when you killed the boss monster the other ones would die," says Jason. "What should we do, Uzma?

Clear out the hive? There must be thousands left."

"I used to watch my brothers playing video games a lot, when I was a kid," says Uzma. "This was just like that. Except the bloody smell. I don't feel anything. Do any of you feel anything?"

"I feel dirty," says Anima. "Not, like, spiritually. Just covered in shit. Can we go home?"

"We're going home," says Uzma. "Wu, can you do some kind of spirit blast thing and take out all the eggs?"

"No," says Wu.

"I suppose someone else will," says Uzma. "Right. Everybody out."

The interior of the hoverjet is a mess by the time they're all seated. Ellis sits at the rear, communicating in urgent, angry whispers with his superiors at the UN. The Unit's heroes skip the traditional post-fight camaraderie, but their ordeal is not over yet. From a seat in the hoverjet that Uzma could have sworn was empty a minute ago, That Guy breaks into enthusiastic applause.

"This was one of our best cases, people," he says. "One for the history books! Ellis, could you get a picture?"

Ellis does not get a picture. But some time later, when the hoverjet has entered German airspace, he holds the phone out towards Uzma.

"I really don't want to talk to your bosses right now," Uzma says. "Later, Ellis. Later."

"It's not the UN," says Ellis. "Wait, I'll transfer to holo-screen."

Tia's face appears on a floating window in the hoverjet.

"What do you want?" snaps Uzma.

"Hi," says Tia. "You look good."

"I thought you didn't want to talk to any of us again."

"I didn't have anything to say then. But I've got some information for you now," says Tia.

"I really don't want to do this, Tia," says Uzma. "If Aman is alive, and wants to talk to me, tell him to get in touch directly. But not now."

Tia looks at her warily. "You know that Rowena girl you're looking for? The power remover?"

Uzma is puzzled, but feels a wild excitement growing within her. If Tia knows about the Unit's top-secret search for Rowena, it can only mean…

"Say yes quickly, love," says Tia. "This call isn't cheap."

"Maybe," says Uzma. "What about her?"

"I'll tell you who has her, if you promise to give me first crack at him when you find him," says Tia.

"Done," Uzma says, lying blithely. "Who is it?"

"A young Japanese billionaire," says Tia. "Human. His name is Norio Hisatomi."

# CHAPTER SIX

"You know what your problem is?" Aman asks Norio.

"Yes," says Norio.

"No, you don't."

Norio's back is turned, and there's a styrofoam cup of tea in his right hand. Aman looks around the hall they're in, searching for an escape route, weighing his options. A quick dash could get him to the door, but he's still drowsy from the drugs, and doesn't know if he can make it, or if there is security outside the door. So he shifts his weight and tries in vain, again, to go online.

Aman has no idea where in the world he is, or what time of day it is. They're in an empty hall, with lots of closed windows. An office? An empty house? There's no furniture apart from a few revolving chairs. They look unused; one is covered in plastic.

"Well?" says Norio.

"What?"

"What's my problem?"

"You've read too many superhero comics. Seen too many films. You were the wrong age when they went mainstream. In fiction, and then in real life," says Aman. "I recognise the signs. Fellow victim."

Norio listens to Aman's words echoing through the empty hall. He turns, smiling.

"And why is that a problem?" he asks.

"Well, it just means that once you become a super, you start acting like your favourites. Sometimes people don't even know they're doing it," says Aman. "I mean, I had a suit of armour once. Gadgets everywhere. It seemed like I only had it for a few minutes, but it was a few months before Tia could get me to stop pretending to be Robert Downey Jr. And you clearly—"

"Interesting," says Norio. "Incorrect as well. I'm not superhuman."

"By choice. You could have afforded the airtime. Like the other Utopic directors."

"Are you stalling for time while you try to get online?" Norio asks, sipping his tea.

"No," says Aman. "You've got some kind of blocker in place, don't you?" His gaze darts around the hall, looking for a weapon, looking for the source of the interference. He finds nothing.

Norio shrugs. "I thought we should conduct our business without the police dropping in," he says. "Or Tia."

"You shot Tia."

"She has other bodies."

"Those are other people. When you kill a Tia, she dies."

"It was necessary. I had to eliminate her, and I knew it

wasn't murder." Norio's tone is casual, but Aman can sense his tension. He decides to push it.

"It actually was. You murdered three people, and you crossed the line," says Aman. "Whatever your plan is, if you see yourself as some kind of hero at this point, you should stop."

"It's really pretty when she dies," says Norio. "That swirl of dust—"

Aman lunges at him.

Norio blocks his inexpert jab, deflects his second wild lunge, and sends Aman reeling with an open palm to his face. Aman lands flat on the grey carpet, more humiliated than physically hurt. He tastes blood, and smells strange chemicals he cannot identify on the carpet.

Norio takes another contemplative sip of tea.

"Did you have any actual point, or were you merely preparing for this lethal attack?" asks Norio as Aman clambers to his feet.

Aman rubs the back of his head. "I had to try."

"You were magnificent."

"What was I talking about?"

"My problem is that I've seen too many superhero stories."

"Yes. And you started thinking you were some kind of real-world Batman. I mean, that's how I got you."

"And that worked out well for you, didn't it?" There's a flash of real menace in Norio's eyes as he steps towards Aman, and Aman involuntarily takes a step back.

"Well, I was wrong about you. I thought *I'd* found *you*, but you were baiting me all along, weren't you?" says Aman. "And it took me a few minutes to figure out you're no Batman. In fact, when you were doing your whole bipolar thing at my island base, I thought you were channelling Heath Ledger. But you're not crazy. You're acting. You're trying to be both Batman and the Joker here. Pick a side."

Norio stares at him in silence for a few seconds before speaking.

"How do you manage this distance from the world?" he asks finally.

"I found the right island."

"You manage to just watch everything, don't you? From a great distance away. It's all like some story happening to someone else. Nothing's real. You're not really here, even now."

"I'm online a lot," says Aman weakly, but he doesn't know how to respond. In any case, Norio isn't really listening. He gestures for Aman to sit. Aman picks the most sturdy-looking chair. It creaks and tilts.

"Where are we?" asks Aman.

"It doesn't matter," says Norio.

"All right. Why are we here?"

"Why do you think?"

"Let's see," says Aman. "You don't want me dead. You don't need me as a hostage, since the whole world thinks I'm dead. You need to use my powers."

"Elementary," says Norio.

"Give me time. Now what could you possibly want? There isn't a revenge angle as far as I'm concerned. I've never met you, or taken money from your family. As far as I know."

"No, you haven't. I've always been a sincere admirer of your methods. And actions."

"Thank you. You might just be a crazy powerist looking for supers to kill, but I don't see why you would go to so much trouble to find me when you haven't even dealt with your principal rival, the Kaiju King. Or when your original nemesis is doing so well. Jai caused your father's death. Almost killed me too, the last time we met. So you'd think we'd have something in common. That's what I thought, at least, which is why I wanted to work with you."

"This is most disappointing," says Norio. "I don't know why, but I expected you to be really intelligent. But that's not your power, clearly."

"No, it isn't," says Aman. "But I work things out eventually. You've brought me here, to what has to be the world's least impressive villain lair—"

"Sorry about that."

"Yes, seriously, you should be. Where are the minions? The aquariums? The doomsday devices?"

"I actually have a few doomsday devices. Thanks to Sundar."

"Where is Sundar?"

"Elsewhere."

"Well, it's insulting, is all I can say. At least when I kidnapped you, you got a nuclear-class submarine. And you would have had a crazy beautiful underwater base after that. And a really friendly interrogator. Also, why is there no security? Where are the underlings in uniform?"

"I don't mean to insult you. But you are no threat. Why would I need guards? My hospitality, though, yes, I should be keeping you in more discomfort. But I work with humans, not supers, so these things take time."

"It's all right. Where were we?"

"You were telling me what my master plan is."

"Yes. So you brought me here because you want to use my

powers. But you're blocking my powers, which gives me a hell of a headache, by the way. You're not even doing a decent monologue telling me what you want. So you've essentially brought me here because you want to put me in a Utopic zoo. Run tests on me, bottle my powers, whatever it is that you people do."

"Wrong answer," says Norio with a shrug.

"Well, then, I don't know, Norio," says Aman. "Why don't you tell me?"

"You got one bit right, though," says Norio. "I do want to kill Jai Mathur. Honour demands it."

"Then you should have asked nicely," says Aman. "And I would have told you I don't know how."

"And I wouldn't have believed you," says Norio. "If anyone knows, you do. And I'm going to find out."

"Are you planning to torture me?" asks Aman. "Because you can skip that. I have a very low pain threshold."

Norio laughs. "No," he says. "Aman, I would have enjoyed being your ally, and putting my hopes and dreams in your hands, but I am afraid I do not have time for that. I am neither a murderer nor some sort of crazed villain, and you should know I regret deeply what I am about to do to you."

Aman sighs. "Tia will find me, you know. She'll save me. Or she'll avenge me."

"She won't need to," says Norio. "When I'm done, I'll let you go."

"You won't," says Aman. "We both know that."

"Well, we shall see. Now can I trust you to sit here quietly for a while? I need to bring some equipment from another room. It'll take a few minutes."

"Sure, go ahead," says Aman.

Norio turns and walks out of the door.

Aman gives it two minutes, and then sprints after him.

The door leads to a landing, there are flights of stairs in both directions, and an elevator. Outside, it's daylight. Aman can see tall buildings. A billboard, with large Japanese letters. A pigeon sitting on it. And Azusa, who's standing by the elevator dressed in a sharp blazer, a resigned look on her face as she walks towards him.

When Aman regains consciousness, he's back in the hall, and back in his chair. This time, his hands are tied behind his back; the knots aren't tight, but they are firm. Azusa stands beside him, idly toying with a long and slender samurai sword.

"Thanks," says Aman. It comes out squeakier than he intended.

Azusa nods.

The door opens, Norio enters, pushing a large trolley on which sits what looks like a computer from a museum. Wires trail behind it, occasionally tangling up with the trolley's wheels. On top of the bulky monitor sits a tin-foil helmet with two wires attached to a chunky cluster of chips on top of it.

"Almost done," says Norio. "I'll just have to set this up. There's an extension cord somewhere. Azusa, entertain him. Tell him some jokes or something."

Azusa subjects Norio to a piercing gaze, and then turns and stares at Aman, who flinches.

Norio swiftly plugs in the extension cord and switches on the computer. It takes ages to start up, with a series of moans and dying-fridge noises. When it finally starts running, the foil helmet lights up, and Norio picks it up and puts it on Aman's head. He walks back to the trolley and stands in front of the large, unwieldy keyboard.

"All set," he says.

"And what new low-budget delight is this?" asks Aman.

"This is a mind control machine," says Norio. "I type in commands, and you execute them."

"That's ridiculous," says Aman.

"Yes, it is," says Norio. "But all of Sundar's inventions are. How long did you and he work together? A few months? I've had him for several years. And your friend is industrious to a point that puts us Japanese to shame."

"Let him go," says Aman. "You know who wanted to use Sundar exactly the same way? Jai."

"Sundar isn't a prisoner. He's the head of my zaibatsu's R and D department," says Norio. "I've given him a life of luxury, a fat salary, and all the toys he needs to be the very best mad inventor he can be. He's happier now than he's ever been before."

"I need to see him," says Aman.

Norio smiles. "No, you don't," he says. "Now, sit very still."

Aman sits in his broken office chair, a tin-foil helmet on his head, feeling like a complete idiot, as Norio types into the keyboard. And then Norio looks up, smiles and hits a key. The helmet shakes and crackles, and Aman smells his hair burning.

Norio watches as Aman's face contorts, and he struggles in vain to free his hands and lift the helmet from his head. Aman struggles in the chair for a few seconds, and then slumps forward, drooling, his eyes rolling upwards.

At a signal from Norio, Azusa extracts a small device from her pocket, and switches it off.

"He can go online now?" Norio asks.

Azusa nods. "How long will it be before he regains control?" she asks. "Should I strike him when he does?"

"Well, it lasts for about ten minutes on normal people," says Norio. "So let's say about two minutes for him, and then just turn the blocker on again. There's no need for violence."

Azusa gives him a very odd look indeed as he starts typing, fast, the sound of his keystrokes incredibly loud. Sundar's machine hums even louder, and a thin trickle of blood flows out of Aman's nose.

Norio feels Azusa's gaze burning twin holes on his forehead.

"What is it?" he snaps. "What do you want to say?"

"It is not my place, sir," says Azusa.

"Just tell me," says Norio. "Our – relationship has never been about master and servant. You know this. You've always known."

Azusa shakes her head. "There are too many questions."

"You want to know what I'm making him do."

"I want to know everything," says Azusa.

Norio glances at her and clears his throat. She's never seen him so nervous.

"Before we can end the superhero plague, I have to know exactly who they are and what they can do," says Norio, his eyes fixed on the monochrome monitor in front of him. "Aman is sending us a list. Everything he knows about every superhero in the world. Powers, weaknesses. Where they are. Teams, free agents, Utopic prisoners, fugitives. How to find them, and how to kill them."

Azusa makes sure her face is perfectly composed before speaking again. She looks away from Aman, whose nose and ears are bleeding heavily now, his moans of pain almost inaudible below the drone of Norio's computer.

"You want to kill all supers?" she asks. "Is that not... excessive?"

"I don't want to kill them *all*," says Norio. "But the world is slipping away from humanity. Out of balance, out of time. I have to find a way to stop this."

Azusa draws a handkerchief out of her pocket and mops up Aman's face.

"Why not just find out where Jai Mathur is, and send a nuclear missile there?" she asks. "No one has tried that before. You will have your revenge. Your honour will be satisfied."

"Because I need to look Jai in the eye when I destroy him. But that is a personal matter. Jai is not the real problem," says Norio. "This war we have entered will not stop until the world is in balance again. This plague – and I call it a plague because it is unnatural, and wrong – must be ended. Killing Jai is just one step. Jai is just one man. There are others like him."

"You think of it as a disease," says Azusa. "But the world thinks of it as evolution. The powered think of it as something that happened by chance, or because they were chosen, by karma or kami. Many with powers never asked for them. They do not deserve to die."

"And I never said I would kill them. But no, this is not evolution, Azusa."

"Why not? A new species of human is here. The birth of any new era has been heralded by bloodshed and violence. But supers have helped the world too. It's a leap into the future.

And yes, the unknown always inspires fear. But you were never one to look back, Norio. You were always the one who believed in better worlds."

"It's not a better world. It's a world where humans have given up. The new super-race does all the real work, and earns all the glory. And humans watch, and stagnate, and die."

"That is not true. The supers are reshaping the world, and humans are richer for it. You are richer for it. Think of the ways Sundar's inventions have helped the Hisatomi zaibatsu alone. Think of the gene-sequencing programme. In a few years you'll be selling augmented limbs and making humans who run like cheetahs and can breathe underwater. You're making bioprinters. Fountains of youth. Cyborgs. Drinking water teabags. You're splicing genes. Birthing new insects. Space elevators. The supers aren't just an improvement themselves, Norio, they're helping us grow as well. If this isn't evolution, what is?"

"If it were evolution, if it were natural, the children of supers would be supers too. This is something else. Something artificial. A contamination. A problem we must fix."

"Why us?"

"Because no one else can."

"I do not agree," says Azusa. "You are giving up your life – and your ancestors' work – to follow this quest, and already it has changed you too much. I do not know you any more."

"Those are strong words," Norio snaps. "You know me, Azusa. No one else knows me better. I've trusted you all my life. Is it too much to ask that you trust me in return?"

Azusa walks up to Norio, and looks deep into his eyes. He looks back, unwavering, solemn.

"I do trust you," she says. "But I don't know if you're right."

"When I am done, the world will be better," he says. "The journey will be rough, and I will need you. I will give you many reasons to doubt me. But can you also believe in me?"

"I think so," she says.

He moves forward, grasping her shoulders, and leans in to kiss her, but she shivers involuntarily, and he lets her go, almost pushing her away.

Azusa stands silent, head bowed.

"What's wrong?" he whispers. "I am still Norio. I haven't changed."

His eyes follow hers as she looks at Aman, now bleeding freely again, shuddering in his tin-foil helmet, his body bent awkwardly, like a discarded puppet.

"Do you love me, Azusa?" Norio asks.

She says nothing.

Norio types in a sentence and looks up at her. "Do you wish to leave my employment?" he asks.

"No," says Azusa.

"Then restore the signal block. He's coming round."

"Yes, sir."


Norio glares at Azusa's back as she strides away. He types in another command, and the machine's humming grows softer as it powers down. He lifts the helmet from Aman's head, and Aman blinks and groans.

Norio looks into his eyes as he wakes.

"Are you done?" Aman asks.

"No," says Norio. "But now, thanks to you, I can finally get started."

# CHAPTER **SEVEN**

A broad, dusty, cratered highway runs through the desolation of Gurgaon, in what used to be north India. Either side of the highway lie clusters of burnt, broken buildings; gigantic hoardings advertising everything from holo-projectors to experimental jetpacks glitter and swivel, displaying their wares to wandering packs of feral mongrels. The afternoon sun is dazzlingly bright; occasional gusts of wind blow swirling patterns of dust across the sky.

In the silence, the sound of an approaching van is deafening, but the lone figure trudging down the side of the highway towards Delhi shows no signs of having heard it. It's a woman, short and shapely, dressed in a kurta, protected from the sun and wind by a dupatta draped over her head and shoulders.

The van is white, and full of lean, hungry boys. They look like teenagers, and the guns in their hands and the rattling van they're huddled inside, look considerably older. Through tinny speakers in the back, a wailing turn-of-the-century British-

Punjabi rap song competes with the noise of the van's engine.

They spot the woman from far away, and their faces light up; pickings for the rape gangs of Gurgaon have been slim, since the mass exodus of five years ago. They scream obscenities at her: ripe fruit ready for plucking is the politest comparison they make.

Tia walks on, ignoring them as they slow down behind her and cruise for a few minutes. It's only when one of the boys in the rear seat slides open the van door that she reacts at all.

Five minutes later, it is over, and the rape gang is but another bad memory. Tias drag the bodies back into the van. Already, a flock of crows has assembled in the sky above them. She'd tried to scare them away, to reason with the last few, but she didn't know if they had even understood her Hindi. Some of them looked like Afghans; they could have been from any of the war-torn fiefdoms that now ran from western Afghanistan to central India.

Tia pushes one of the bodies into the driver's seat, merges back into a single body, puts the dead driver's foot on the accelerator and starts the vehicle. The van drives off the highway, runs into an abandoned petrol pump and crashes into a vending machine. Tia walks away, imagining herself in slow motion, waiting for a huge explosion behind her. But there is none, the pump has been abandoned for years.

She walks for two hours, pausing occasionally to take a swig from the NutriPac in her bag. She passes broken housing colonies, burnt malls, cracked flyovers. The ruins of Gurgaon do not impress her, she's seen worse. She does, however, take pictures in passing of the craters left by Indian Army artillery; she has a separate photostream for craters and cacti.

It's almost sunset when her search finally ends. She walks by the old, abandoned international airport, remembering a day that seems so long ago now, a flight that had seemed noteworthy only because she'd thought her love life had reached rock bottom, that it was time to begin again. She laughs out loud.

Her laughter dies when she sees the SUVs pulling out of the airport's parking lot. It's another gang, but one of the richer ones: the cars are newer, the wheels equipped with cutters, there's a rocket launcher on the roof. This is no casual rape-gang; these cars have seen battle. Tia replicates herself quickly; two Tias run into the airport, pulling out their slender pistols. Another takes cover behind a pillar. One Tia, resigned to a gruesome death, turns and runs down the middle of the road. She hears the inevitable war-whoops. The SUVs swerve towards her.

And then comes the sound she's been waiting for: a tiger's roar, played over tinny speakers, not too far away. She hears the thunder of motorbike engines behind her. She turns.

Five ancient Bullet bikes, painted orange and black. One driver, one rifle-toting pillion rider each. Behind them, three hybrid auto-rickshaws, fronts loaded with pointed bars and barbed wire. They move fast, streaming dust behind them. The SUVs, now just a few seconds away from Tia, swerve, screeching, leaving burn marks on the tarmac, and power off into the distance. Tia keeps a close eye on them, wary of a stray rocket, but escape from Sher's warriors is clearly the only thing on the gang's mind.

The warriors break formation as they reach her. She sees the striped tattoos across their faces and arms and sighs in relief.

"Why are you here?" their leader demands.

"Just taking a walk," says Tia.

"You shouldn't be here," he says. "It's not safe."

"A girl should be able to go for a walk when she feels like," says Tia. "Do you know what year this is?"

"It's asking for trouble."

"If I hear any variation of the asking for it line," says Tia, stepping towards him, "you and I are going to have a problem."

"I didn't mean because you're a woman," says the leader, stammering a little. "I meant because you're a human."

"Good," says Tia.

"We just saved your life, sister. Aren't you going to thank us?"

"You made me wait for hours before showing up. Presumably because it takes you that long to put on your makeup. So no," says Tia. "And I don't need saving. Now take me to Sher."

The leader refuses to do anything of the sort, but then an elderly Sher acolyte sticks his head out of one of the autos and tells the offended biker this strange woman has visited their lands before. He pushes the tiger-tattooed AK-47-toting teenager in the auto's rear seat out, and offers Tia his place with something approaching gallantry.

The auto's seat is upholstered with, predictably, tiger-skin patterned leather. As Sher's boys restart their engines and roar off, back towards Gurgaon, Tia leans back and watches the dead city flash by.

The last time she'd come to the urban warzone was just after Sher quit the Unit, and disappeared from the world. They'd thought he'd gone off to find himself, like Vir, but Sher's quest hadn't been anything so high-minded: all the women in his village in Haryana had been killed or carried off in a caste war, and the one thing Sher wanted was blood. No one knew the whole tale of Sher's rampage through the wild lands of north India, or how he'd built his army after that, but Sher's name quickly became legend, a whisper of dread that ran from Varanasi to Kabul. More than the armies that tried to redraw their countries' borders, more than the warlords that ruled the new provinces, more than the supers who'd tried to build their own territories in the beautiful ruins of Kashmir and had failed, one by one, the rumour of Sher's approach sent men scurrying back to their bunkers, and let women walk the streets without fear.

Tia's auto is assigned two bikers for security, despite Tia's protests. The rest of Sher's squadron returns to its patrol. Their sworn enemies are the rape gangs, the local warlords are safe as long as they leave the villages alone, and pay Sher their tribute. They play their roar proudly as they charge through a broken highway toll booth. Tia watches them leave, and wishes them well.

By the time Tia's convoy reaches the entrance of Sher's present headquarters, the sun has already set. Gurgaon in the evening is neon-lit and deadly; smugglers, arms dealers, and shady characters from all over the world lurk in garish bars, ogling rich kids who have bribed their way out of Delhi's walled cities to see exotic dancers from Central Asia gyrate to remixed qawwalis. Tia had met Sher in a delightfully sleazy pleasure palace the last time, but clearly the tiger-man has grown more ascetic in his tastes.

The MegaMall was built a few months before the war that broke Pakistan and took a huge bite out of India's north-west in 2014. Uzma had ended the war after a week with a stern closed-door summit meeting, but no one could have healed the damage of that week easily, and sticking around to watch nations heal wasn't the Unit's style.

The MegaMall had been, for a brief and glorious period, a towering temple to high-end retail that rivalled the best in Dubai, but a Pakistani plane piloted by a rogue supervillain had changed all that. The F-16, one of the last of its kind, is still embedded wing-deep in the mall's eastern side, a dagger in the heart of the region's aspirations. The deluxe farmer's market in front of the mall now crawls with tattooed militia, and a wide range of modified combat vehicles stand in front of the grand entrance, ready to roll out at a moment's notice. Tia whistles appreciatively as she spots a line of tanks and artillery vehicles, bright orange and black, glittering in the mall's neon lights, reflecting large signs offering cheap pizzas and expensive massages. Sher's soldiers stand outside, waiting for their orders. Among them are women in sleeveless vests, proudly displaying tiger-tattooed arms with bangles on them. They wave at Tia as she drives by.

Tia notes with some amusement that the mall entrance's metal detectors are still in place. Utopic logos on them, even here, even now. Sher's soldiers take her bag, and march her inside. Some of the shops are just empty rooms full of rubble, shattered glass and mannequin limbs; others have been turned into offices and living quarters. Tia is taken to the grand movie theatre that occupies several floors on the west side of the building. She walks through corridors full of tattered movie posters.

Sher meets her in the lobby. He's in tiger-man form – legend has it that he has sworn not to wear his human face again. He's using human hands, though, to dig deep into a large carton of popcorn. As Tia enters, he tosses his snack to an aide and lumbers towards her.

"What are you doing here?" Sher rumbles.

"It's good to see you too," says Tia. "We need to talk."

Sher walks up close to her. He's even larger than she remembered, but there's something about him that seems slower, older – did he age in tiger years? Tia remembers the first time she met him, in Aman's old Versova house, standing in the living room behind Jai, radiating danger. There had been so much going on then that she'd forgotten to be scared. There's no question of being scared now. She leaps forward and hugs him, flinching a little from the tiger-man's rank odour.

Sher growls from his stomach, and steps back.

"Wait outside," he commands, and his troops file out of the lobby, trying not to grin.

When they're all gone, Sher looks sternly – not that he ever looks anything but stern – at Tia.

"Don't do that in front of my soldiers again," he says. "I'm trying to run an army."

"I'm sorry, love," says Tia. "I suppose they won't find you intimidating any more? How nice it would be if you had a tiger's head or something."

Sher emits something between a bark and growl; Tia has made him laugh before.

"I have an ammunition raid to plan, three captured rapists to kill and an ISI spy who wants to bribe me," he says. "So tell me what you need."

"I need to see Kalki," says Tia.

Sher's whiskers twitch. "So why come to me?"

Tia shrugs. "I don't know," she says. "I thought I'd try you, since you've been hiding him for years now."

"No," says Sher. "You can stay here if you like. I must leave you now."

He turns, and strides towards the exit.

"You owe me," says Tia, and Sher spins around and roars, a deafening sound that shakes the whole lobby. Tia flinches and replicates herself nervously.

"I owe you?" Sher demands. "For what? For standing by all these years while I tried to save our country *alone*, when you could have been the army I needed? Do you know how many lives we could have saved?"

Tia composes herself, and blends into one.

"I really don't have time for this, Sher," she says. "Aman's been captured, and the world's supposed to end in a couple of weeks. I don't know what to do. I'm tired of sparring."

Sher stands, breathing deeply, staring at her.

"Why did you say I owed you?" he asks finally.

"Who cares? It doesn't matter. Just help me now."

"What can I do?"

"Kalki. I need to see him."

"Even if I could take you to him, what do you need from him?"

"Well, Kalki grants wishes, right? That's what I've heard," says Tia. "I need to save the world. Or at least find out how."

Sher shakes his head. "You know I never lie, Tia," he says. "So this is how it is. You cannot see him."

"Why?" Tia's eyes sparkle. "What do you want from me, Sher? You want me to cry? Beg? Break down? I don't have time. I need this."

Sher tilts his head to one side. "And you would do anything, wouldn't you. You'd fight me, even."

Tia grins. "Oh, fight you? Of course I'd fight you. We both know I'd win. But why are we even talking about this?"

Sher paces about the room, his tail twitching slowly.

"The reason you cannot see him," he says after a while, "is that it is too dangerous."

"Why?"

"What Kalki does is more than grant wishes," says Sher. "He changes words into truths."

Tia frowns. "He changes reality?"

"Yes," says Sher. "And because of the way he was born, and the way his powers have been growing, I do not know what he is capable of."

"And that's why you don't want me to see him," says Tia. "Because you don't know what I would ask for."

"You will have to ask through me," says Sher. "That is not the problem."

"What is?"

"I cannot afford to trust anyone," says Sher. "And there are too many people trying to kill him."

"You can trust me," says Tia.

Sher snorts. "What if you are the one Tia who chose to work for Utopic?" he asks. "My answer is no."

He looks up, to see seven Tias in a row.

"Then we have a problem," says one.

Sher pops his claws and studies them lazily.

"Have I ever killed you?" he asks.

Tia looks offended. "You don't know?"

"The faces blur after a while," says Sher. "Just go away, Tia. This hunt would bring me no joy."

"Actually, I wasn't even threatening you," says a Tia. "I was offering you an army."

Sher bares his fangs, and they glitter in the light of a neon cola advertisement to his right.

"Well if you grant my wishes, I suppose it is only fair I grant yours," he says. "I will take you to him."

"Does this involve blindfolds and helicopters?" asks Tia.

"No," says Sher. "We can use the escalator. He's upstairs."

The problem with Kalki, Sher explains as they leave the lobby, is that he still can't speak any human language, or write. Over the last eleven years, all of his foster parents have tried to get him to talk, or learn any kind of sign language, but they've failed entirely. Even now, Sher does not know whether Kalki reads minds, or just blunders his way through the world on instinct. Despite his godlike powers, Kalki was dealt a horse's language skills with his horse's head.

"But *you* can speak," says Tia. "Animal head or whatever."

"Yes, but I knew how to before I turned into this," says Sher. "And it was difficult. I had to learn everything again."

"But he must understand what people tell him," says Tia. "How would he grant wishes otherwise?"

"I don't really know what he does," says Sher. "Sometimes people find their way here, and he gives them what they want."

"How do they find him?"

"It is a mystery to me. Dreams."

"What has he given you?"

"Nothing. I won't ask for new realities. I will change the one I'm in."

Tia pats Sher's shoulder. They stand outside a large pair of doors. Sher is about to swing the doors open when he stops and turns to Tia again.

"What will you wish for, Tia? You need to be very sure. I don't know whether he understands my words, or whether he reads the asker's mind."

"Well, can't you figure that out from what happens when he grants his wishes?"

"No."

"Why not?"

"Because Kalki does what he wants. And he doesn't always give people what they ask for."

Tia's eyes narrow. "What do you mean?"

Sher shrugs. "I think he really is a god, Tia. And we're not supposed to understand gods. Kalki gives people what he feels like giving them. Not what they want. But perhaps what they need."

"Example."

"A few weeks ago there was a businessman who had walked all the way from Gujarat to meet him. Barefoot. Led by dreams. A super. Could spout cash from his hands."

"What did he ask for?"

"He wanted a son. I didn't want to ask Kalki, but there was something magical going on – there was no logical way this man could have found us, or survived his walk. So I asked Kalki to give this man a son."

"And what happened?"

"Kalki took his power away."

"Why?"

"I don't know." Sher looks Tia in the eye. "So. Are you sure you want to do this?"

Tia scratches her head. "Ask a crazy pre-pubescent god for a boon?" she asks finally. "Yes. Yes, let's do this."

Sher swings the door open, and Tia is immediately assailed by a strong cocktail of smells and sounds. At least four different songs are playing, and the air is filled with marijuana-flavoured smoke, but Tia doesn't notice any of this: her ears and nose are in the queue, waiting for her eyes to recover.

It's a small film theatre with a large screen, an exclusive viewing hall for rich patrons. A playlist of Bollywood trailers is playing on mute on the screen. It's been sped up, and Tia sees one of Wingman's summer blockbusters flash by. Most of the seats have been stretched back all the way, like a bumpy red velvet carpet. The occupants of the seats are mostly stranger than the images speeding by on the screen in front of them: Tia spots a young boy doing chemistry homework, a couple of Chinese gamers with little holo-screens, a full-bearded Hindu ascetic meditating on top of a wrestler doing push-ups, and a maglev-emo band that seems very close, given how entwined they all are. Assorted limbs can be seen moving rhythmically over the seats at the rear, and a group of women in what appear to be football uniforms lie in a huddle near the entrance. What really gets to Tia, though, is something that she cannot quite define: a strange, cloying, grasping feeling, as if some presence had its fingers in her brain and was prodding around – and not too gently.

"I thought this was supposed to be a top-secret hideaway?" Tia whispers.

"They find us," says Sher. "We lose them. We keep moving."

Kalki sits on a tall red velvet chair, the only one with the seat up, in the centre of the theatre. His body is an eleven-year-old boy's, normal except for the fact that it's blue and he has four arms, all of which hold bright red glasses. Four straws channel streams of cola into Kalki's mouth. When Kalki was a baby, his horse's head had seemed too big for his body; it had lolled grotesquely, and he'd been incapable of controlling it. Now it's up, and he moves it from side to side, watching Tia and Sher as they enter. His eyes are incredibly large, shining black pools, Tia can see the screen reflected in them.

"Do you think he might remember me?" she asks. "Some kind of special deal for old babysitters?"

"Be very careful what you say here," says Sher. "Anything you say or think could change the world."

Kalki throws his cola cups aside, tosses his electric-blue-dyed mane, whinnies enthusiastically and beckons them forward.

"So what do you want, Tia?" asks Sher.

"Is there a three-wish deal?"

"Pick one thing. You don't want him confused."

"Well, I want Aman back, and I want to know what ends the world, and I want to know how to stop it. Do I just go and ask for these things?"

"No, I'll do it," says Sher.

"What if three of me ask him? We could each do one."

"This isn't a game. Come on. He doesn't like to wait."

Kalki greets Sher with a warm nuzzle, sits again, and stares curiously at Tia. Sher bends and talks into his ear, his low growl echoes through the theatre. Midway through Sher's message, Kalki jerks back, snorting, and feebly pounds Sher's chest with all four hands. Sher steps back and beckons Tia forward.

Tia walks up, slowly, barely noticing that all the smoke in the room has now gathered above Kalki's head in an upside-down rotating pyramid.

Kalki waits until Tia is close, and then leaps off his chair onto her. After her initial shock, she holds him easily, though he's heavy for his size. He nuzzles his horse-head into her neck and clasps her firmly. After a few minutes of standing still, Tia puts him down gently. Kalki points at her, shakes his head up and down, and snorts.

"I think he wants you to tell him yourself," says Sher. "There's no real point asking where Aman is – he has no way to really explain. Ask him your other questions."

"How does the world end?" Tia asks.

Kalki stares at her for a few seconds, and then neighs loudly. The room is suddenly silent. The music stops, the screen goes blank. Kalki's devotees fall unconscious with low moans and whispers. The theatre is dark.

And then the smoke above Kalki's head starts to glow, and swirl around. Tia makes out a growing shape, a human shape, but more smoke gathers around its head and shoulders until it is clear the man in the smoke is Kalki himself, a grown-up Kalki, rippling with muscles, his mane rippling and billowing. He holds smoke-swords in all his hands. Three slashes appear in the air behind him, stripes of utter darkness that burst into flame.

"All right," says Tia. "How do we stop this? How do we stop you?"

Kalki giggles, a shockingly human sound. A beam of light from the projector cuts through the smoke, and the screen comes back to life. His devotees awaken, and there's music everywhere. Kalki leans back in his chair and closes his eyes. Some way behind him, someone starts playing bagpipes.

"We should go," says Sher.

Tia is silent all the way back to the lobby. Sher seems pleased by this; he offers her a cup of coffee, and pats her head encouragingly.

"I don't get it," says Tia. "Did he really just say *he* was going to end the world?"

"He might have just been playing with smoke," says Sher. "Come with me now. We have raids to plan."

"How can you be so calm about this?" Tia yells. "What is going on?"

"I try to focus on things I understand," says Sher.

"Has he done this before? Actually claimed he's going to end the world?"

"No."

"Suddenly I see why so many people want him dead," says Tia.

"And for the first time," says Sher quietly, "I do too."

"Are you going to let them kill him?"

"No," says Sher.

# CHAPTER **EIGHT**

Aman is quite used to this routine by now: waking up in a strange room with absolutely no idea what time of day it is or what part of the world he is in. He checks himself, as usual, for body modifications or mind control devices, and is relieved to find none. He tries to go online, and isn't surprised when he can't. He looks for the camera, and finds it on the ceiling fan. He waves, cheerily, and gives it the finger, in case his captors aren't sure how he feels about his stay. What concerns him most are the physical symptoms he's beginning to display from his internet withdrawal: twitching fingers, compulsive blinking, dry mouth. Of course, it could be the drugs, but Aman remembers feeling the same way during the long power cuts in his Delhi home many years ago, when his broadband connection was new and shiny, and realises he's the world's worst internet addict.

Norio enters the room a few minutes later, full of good cheer.

"Good morning, good morning," says Norio. "You

couldn't have woken at a more convenient time. We're about to run the test."

"Some kind of sanity test, and if you fail you'll hand yourself in?" asks Aman.

"No. And speaking of handing myself in, you'll be glad to know Tia has the Unit looking for me. She must have given up on finding you alive."

Aman stirs. "I should worry a bit more about the Unit finding me if I were you. Especially given the history of your family's health."

Norio moves so fast Aman barely has time to flinch. He has plenty of time to roll about on the floor rubbing his jaw afterwards, though.

"Sorry about that," says Norio. "I was sparring with my bot when you woke up. Still a bit wound up."

Aman thinks of a few good lines concerning the Unit, but decides to save them for later. Norio looks as if he wouldn't mind a little more exercise.

"Anyway, you must remind me to thank Tia when we meet," says Norio.

Aman gets up, still rubbing his jaw, idly trying to make Norio's head explode with the power of his mind. Norio does not seem bothered by his silence.

"I suppose she expected I might have to go into hiding," says Norio, "She was quite right. I have been, what's the word? Foiled. All those TV crews parked outside my tower. Very annoying."

"But all part of your cunning plan?"

"No, but it's an interesting new angle. They want to interview me not because of ARMOR, which Tia seems to have forgotten to mention, but because they think I am about to join the Unit. Stand side by side with the glorious Faceless. Hisatomi stocks have been shooting upwards, and I have you and Tia to thank for that."

Aman settles for glowering.

"The thing is, now that I have the world's attention, what should I tell them?" Norio's eyes gleam. "Should I tell them the great Aman Sen is alive, and thousands, maybe millions of people have been wearing the wrong T-shirt all these years? Should I tell them I captured him single-handedly? Weren't you the world's biggest supervillain at some point?"

"Yes, in 2011, but I wrote that list myself."

"You know, I was really looking forward to bringing Tia and you back together. I'm most disappointed she gave up on you so early."

"The Unit doesn't know you have me. They probably don't know I'm alive," says Aman. "This is just a warning shot."

"Well, consider me warned. I feel hunted, Aman. I'm shivering in fear. What should I do now?" Norio flings his hands in the air. "Should I give you to the Unit on live TV? They'd probably make me team leader. Can you imagine what that would do for my company? I could probably control Utopic!"

"But you despise Utopic."

"Well, now you know why I miss most of the meetings," says Norio. "But imagine how well I'd do if I handed you over. You've stolen from all of them. They might want to spent a few centuries finding innovative ways to keep you alive and in pain."

"Once you're done with the really bad acting, you'll tell me you're not going to do any of those things and you'll stick your stupid helmet on me again," says Aman. "You should just get to that, I think. The last time I was kidnapped, at least I didn't have to take part in endless conversations."

"I wish I could use the controller on you again," says Norio. "But that was just a one-time thing. The mind builds its own defences, or collapses; either way, the helmet would be of no use now. No, if I wanted to make you bleed, I'd just put you up for auction on the internet. A lot of people want to get their hands on you, Aman Sen. But, no, I'm a nice guy. And I promised I'd let you go."

"Can we skip to that part, then? I like this threatening monologue, but I have work I need to get back to."

"In a bit, in a bit." Norio rubs his hands together. "But I need to thank you for a few things. First, that list. What a list! So many famous people just hiding their superpowers. If knowledge is power, you've done very little with yours."

"What have you done with Rowena?" asks Aman.

"Yes, that's the other thing I need to thank you for. Rowena! I find the one power I need most on your list, the one power I was willing to risk all my wealth to acquire. And she's already with me, a free prize. I didn't even need to use the controller on her, you know. Rowena works for me now."

"What are you going to do with her?"

"I'm going to give her access to the world's finest research facilities and find exotic patients for her to heal. All the things you couldn't give her, in fact."

"And you're going to remove Jai's powers with her blood and then kill him."

"Yes," says Norio.

"Despite the fact that your father's death was an accident. And that Jai's spent eleven years in slavery doing nothing but good. And that he keeps the world's greatest superhero team safe. And probably suffers more doing it than he would if you killed him."

"Yes," says Norio.

Aman remembers fighting Jai. He remembers running, breathless, through London's tube tunnels, remembers swinging a lamppost through the air, remembers watching Jai falling from the sky, smashing through the street, lying in a crater, and then getting right back up again.

"He'll kill you, you know," he says.

"We'll see."

"All right, then," says Aman. "Are we done?"

"No," says Norio. "Come with me."

Aman hopes the journey to Norio's lab will yield some clue as to their whereabouts, but all his plans for subtle detective work are doomed to disappointment. Norio leads him down a corridor and up a flight of stairs. There's a brief flash on the stairwell when Aman's head clears up, and for one glorious moment he's online again: unfortunately, he's distracted by social media for the second it takes for Norio to realise this and push him forward into another blocked zone.

They enter a large air-conditioned hall. There's a cube of reinforced glass about seven feet across under a blinding spotlight in the centre of the room. Aman blinks at the strength of the light, and then goggles open-mouthed at the ugliness of the creature it illuminates.

The naked man is covered in scales and spines; he looks like a down-on-his-luck deep-sea predator. His huge, translucent eyes and incredibly toothy mouth certainly fit that description. His belly is bloated, and his arms spindly and end in strange blobby fins. His legs, grey and scaly, have fused together into a blob that might serve as the world's ugliest fishtail. He sits, looking around the room, gulping occasionally.

"I went fishing a few days ago," says Norio. "Meet Spiny Norman."

Spiny Norman looks miserable, perhaps because his mouth is curved downwards and has drooping tentacles on either side, or perhaps because he is on display in a glass cube. As Norio and Aman approach, he stares balefully at them and emits copious quantities of green gas from his nether regions.

"Poisonous, of course," says Norio. "He also has big spines hidden under those lovely scales of his, and will stick them into you if you come too close. It's all in your list."

"Whatever it is, it clearly was his deepest desire," says Aman.

"Every wave of supers confirms a suspicion I've had since my teens," says Norio. "People are all mad."

"Yes."

"Why would a man want to be like this? What would drive him to it? What does he want now? Wealth? Power? Fame? Children?"

"I have no idea," says Aman. "If you're asking me to volunteer for some kind of Nazi sex experiment with him, the answer is no."

Norio laughs. "No, I just want you to watch," he says.

Azusa emerges from the shadows behind the cube, carrying a rifle. Aman squints and looks around the hall. In the shadows at the far end is a hulking shape: a ten-foot-high man with a bullet for a head.

"I see you have another friend there," he says. "Who looks a bit like a super to me. You've changed your hiring policies."

"I see you've spotted Awesome Boy," says Norio. "We're in his room."

"Robot?"

"Yes."

"Sundar?"

"Yes."

"Does he do anything besides lurk?"

"Oh, he does a lot," says Norio. "Mostly security work for the less, shall we say, legal, aspects of my business. Fortunately we don't need protection from you."

"I'd like to meet him."

"But we'd have to enable networks to show you. And then you'd hack into his control system, and make a mess. Your plans for escape would be brilliant if they were less transparent. Now. Observe."

Azusa moves a lever and Spiny Norman's glass cube is suddenly full of white smoke. The creature thrashes about a bit, looking even more depressed then usual, and then flops on to the floor and is still, barring the occasional twitch. Azusa pulls another lever, and from the top of the cube sprinklers start raining water on the smoke and Norman. Water collects at the bottom, full of clumps of slime, hair, scales, and other assorted mulch that makes Aman feel vaguely sick.

"Where did you find this handsome fellow?" Aman asks Norio.

"He was on your list. And in the neighbourhood."

"Convenient."

Norio looks at him sharply. "Yes. Too convenient. I'm going to ask you a silly question now."

Aman shrugs. "Whatever it is, I've heard sillier."

"When you become a superhero…"

"Hero?"

"Superbeing. Super. Alpha. Proton. Mutant. Meta. Whatever it is. When you become one, do you receive instructions? Are there superiors who guide you?"

"No," says Aman. "And you're right. That is a silly question."

"So I thought," says Norio. "Not that you'd tell me in any case, of course."

"There's no secret plan," says Aman. "There's no council of guardians. It's just… random. Evolution. Chance. No one knows. We know very little about why, or how, but it's been eleven years, and this is the one thing we know."

"Explain Sundar, then."

"I can't. I can't even explain myself."

"I used to be suspicious of coincidence before I started hanging around supers," says Norio. "But you people are so ridiculous that eventually us humans just get used to it. But Sundar? Out of all the supers in the world, he's the most sinister. Everything he does has a *deus ex machina* smell. Why does he design what he does? Who's pulling his strings, who's issuing his orders?"

"I don't know," says Aman. "Neither does he."

"Yes, but how did he design you a suit of armour the very moment you needed one? This isn't a James Bond film. It points to the existence of a larger observer with a larger plan."

"Sundar spent a few months with me before he disappeared," says Aman. "In that time, he built a few things. I used what I could. There were other things I couldn't use. Are you trying to tell me there isn't a whole heap of random stuff he's made that you can't figure out at all?"

"Do you know why I refuse to get superpowers?"

"Because your father was killed by supers."

"No," says Norio. "It's because I can't shake the feeling that there are larger forces at play. That all of you are rats running around a maze for someone's amusement. And I refuse to be part of that system."

"Fine by me," says Aman. "I really don't want to imagine you with superpowers. You'd probably be like Jai."

"I'd be nothing like Jai."

"Well, in any case, there's no secret plan. No aliens, or gods, or secret societies. This is just something that happened. One day we'll know why and how. We didn't stop being apes and immediately start making documentaries about it. This whole obsessive self-analysis thing is just the last few generations. Our ancestors didn't take selfies. Until someone finally understands the science behind what's going on, it's just a bunch of people trying to live their lives. And it would be much easier without billionaire conspiracy theorists with revenge on their minds."

Norio sighs. "You must have had an interesting time when the First Wave hit you," he says. "But I am afraid we must interrupt this conversation now. Azusa, is it ready?"

Azusa nods, and slides one wall of the cube open. A slight hiss sounds as the air inside the cube enters the room, but Norman does not move. Without any ceremony, Azusa raises her rifle and shoots. A dart pierces Norman's shoulder.

"Before she left for the hospital she now runs, Rowena was kind enough to give us a few samples of her blood," says Norio. "This should be interesting."

They watch in silence as Spiny Norman changes. His bloated body shrivels, his spines retract, his eyes and mouth transform.

His hindquarters wriggle and split, showering the cube with filth, but leaving two distinct legs, pink and quivering. His scales slide off his body, leaving a trail of fine gel. One extended, potent expulsion of gas, and Spiny Norman is a thin, wrinkled, bald man lying in a pool of sludge, unconscious but clearly alive.

Azusa wrinkles her nose and shuts the cube.

"Aman, may I present Normal Norman," says Norio with a smirk. "See how cheerful he looks."

"That's just because his tentacles have fallen off," says Aman. "Tell me, did you ask him if he wanted his powers removed?"

"No. But considering that the reason we found him was that he had been keeping a fishing village up all night with screams of pain, and trying to kill himself by swimming into sharp rocks, I think he's going to thank us when he wakes up."

"You could be wrong."

"I'm right. We have freed him from the superhero curse," says Norio. "When he wakes up, he will look back on his days as a super as if they were a bad dream, and go on with his life. Soon, I will liberate Jai from his powers as well. It might not be what he wants, but I think I will be happy enough for both of us."

Aman says nothing for a while, as he watches Norman in the cube. He seems to be sleeping peacefully now.

"So this is your plan," he says finally. "Kill Jai, and then remove the supers, one by one."

"No," says Norio. "How could that be my plan? I only just found out about Rowena."

"It'll never work, you know," says Aman. "There are just too many supers now. There's no way you could get to all of them at once."

"Yes, that's the whole problem with supers, isn't it? Unique gifts, unique tech, just for that one special person. You know, I haven't been able to mass-produce a single one of Sundar's inventions. I've even ruined a few things trying to reverse engineer them. And yes, I have the same problem with Rowena's blood. I can't synthesise its powers. But I was wondering – do you know anyone who could help me fix this?"

"I do, but you killed three of her," says Aman. "I don't see Tia being very eager to help you out."

"I was actually thinking about you fixing it," says Norio. "You could make Tia do it."

"Get the only person I know who really loves her superpower to help you make all powers go away? Unlikely."

"Not all powers. As you've pointed out several times, there are powers that help the world. I'm a reasonable man, Aman, and my management style is very flexible. The good powers can stay. But there are supervillains and others whose powers need to be taken away. For the greater good."

"And you get to decide which. And you want Tia to deliver your verdicts for you. She'll never do it."

"But perhaps if the life of someone she loves were under threat…"

Aman shrugs. "Good luck," he says. "I'd really like to watch you and Tia have that meeting."

"I see. Well, if that's your attitude, I suppose you won't help me," says Norio.

"No," says Aman. "I'm not as flexible as you."

"Very well. Azusa, did you have anything to ask Aman?"

Azusa does not.

Norio sighs, and stretches. "Well, then, I suppose it is time for me to let you go, as promised," he says. "Thank you for all your help. Maybe one day we'll meet again, on your island. Maybe we'll be friends then. I'd like that."

Aman looks at him, then at Azusa. He stays where he is.

"I can't offer you a lift home, I'm afraid. Do you speak Japanese?" asks Norio. "Do you need money?"

"I'll be fine," says Aman. "Are you... actually letting me go?"

"Don't get emotional now, Aman. It's been good, but we're done."

"I don't believe you."

"You don't know anything about me. One day you'll learn. One day you'll see, and you'll thank me."

"Maybe," says Aman. He glances around the hall nervously, waiting for the punch line, or the punch, but both Norio and Azusa seem completely calm.

"Seriously, get out of here before I change my mind," says Norio. "I've grown quite fond of you, and I'm already beginning to regret my decision. All the chats we could have. I am also excellent at word games."

Aman decides not to push his luck. He walks towards the door, faster with each footstep.

Norio waits until Aman's actually got the door open, and then clears his throat.

"One moment, please," he says with a smile. "I almost forgot. Azusa?"

Azusa raises her rifle and shoots Aman.

Aman stares at the dart on his arm in disbelief. A strange, sluggish coldness flows up his arm.

"I'm afraid I can't let you keep your power," says Norio. "You'd be far too much trouble online."

Aman tries to pull the dart out, but his hands don't move. He wants to run, but his legs don't listen. He crumples up in a ball on the floor, and feels waves of numbness sweep over him.

"Switch off the blocker now," says Norio. "I need to check my email."

Aman watches in quiet fascination as the hall blurs around him, the only sounds he can hear are the slow beat of his own heart and the incredibly loud clatter of Norio's boots as he walks towards him. Norio's got his phone out, and is absorbed in it. Aman senses nothing. The world throbs, fades, and he falls into darkness.

# CHAPTER **NINE**

A giant bear swims through the waters of Tokyo Bay, its muzzle pointing towards the island of Odaiba.

There's nothing warm or fuzzy about this bear, no animation artist in the world could make it cute. It doesn't look as if it wants to dance or wear a T-shirt and look for honey; it could only be used as a mascot for an extremely kinky underground Olympics. Giant mammals have always been, aesthetically speaking, the Kaiju King's weakest creations: he deals best in reptiles, insects and floating human body parts. This bear kaiju is clearly a work in progress rushed out to meet demand. The King hasn't bothered much with the details: its fur is patchy, clumps of black and brown hair over a mountain of pink, veined, exposed leathery skin. Only its head is above the surface of the water, it looks like an extraordinarily ugly island.

Far above the bear, helicopters dot the sky, massive cameras streaming this new kaiju's image across the planet.

The spotlights haven't come on yet, as the sun is still up. The giant bear is unfashionably early.

In Kabukicho, Oni's client huffs and puffs above him. An energetic cartoon theme song plays in the room, but Oni can hear over it, in the room next door, an excited news presenter describing the giant bear.

"It's too soon," he mutters.

"But you told me to hurry!" moans his client, wiping her sweaty brow with a well-manicured palm.

Oni has an excellent view of his own perfect legs. He stares at his demon tattoo, hoping it won't glow, hoping it will. The tattoo stares back at him. He pats his client's head gently.

"Take your time," he says.

In Shibuya, Baku is far too busy to look at the news. In any case, there's a high-stakes football game on TV: Kashima Antlers are playing Jubilo Iwata.

In Akihabara, Raiju enters her cubicle and waves the pass-gesture at the camera above her.

"Raiju online," she says.

She waits a while. The cubicle door stays open. She slides it shut manually, and calls out again, her voice louder. She sits on the floor, tapping the side of the cubicle with her fist.

"Come on, Amabie," she mutters. "Where the hell are you?"

"Sorry to keep you waiting," says Azusa. "It is an honour to meet you."

"Thanks," says Uzma. "We should have called first, but we're in a hurry."

"I know how busy you must be," says Azusa. "Welcome to Hisatomi Tower."

The giant bear rises out of Tokyo Bay. Its claws are long, thick and yellow, its eyes a startling green, its genitalia conspicuously absent: presumably the Kaiju King wishes to appeal to younger audiences.

It is greeted by missiles: four Tan-SAM Kai IIs sizzle as they hit it, and four fireballs blossom on its chest. It reels, roaring, and splashes its chest with water. Apart from four singed circles on its torso, and a slight increase in the intensity of its scowl, it appears unaffected.

The bear clambers out of the water and shakes itself vigorously. It stands on the same docks where the ARMOR mechas recently battled the giant lobster, but ARMOR is not here. Some Air Force jets are, though, and they strafe the bear's body with fire, but it seems not to even notice them. It rears up on its hind legs, and with one wild sweep of its paw sends a huge pile of containers flying into the air. They burst open and pour out their contents as they arc out over the bay and splash into the water. The bear turns, sniffs the burning air, and shuffles around. It sees the glittering buildings of Odaiba before it, the new dome of the Museum of Emerging Technologies holds its attention for a while, but behind the museum, taller and shinier, stands the never-ending spike that is Hisatomi Tower. It goes to work.

In the lobby of Hisatomi Tower, the Unit is getting restless. Uzma looks around; Anima's playing a game on a holo-screen,

Wu stares blankly into space, and Jason and Wingman sign autographs for a group of giggling schoolgirls who have just emerged from a massive elevator after a tour of the tower. The lobby is full of guards, most of whom are engaged in nothing more threatening than occasional glances at her legs. The annoying fusillade of flashing cameras from the paparazzi huddled outside the building has fortunately stopped – the photographers all ran away a few minutes ago. This had nothing to do with the fact that Jai had been sent out to discourage them. Uzma can see from a screen, with a growing sense of mind-unravelling disbelief, that a three-hundred-foot-tall bear appears to be making its way towards Hisatomi Tower, smashing every building and street in its path. She turns, again, to the pretty young woman in a close-fitting business suit in front of her.

"So where is Mr Hisatomi?" she asks.

"I'm so sorry," comes the reply. "But Mr Hisatomi's appointment calendar is very full."

Wingman and Ellis had both cautioned against the direct approach; they had pointed out five other ways to tackle this whole Hisatomi business. But Uzma has been feeling itchy and restless ever since Prague, and is in no mood to be stopped by lackeys.

"Where is Norio Hisatomi?" she Asks the young woman.

"In the basement of this building," she replies immediately. Her eyes widen, and then narrow. "I see you just used your mind rape power on me," she says.

"What did you just say?" thunders Uzma.

"I apologise. My English is not perfect. Mr Hisatomi will see you, of course, but there is one small problem."

"What is that?"

The young woman points at the giant bear on the holo-screen above the reception desk.

"There seems to be a minor security alert," she says. "Now if you could please excuse me, I must make arrangements for the children."

Uzma finds she has nothing to say as the woman walks off to the reception and starts issuing orders to guards.

"Any of you want to go kill a bear?" she asks her team.

"I like bears," says Anima, not looking up from her screen.

"Do you like killing things?" ask Uzma.

"Yes."

"Well, then get on it, people. Faceless, stay with me."

"I don't think we should get involved," says Wingman. "It might rake up some bad memories in this part of the world."

"That was years ago," says Uzma. "If you get it right, it'll help us."

"They have a giant robot for this sort of nonsense," says Wingman. "I really think we should stick together, Uzma. We don't know what we're up against here with this Norio fellow."

"They're just humans."

"But if they have that girl—"

"Go," Says Uzma.

As the Unit races out of the lobby, the young woman returns to Uzma. She's wearing AR glasses and headphones.

"You clearly have a lot to hide," says Uzma. "What is your name?'

"Azusa. I work for a large company, and am in possession of a lot of confidential financial information," she replies. "I am afraid this is necessary."

"I understand," says Uzma. "I've sent my team to take care of your monster. Do let Mr Hisatomi know I'm waiting."

"He knows, but I'm afraid you will have to wait a while longer. This tower was destroyed the last time the Unit fought one of the kaiju, and Mr Hisatomi's family was killed during that battle. Since then, we have a very strict security protocol to follow."

"We have a jet that can get him wherever he needs to go. We'll talk on the way."

"I'm very sorry, but Mr Hisatomi has no heirs and so is honour bound to follow the protocol. He will meet you after the kaiju is dead."

"That's fine," says Uzma. "Is there a room where my associate and I could wait?"

Azusa casts a look at Jai. "I am afraid I must insist that the gentleman remove his armour," she says.

Uzma sighs, and begins the usual story. "The Faceless has sworn by his clan's rules that—"

"We are prepared to sign a confidentiality agreement regarding Mr Mathur's identity," says Azusa. "But he may not go past the lobby with his helmet on. Please do us this favour, Ms Abidi. We are making every attempt to cooperate with you."

She meets Uzma's baffled gaze with a completely bland expression, and smiles with what appears to be genuine gratitude as Uzma nods, and Jai removes his helmet.

"Welcome, once again, to Hisatomi Tower," says Azusa. "Please follow me."

What the Kaiju King's new bear lacks in beauty, it makes up for with agility. The kaiju usually specialise in standing in one place, wiggling their arms around and screaming – though that is usually because they spend all their time on land being pounded into bits by ARMOR. The bear moves from building to building, smashing each in innovative ways: some with huge swipes of its paws, others with police vans picked up from the street. There's a hail of gunfire hammering into it from all sides; the bear does not let this get in the way of its rampage. It smashes through a glass tower belonging to an insurance conglomerate, then picks up a police car, shakes it until all the screaming policemen inside it fall out, and tosses it into the sky, where it hits a helicopter. Both vehicles explode in a spectacular mid-air fireball.

A speck of green light catches its attention – a little ball of green that darts from side to side. The bear bats at it with its paws, but the light dances out of its reach. Roaring in frustration and delight, the bear leaps at it, and chases it down a street, back the way it came. But after a minute or so, something stops it. It turns, losing interest in the light, and trundles back towards the Museum of Emerging Technologies.

Anima does not enjoy being ignored, and the bear kaiju discovers this the worst possible way. She charges herself up, bending the city around her as waves of green energy gather into her body. Then she shouts a challenge, and the sky lights up. From above the bay, the newsfeed cameras capture, for an instant, what looks like a giant lightsaber, a solid line of green energy as Anima flies forward and up, then charges full-tilt into the kaiju. She passes, burning, shining, right through it, and straight out of its chest where its heart should be. She bursts out like a comet, a black blob of kaiju slime that gives birth mid-flight to a shining green ball trailing an arcing stream of blood. Anima flies on until she is spent, a floating waif far above the shattered Odaiba skyline, and then her power runs out, and she is suddenly alone, floating in the sky, surrounded by fading green sparks.

The kaiju stands perfectly still, a human-sized hole burnt out of its torso. It staggers, too shocked to roar, totters, sending police cars screeching backwards.

Anima's body folds up, twists. She falls like a stone. Jason runs towards her on a stairway in mid-air he builds as he runs, of chunks of steel, plaster and furniture ripped out of broken towers.

The kaiju falls. It smashes into yet another tower, sticks its head into a gigantic advertisement hoarding for beer, and lands with a *whump* that shatters every window on the street, fills the air with the caterwauling of car alarms, and sends a mushroom cloud of dust and debris into the sky.

Jason sends an endless sheet of metal and glass twisting through the air, and breaks Anima's fall. She slides down the twisting slope, limbs flailing and he builds the slide below her, faster and faster, until he twists the metal in mid-air, and Anima is safe, sliding in circles in the bowl of a nineteen-foot-long spoon Jason builds in a second out of the side of a tower. Jason's shoulders sag, and he stumbles, but before he can fall to his death Wingman plucks him up, soars into the air, and tosses Jason into an office.

The kaiju roars. It flings its forelimbs up, and rises again, slowly, its body creaking and shuddering like a tree in a gale. In a matter of minutes it stands again, holding on to a tower, its eyes burning as bright as before.

Wingman flies in sending bursts of plasma fire with deadly accuracy into the beast's eyes. The kaiju swats at him, paws much larger than Wingman's body flailing about with surprising speed, trying to squash him like a mosquito. His seventh strike connects; Wingman is caught in mid-flight. He scrambles, and in a desperate burst of speed flies out of the beast's paw a second before it smashes it through a wall. Wingman is caught in a hailstorm of steel and concrete. Dizzy, bleeding, completely exhausted, he hovers, waiting for the killing blow. But it does not come.

Instead, Wu emerges from above, eyes glowing a blinding, pupil-less white, bringing lightning with her. A direct hit on the kaiju's skull hurls it back, making it forget Wingman altogether. Above the beast, clouds gather and dance. Caught in the gathering storm, the newsfeed helicopters make desperate attempts to escape, but several are caught and tossed about in the howling wind.

Wingman calls out to Wu, but Wu is well past hearing him now. Fortunately for the intrepid journalists above them, the spirit riding Wu chooses to let them live. It leaves Wu, and the light in her eyes dies out. Wingman flies up and catches her – just in time. The kaiju makes a great leap towards them, and Wingman evades its wild strike with one second to spare.

The bear lands heavily on its hind limbs, and calms itself. It calls upon whatever unearthly force powers it, and blood stops pouring out of the hole Anima burnt in its chest. It thumps first one foot, then the other, like the universe's largest sumo wrestler, then looks at its feet, and takes a deep, slow breath.

Then the giant bear looks up sharply, and opens its maw. A torrent of fire streams out of its mouth, up into the sky. The few helicopters still left above it burn instantly. As they fall flaming around the monster, it looks down again and strikes the nearest towers, roaring a challenge that echoes through every corner of Tokyo.

Wu answers. She has a new spirit in her now. She floats towards the kaiju, arms outstretched, talons of light extending from her fingers. A cold wind blows down the street, picking up clouds of debris and tossing them about, blasting the bear with torrent upon torrent of supercooled dust. Jason darts behind her, riding the storm surfer-style on an ad hoarding he's shaped into a board. Wu flexes her spirit talons, and the dust storm turns into a tornado that spins into being in front of the kaiju. Jason sends a range of objects spiralling into the mix: cars, furniture from shattered towers, glass, girders, potted plants.

The kaiju ignores the twister, and thunders towards Jason and Wu. They retreat, and the beast chases them, smashing through the buildings in its way. But they are too fast, and it is too tired. Soon the beast stops again, and focuses itself. It squats into its sumo stance and prepares to bathe them in fire. One stomp. A second stomp. It looks to earth. It stares balefully at its opponents. It opens its mouth. Fire blossoms in its throat.

Wu brings her hands together, and the tornado rises and flows into the kaiju's gaping maw.

The bear snaps its jaws shut. Its cheeks swell. A ripple runs down its body. Its eyes bulge.

The giant bear explodes.

The Unit's heroes sit on the broken edge of a fiftieth-floor office in silence, breathing deeply, watching chunks of burning kaiju flesh rain down from the sky. They rub their eyes occasionally, and cover their noses.

Jason's phone rings. It's Uzma.

"If you're done playing, could you get back to Hisatomi Tower? We have work to do," she says.

"On our way," says Jason, and disconnects. He looks at his teammates.

"Meeting," he says.

"Can't she handle one human on her own?" asks Anima.

"She might need us," says Wu. "I sense danger."

"Do you? I wonder why," says Wingman. "Is it the danger of yet another Uzma Abidi master plan?"

"Or an epic Wingman whining session," says Anima. "I like you so much when you're fighting, Wingman. You should be in more fights."

"I've had enough of this," says Wingman. "I'm going home. You three are welcome to come along, if you like."

"You smell," says Uzma, as her warriors trudge into the waiting room. Anima grins, but the other three simply slump into the sofas, looking mostly dead. There's an empty cup in front of Uzma, and an untouched full cup beside it. Jai stands silently behind her.

"Did you watch our fight?" Jason asks Jai. "We really didn't need you out there today."

"Jai was busy," says Uzma. "We've been trying out the office facilities. The steam room is excellent. So is the spa."

"When you investigate a company, you're really thorough," says Jason. "Could we get, like, a massage or something while you do your meeting?"

"This isn't a time for luxury, Jason," says Uzma, a massive grin finally breaking through. "We're working."

As two kimono-clad assistants serve the others steaming cups of sencha, Azusa joins them.

"Mr Hisatomi is on his way," she says. "He asked me to convey his congratulations on your magnificent victory. You have saved our city."

"Is ARMOR on holiday?" asks Uzma. "Why didn't the robot show up?"

"ARMOR is a mecha, not a robot. It is a matter of shame that he could not give our guests a display of his abilities today of all days."

"Well, he could do the city a great favour by cleaning it up, I suppose," says Wingman. "We made a pretty big mess out there."

"Your team is called the Unit, not the Cleaners," says Azusa with a smile. "I hope the tea is to your satisfaction. Mr Mathur, would you not like to try some? We take great pride in our tea at Hisatomi Towers. It is from our own gardens."

Jai refuses tea.

A panel on the wall behind Uzma slides to reveal a large screen. Norio appears on it.

"Thanks for waiting," he says. "And thanks for not letting that creature break my tower."

"I'd prefer to talk face to face, Mr Hisatomi," says Uzma. "We've come a long way."

"Indeed you have," says Norio. "And yes, it's time we met."

Azusa takes them up to the very top of Hisatomi Tower. They walk out onto the roof, past a helipad and what looks like a miniature golf course. On a day involving less smoke, dust, fire and jagged dystopian cityscapes, Uzma could have spent hours absorbing the view. Instead, they follow Azusa to a magnificent Zen garden in the eastern corner: weathered rocks standing like islands amidst white gravel arranged with delicately raked ripples.

Norio stands outside the garden, at a vantage point where he is able to observe it all. As the Unit approaches, he turns and welcomes them with a formal bow. One by one, the heroes bow awkwardly, suddenly aware how shabby their clothes look compared to Norio's suit, which is as sharp as a katana. Uzma notes he's also wearing AR glasses and earphones.

"My father had a garden much grander than this," says Norio with a smile. "It perished with him, unfortunately, when the last tower that stood here was destroyed. He loved his garden, and found harmony in it. I like to think he was near it in his last moments."

"We are sorry for your loss," says Uzma. "The Kaiju King has a lot to answer for."

"It was a long time ago," says Norio. "How may I help you?"

"We have reason to believe that a super we are looking for is in your custody," says Uzma. "Her name is Rowena Okocha."

"At the Hisatomi zaibatsu, we like to employ humans before supers," says Norio. "It is not a matter of prejudice, I hope you understand: we just like to make sure humans are not forgotten."

"We didn't say you employed her," says Uzma. "We said you abducted her."

"I have never heard of this woman," says Norio. "I abduct so many people, though, that I might have forgotten your friend. Could you perhaps show me some evidence of my misdeeds? It might jog my memory."

Uzma senses a sudden movement behind her. It's Wu: she seems unwell. She leans on Jason, rubbing her head.

"What's wrong?" asks Uzma.

"I don't know," says Wu. "I'm really tired."

"Me too," says Anima. "Can we go to that spa you talked about while you flirt with the hot suit?"

"Give me a minute," says Uzma.

She turns to Norio, who has been watching this exchange with quiet fascination.

"You know, there's one way to settle this quickly," she says. "Take off those headphones and those glasses. I'll know you're telling me the truth, then, and we'll leave you to your business."

"I have shown you nothing but hospitality," says Norio. "Accusing your host of being a liar is usually considered bad form."

"Look, I'm tired," says Uzma. "Nowhere near as tired as some of these guys, but tired enough. I have a headache, and my back still hurts, and you're not as smooth as you think you are. You're, what, twenty-two?"

"A little older," says Norio. "Why?"

"You have time to talk as much as you do," says Uzma. "I don't. Our informant may have been wrong, or lying. The easiest way to find out and end this matter is if you help me out."

"You must accept my word."

"I cannot do that."

"You insult me."

"Sorry about that," says Uzma. "Take off the damn glasses."

There's a soft hiss behind her, and a thump. Uzma turns, and sees Wu has slumped forward and fallen face first on the roof. Jason moves to pick her up, but he's clearly very tired too; he staggers.

"Perhaps the rest of your team would be more comfortable

inside?" says Norio. "Jai here should be more than enough to protect you from Azusa and myself."

There's another crash behind her. Anima has fallen into the Zen garden.

"What did you do?" Uzma asks.

Norio smiles. Uzma blinks: he looks a little blurry.

"Jai, hold Norio upside down from the roof's edge," says Uzma.

Jai moves forward.

"Wait," says Norio. He pulls off his glasses and earphones. "Ask away," he says.

"Where is Rowena Okocha?" Asks Uzma.

A grunt behind her, and Wingman falls down.

Azusa and Norio are both perfectly still.

"Rowena is in Hiroshima. In a hospital I own. As a doctor, not a patient."

"What have you done to my team?"

"Nothing. I did not bring them the tea, or force them to drink it."

"You gave us... Rowena's blood?"

"I won't tell you."

"What?"

Norio looks concerned. "Is your power working?" he asks. "Are you all right?"

Uzma realises suddenly how sleepy she feels. Her tongue seems to have grown to twice its usual size. She turns to Jason, and the world spins as she moves, and Jason is of no use to her, lying flat on the floor like that.

"You forget... Jai... didn't drink your tea," she slurs.

"No, he didn't, did he?" Norio smiles at Jai.

"Jai, take him out," gasps Uzma, and sinks to the floor.

Jai takes a step forward, and his eyes glaze over.

"But Jai went to the steam room," says Norio to the fallen Uzma. "And even Jai has to inhale."

Jai takes another step forward. His face is contorted with effort; he raises a swaying arm.

He slumps to the ground. Azusa steps forward, extracts a pistol from a pocket, and shoots three more darts into Jai's neck. Instead of bouncing off, the darts sink into his flesh, and Jai twitches and convulses on the floor.

"Kill him," says Azusa. "Finish it."

Norio laughs. "First I'm going to make him remember," he says.

"What he did to your father?" asks Azusa.

"No," says Norio. "What it feels like to be human."

# CHAPTER TEN

Jai doesn't waste any time blinking and looking around groggily, wondering where he is. A second after his eyes open, he's on his feet, in the warrior stance, wholly alert.

He's in a cube made of reinforced glass, lit up with a spotlight from above. The cube is in a large hall. Squinting, he scans the hall. His armour lies dismantled a few feet away from the cube, helmet sitting on the breastplate. Norio is passing the time fencing with a bullet-headed robot. Jai waits patiently for a few seconds until Norio notices he's up; Norio issues a command to the robot, and hands it his katana.

Norio walks up to the cube and stares at Jai in silence.

Jai stretches slowly, shaking the fatigue out of his muscles. He frowns.

"I feel different," he says.

"Haven't been beaten in a while, have you?" says Norio.

Jai looks him in the eye, and Norio almost flinches.

"Is it difficult, knowing your powers have gone? You've

been superhuman for eleven years," says Norio. "Do you feel older?"

Jai isn't listening. His eyes are closed now, his face screwed up in concentration. He breathes in, deeply, and shakes his arms and shoulders.

"Let me bring you up to speed. You killed my father," says Norio. "And now you're here, and about to die. If you're in pain, don't worry. It won't last long."

Jai opens his eyes and grimaces.

"You talk a lot," he says. "I don't like that."

Norio smiles. "I don't like it either," he says. "Sometimes I hear the words coming out of my mouth, and I think, is this really me? I used to be really quiet. I'm still quiet at work, and at parties. But all this dealing with supers and what's basically magic – I change into someone else. Have you ever kept a diary? Or written a secret blog?"

Jai says nothing, but his expression makes clear that he has not.

"Anyway, so it's a whole other me. I get talkative. And then I get surprised. But I'm sort of committed to this now. And you should really be trying to keep me talking as long as you can, you know. Assuming you want to keep living as long as possible."

"I used to talk a lot too," says Jai. "I must have enjoyed it then."

"More than killing innocent people, or less?"

Jai examines his prison.

"I've done a fair amount of research about you," says Norio, "but I didn't realise you failed as a supervillain because you were boring."

Jai looks puzzled. "You want a conversation," he says.

"Yes."

"Why?"

"Because I want to know the man who killed my father. To look him in the eye as I take my revenge."

"You kept me alive so you could talk to me before killing me?" Jai considers this for a while, and a smile spreads slowly across his face. "You're new at this," he says.

"I am," says Norio. "But I spent a lot of time planning our meeting, and you're letting me down."

"All right," says Jai. "What is the point of this?"

"Well, you have a lot of enemies," says Norio. "I wanted you to know exactly which one of them beat you. I wanted you to know that it was an ordinary human that took the whole Unit's powers away."

"I see," says Jai. "What is your name?"

Norio grits his teeth and tells him.

"Who was your father?" asks Jai.

"A great man. He deserved a better death." Norio's hands are shaking.

"Yes," says Jai. "Yes. You were talking about this earlier. I wasn't paying attention. He was killed when I threw a monster at your tower."

"I suppose it means nothing to you. You've killed so many people."

Jai shrugs.

"You've removed my powers and brought me here to kill me," he says. "Is that negotiable?"

"No," says Norio.

"Have you ever killed anyone before?" asks Jai.

"Yes," says Norio.

"Was that for revenge too?"

"No."

Jai turns away, and sits, cross legged, on the floor of the cube. Norio waits for a whole minute, his irritation mounting.

"What?" he asks.

"I haven't had a real conversation in eleven years," says Jai. "And this one is pointless. I am tired."

Norio pounds on the glass. "Face me!" he yells.

Jai turns around, and looks at Norio with something approaching interest.

"Did you really take the whole Unit's powers away?" he asks.

"Yes."

"Good."

The first thing Uzma feels is a hand on her forehead. She grabs it, twists, and opens her eyes. It's an elderly lady in a white coat, and she's squealing in pain. Uzma lets her go, feeling most sheepish.

She's in a low bed, one of several in a long, narrow hall. Soft light filters in through paper walls. Her teammates lie on four other beds near her. Anima stirs as the woman shouts at Uzma in hoarse, angry Japanese, the rest are remain unconscious.

"Where are we?" Uzma Asks the woman. Or just asks, she remembers, as she gets no answer. Her heart sinks.

"Where is Jai?" Uzma Asks. Silence, again. Uzma rubs her throat, fighting back tears. Her voice sounds different, hoarse, older.

A panel at the far end of the room slides open and Azusa walks in.

"Are you all right?" Azusa asks. "We were very worried."

"What?" Uzma splutters.

At a gesture from Azusa, the nurse rushes out of the room.

"You seem weak. Save your energy," says Azusa. "You will experience occasional bouts of dizziness and nausea for the next few days. Other visitors who experienced similar symptoms did. And please keep your voice down. This is a place of business."

Uzma's head spins, she doesn't know if it's Azusa's words, or if the realisation that she's lost her power is beginning to set in.

"First of all, I would like to apologise for the recent unfortunate events," says Azusa. "You are not in any danger. As soon as your teammates have woken up, we will escort you to your hoverjet and you can be on your way."

"Where is Jai?" asks Uzma.

"Who?" asks Azusa.

"Jai!"

"You speak of Jai Mathur, the super-terrorist and war criminal? He was killed by the heroes of the Unit eleven years ago in London."

Uzma takes a deep breath. "My teammate. The Faceless."

"He left after your recent accident," says Azusa.

"Accident?" Uzma fights back tears of rage. "You poisoned us!"

"Not at all. We were unaware that you were all allergic to our special tea," says Azusa, her voice perfectly level. "But we provided you with immediate medical care. I hope your report to your superiors will reflect that."

Uzma gets out of bed. Her legs shake, her head spins. But the only thing she's aware of is world-destroying fury.

"What the hell are you trying to pull?" she yells. "You took away our powers!"

Azusa nods. "An unfortunate incident," she says. "I urge you not to be angry, and once again, do keep your voice down, you are disturbing our employees. There is nothing to be done now, we should all move on and remain on cordial terms."

Uzma has many things to say, and they all try to come out at once. What emerges is an incoherent splutter.

"Please be advised that the removal of superpowers is not illegal in any country," says Azusa.

"Oh it will be, soon enough," snaps Uzma. "You're going to pay for this."

"Though of course the unauthorised *acquisition* of superpowers is punishable by death in several parts of the world," says Azusa. "The Hisatomi zaibatsu's legal team are prepared to make any clarification you require, but I can tell you informally that legal action will prove futile. I do not understand why you seem offended: you are still human. Like myself, and everyone who works here. Do you find that repugnant?"

Uzma stands up.

"You have no idea what you've done," she says. "We are the world's greatest superteam. We've saved millions of lives."

"I watch the anime," says Azusa. "All shows get cancelled eventually. I'm sure you will be remembered fondly by your many fans."

"We're going to beat this," says Uzma. "This is not over."

"Speaking of beating things, I must warn you that further disorderly conduct will give us grounds to restrain you with necessary force," says Azusa. "I advise you to rest until your colleagues are up and about, and then depart in an orderly fashion."

"What have you done with Jai?" asks Uzma again, trying to match Azusa's calm and failing utterly.

"I do not know of any Jai," says Azusa. "I must warn you that this conversation is being recorded, and your repeated references to a super-criminal would cause a great deal of harm to your team's reputation should these recordings be accidentally leaked to the media. Especially considering that you will be rendered irrelevant to the world after your unfortunate loss of power. Perhaps the acquisition of more enemies would be unwise."

"I see," says Uzma.

"Thank you," says Azusa. "Would you like some tea while you wait?"

Uzma takes a step forward, fists clenched. And then she sees a flicker of pure joy in Azusa's eyes – something tells her Azusa is dying for a reason to beat her senseless. Uzma sits down on her bed instead, steeling her face into perfect composure, and waits for Azusa to leave. Then she starts shaking her teammates awake.

At a gesture from Norio, Awesome Boy stomps up to the cage. Jai observes the robot with interest; its arms and legs extend and contract as it walks, like pistons. It isn't a robot built to care for the elderly or the young; it's a warrior. It stands in front of the cage and transforms: one of its hands retracts its fingers, and sprouts spikes in its place; the other transforms into a plasma cannon.

"I'm offering you a choice my father never had," says Norio. "Would you like my robot to kill you, or should I do it myself?"

"You," says Jai.

"It will be slower," says Norio.

"I'm in no hurry."

Norio steps up to a lever, but sees Jai smiling and stops.

"What's so funny?" asks Norio.

"Life," says Jai. "I was supposed to rule the world. To think I should meet my end in an empty room, at the hands of some nobody. Life is strange."

"Believe me, Jai," says Norio. "When I am done, the world will see your death as a footnote in the tale of my adventures."

Jai smirks. "Trapping me like this was a fluke, boy. Caused by Uzma's poor planning, not mine. You wouldn't stand a chance against me."

"When you were a super. Which was another fluke, wasn't it? Right now, we're here. We're on equal terms. You can show me what you're made of."

"Oh, I'm not making excuses," Jai snaps. "But if you're planning more than just revenge, then killing me is a very stupid idea. You should employ me instead."

"And why would I want to do that?"

"Because I have seen how this world really runs, boy. You have no idea. You're just a rich kid with lots of fancy toys who thinks he's ready to play in the real world. You'll get crushed. You need me to survive."

It's Norio's turn to smile.

"I wonder what inspires this sudden concern for my well-being," he says. "Does it have anything to do with your impending death?"

"I was thinking about it," says Jai. "I took your father's life. It was an accident, and technically it wasn't even me, since my mind was controlled by someone else. But let's say it is my fault, and all the years you've spent plotting your revenge weren't a waste of time, if we became allies, I could save your life, and then we would be even."

"No," says Norio.

"Think about it," says Jai. "You say you have a larger plan. I would guess it has something to do with defeating supers. Forming a human resistance. Depowering more supers."

Norio says nothing.

"Well, you've made me human. I have many enemies. Supers. That means my side is picked for me. I have lived in slavery for eleven years. My every thought dictated, my every action controlled. They made me – me, Jai Mathur – a puppet. How do you think I feel about that?"

"I would imagine you feel pretty angry."

Jai's anger is evident now; the veins on his neck stand out.

"Let me get my revenge first. Then kill me as you please."

"Why should I?"

"Because I know enough to bring down every superhero organisation in the world. I haven't slept through these eleven years, Norio. Uzma controlled me, but I was awake, I was alive. I was watching. Together we can end the age of supers. And that's what you want, isn't it?"

"I just want a world where people are equal, or at least not more unequal than when this all started," says Norio. "I know it sounds naive, especially coming from me, but an elite group running the world doesn't work. Nothing changes."

"Because if the First Wave had never happened, you would have been in that elite group," says Jai. "I understand."

"No, that's not it at all," says Norio. "I could become a super if I wanted – the Utopic board has already upgraded. But if some people are super and others aren't, people like my father die unnaturally. This has to stop. And I will stop it."

"And I will stop it with you!" says Jai, his face aglow with enthusiasm as he pounds the glass wall enthusiastically.

"No you won't," says Norio. "I'm almost flattered by how stupid you think I am. That was some of the worst acting I've ever seen."

Jai grins ruefully. "Worth a shot," he says, and steps back.

And then they both notice the huge crack on the glass cube's wall.

As they watch, the crack grows, like lightning in super-slow motion. It spreads, slowly, sending tributary cracks off in every direction.

Jai punches the reinforced glass. It shatters. Jai looks at his fist.

"Interesting," he says.


The first thing Anima does on waking is turn into her cartoon princess form, and send green sparks shooting across the room. One strikes Wingman, who leaps up and covers himself with what looks like an armadillo shell. Jason and Wu are up as well, rubbing their eyes, taking in the room.

"I'm an idiot," says Uzma.

"We know," says Anima. "Why exactly?"

"That nurse didn't speak English." Uzma smacks her forehead. "I could have made that bitch dance the Macarena instead of taking all that shit."

"That's nice," says Wingman. "What now?"

"Get up, all of you," Says Uzma.

The other four stand up immediately, startled and immediately disgruntled.

Azusa bursts in with four armed guards. A flick of Jason's

wrist, and they are disarmed. The guns bury themselves in the ceiling. Anima sends sizzling maces into the guards' foreheads; they fall, stunned.

Two seconds after entering the room, Azusa finds herself alone, facing the Unit.

"Slap yourself," Says Uzma.

Azusa does, her eyes blazing.

"Your poison didn't work on us. Why?" Uzma Asks her.

"I don't know," says Azusa. "I personally tested the tea and the steam on other guests."

"And your other victims didn't recover like we did?"

"No. We held the first two subjects for a week to make sure."

"What did they have in common that we don't?"

Azusa looks thunderstruck. "Physical deformities. Powers that brought them pain."

"Just like the Utopic subjects. And Rowena's blood fixed them."

"Yes."

"So you gave us a healing potion. Not necessarily a power removal portion."

"Yes."

"And how stupid does that make you feel?"

"Very."

"Good. So, Norio. Where is he?"

"In Awesome Boy's dojo."

"I don't know what that means, but take us there. No, cancel that, mark it on your phone and give it to us."

Azusa busies herself with her phone.

Uzma turns to Wingman.

"You take her to the hoverjet. Wu, go with them. Jason,

Anima, we need to move fast. I want Norio alive."

"Aman Sen didn't have any physical deformities," says Azusa, mostly to herself.

The room goes very silent.

"Slap yourself again," Says Uzma.


Awesome Boy's pulse cannon keeps up a constant barrage of blasts. Each pulse lands squarely on Jai's chest, and Jai's body shudders, but stays upright. His clothes are in rags, but he's healing at incredible speed.

Norio races around the hall looking for Azusa's rifle, praying she left it somewhere in the room. *One shot,* he tells himself as his search grows more frantic. *One shot wins it all.* The stench of burning flesh and hair fills his nostrils, he wants to vomit.

Jai walks closer and closer to Awesome Boy, energy pulsating off his chest, deflected blasts shooting all over the room. The glass cube is in smithereens now, broken sprinklers raining water on a lake of shards.

"I'll give you a choice," Jai shouts, above the whine of the pulse cannon. "Would you like your robot to kill you, or should I do it myself?"

Norio's heart pounds. Finally he spots the rifle, stacked neatly on a shelf in the darkest corner of the hall. He races towards it.

"Not feeling so talkative now, are we?" calls Jai, watching Norio's progress with interest.

Awesome Boy's pulse cannon spins, completely discharged. Jai's not prepared for this, and stumbles. Awesome Boy's right arm pistons forward, and Jai gets a face full of spiked club. The impact sends him flying backwards. He lands with a crash in the remains of the glass cube.

Awesome Boy retracts his pulse cannon. His left arm shifts, and a chainsaw emerges.

"Nice," says Jai.

Norio fires his rifle. The dart hits Jai on the shoulder, and bounces off.

Jai turns towards him lazily.

"Keep doing that," he says. "Don't go away."

Awesome Boy stalks forward, chainsaw extended towards Jai, club raised above his head. Jai grins, and tilts his head, cracking his neck. He claps his hands together.

"Come on, then," he says.

Snaking under the chainsaw thrust, Jai goes for Awesome Boy's leg. But he hasn't factored in how heavy the robot is. Awesome Boy stumbles, but gets a solid hit on Jai's back with the club. Jai roars in pain, and, as his body convulses, Awesome Boy swings the chainsaw into Jai's neck with a swipe that would have beheaded a full-grown bull elephant.

A fountain of blood and tissue spurts into the ceiling, but Jai's head stays attached to his body. He screams in agony, and skids on his own blood. In mid-slide, he leaps up, and vaults far away from the charging robot. His neck is a mess of ripped muscle and exposed bone; every gulp of breath he takes makes a horrible whistling noise. But as he turns – his body, not his head – to face Norio, his voice is calm.

"What is your big plan?" he asks. "Where are you going with this?"

Norio watches in disbelief as Jai's neck stops bleeding, and new muscle knits itself over his bones. Jai's not at full strength, though. He moves lightly on his feet, retreating, keeping a safe distance between himself and the advancing Awesome Boy.

Norio has two darts left in his rifle. He shakes them out on to his hand, and races towards Awesome Boy.

Jai starts growing new skin on his neck. What worries Norio more is the smile on his face.

Norio reaches Awesome Boy. "Chain gun, empty two chambers!" he yells.

With a mighty clang, Awesome Boy extends his right arm, and a chain gun replaces the club. Two chambers open; shells drop out. The robot pistons its hand forward, and Norio stuffs the last two darts into the empty chambers.

Jai rolls his head around his neck. "Good as new," he says.

Two darts, loaded with Rowena's blood, stream towards him. Time slows down for Norio, as if he can hear the blood sloshing about inside the darts, feel the air heating up around them as they hurtle towards Jai, hear the never-ending growl of Awesome Boy's chain gun rotating, new shells clicking into place.

Jai catches the darts in mid-air and tosses them aside. He charges at Awesome Boy. The robot fires the chain gun and raises the chainsaw to strike, but Jai is unbelievably fast. He leaps at the robot, shells ricocheting off his body, and slams into its breastplate.

Awesome Boy goes down. Jai springs to his feet and rips out the dented breastplate, ignoring the chainsaw that's hacking into his thigh, and jettisoning a fine spray of blood into the air. Then he grabs Awesome Boy's left arm and rips it off. The chainsaw is still whirring as he plunges it into Awesome

Boy's innards. Circuits and wires and sparks fly everywhere as Awesome Boy shakes, rattles, and shatters.

Norio's heart seems to stop for a few seconds as Jai, matted with blood and dotted with pieces of robot shrapnel, looks up and into his eyes.

"Run," says Jai.

Norio wants to, but his feet cannot move.

"Game over," he says. "Kill me. I'm not afraid."

Jai plucks a few shards of metal out of his body.

"I want you to understand something," he says. "I don't really care whether you live or die. You mean nothing to me."

Norio bows his head.

"I did what honour compelled me to do," he says.

"Spare me that nonsense," says Jai. "You have no idea what honour means. You're a foolish boy who read superhero comics and thought he understood power. A fat little sheep who thought he could play wolf. What was your plan?"

"It doesn't matter," says Norio.

"You found a way to trap me," says Jai. "If your trick with the steam had not failed, you would have killed me. I'm almost impressed." He picks up Norio's sword from the floor.

"Your days are numbered," says Norio. "I might have failed, but there will be others. Mankind will survive you."

Jai swishes the sword around. "I used to be a leader of humans," he says. "I used to inspire them to do things. Up in Siachen, where it's so cold that you could die of exposure before taking three steps, I used to make them do what I wanted."

He points the sword tip at Norio's throat.

"People used to go mad up there, you know," he says. "Young boys, stupid killers from some godforsaken village. It didn't matter what side of the border they were on. They'd play games with each other. Collect heads."

He nicks Norio's throat with his sword. A slow trickle of blood runs down Norio's neck. He's amazed at how warm it feels.

"I am not going to kill you," says Jai. "I gain nothing from your death. A life for a life: we are even. But before I let you go, tell me how you planned to defeat all the superhumans."

"Step away from him," Says Uzma from the door.

Jai lowers his sword slowly, and looks at his teammates as they run in.

Jason stands behind Uzma, Anima hovers in a green energy field in front of them.

"Are you all right?" he asks.

"We're fine," says Uzma. "There's no need to torture him. He'll tell us everything he knows. Let's go."

"So no one lost their powers?" asks Jai.

"No," says Uzma. "Rowena's blood doesn't remove superpowers. It just heals people. We'll find out more when we pick her up. Where is she again?"

Norio stands silent, head bowed. Uzma sighs and clears her throat.

"Wait a second," says Jai.

He brings the sword up again, and points it at Norio's throat.

"What are you doing?" asks Uzma.

"I thought I felt different," says Jai.

"Put the sword down."

Jai smiles. "Ask me properly," he says.

"Put the sword down and step away from Norio!" Shouts Uzma.

The team stares at Jai, horror slowly dawning in their hearts.

He flicks the sword at Norio's throat: another thin line of blood wells up.

"I don't think I want to," says Jai.

All hell breaks loose.

Norio dives for cover as Jason sends a swarm of jagged metal and glass hurtling towards Jai. Anima, screaming in horror, hurls a barrage of light-spears. Jai reels under the onslaught, but stays on his feet, bleeding from every possible part of his body.

"Get Uzma out of here!" shrieks Anima.

Uzma's already running for the door, too shocked to speak, Jai's fierce smile burning in her eyes.

Jai begins to laugh. A rich, rolling laugh that echoes around the hall as a swarm of glass and metal rakes across every inch of his body, as he twitches and shudders in an endless stream of light-spears.

Norio's face and arms bleed as he rolls away into the shadows.

Jai grabs a piece of the robot's breastplate and hurls it at Uzma. Jason, exerting all his strength, sends it slicing into the ceiling. Anima retreats, flying back in terror as Jai races towards her.

As soon as Uzma's out of the hall, Jason rushes back in.

Anima hits Jai with every weapon she can think of, but nothing can stop his charge. Jason, roaring, sends another cloud of debris smashing into him, piling around his legs, until he trips and falls heavily. In an instant, Jai is buried in a pile of rubble. Anima flies around the hall, sending green daggers pounding into the walls. As they break, Jason adds to the rubble around Jai until he's completely encased in debris; he rolls the pile around like a snowball gathering mass. Anima, screaming unearthly anime-princess battle cries, sends twin beams of light arcing around the sphere, covering it in a force field.

After a minute or so, the sphere stops shaking, and Jason pulls Anima down to earth. She reverts to human form, shaking uncontrollably, tears rolling down her cheeks.

"Uzma?" calls Jason.

"I've called Wu and Wingman in," says Uzma from the door. "It'll take all of us to keep him down."

Jason looks around. "Norio's gone," he says.

"He is the least of our problems at this point," says Uzma. "Stay focused on Jai. Believe me, you'll need to."

"Kind of you," says Jai's voice from within the sphere.

He bursts out of the pile, sending metal flying in every direction. He's naked, covered in blood, and looks more like a porcupine than a human, but they all take an involuntary step back at the sight of him.

Immediately, Jason and Anima flow into a joint attack stance, but Jai raises a hand.

"Not here," he says. "Not today."

He turns and runs across Awesome Boy's former dojo, trailing blood, glass and metal. He smashes straight through the far wall, out in mid-air, and disappears.

The Unit heroes stand in shocked silence, trying to catch their breath, hearing screams and sirens outside, but unable to summon the courage to go and stop them.

# CHAPTER **ELEVEN**

The sunsets over Mar Bella beach are among the most beautiful in Barcelona, and today is no different. It will be dark soon, and the sea is turning from brilliant blue to smoky grey, but Uzma's gigantic sunglasses stay resolutely on. Down the years, she's accepted the fact that there is nowhere in the world where she can stay unrecognised for any reasonable period of time.

No one left on the beach has any interest in lounging about: the sea is empty, and the boats have left. Uzma is surrounded by large numbers of incredibly toned young bodies cavorting in the sands, and the trendy bars now blaring turn-of-the-century dance music. Since she's wearing a bikini, she's one of the most conservatively dressed people on the beach, but she's getting stares from all sides as usual. She doesn't know whether it's her powers or just her demanding workout regimen, but several men have already managed to summon up the courage to ask her to accompany them across a large dune to the nudist section. She sips slowly from her fourth glass of sangria, and wonders, for the thousandth time, whether this whole solo excursion is her worst idea yet; worse even than charging into Hisatomi Tower without wondering what that annoying Japanese maniac might have done with Rowena Okocha's blood.

But it's difficult to keep thinking about blood and violence and intrigue on the sands of Barcelona. Uzma stretches and yawns, and looks around again, taking in the parties that are starting around her. She idly watches two Adonis-like men throw a large beach ball around, clearly for her benefit, and when there's a soft cough behind her, she waits a good minute before she turns and acknowledges the man in his mid-thirties who's standing nervously in the sand near her towel.

"I feel like I should beat you up," she says.

"How long do you have?" asks Aman.

Uzma smiles, and shakes her head. "You let me think you were dead," she says. "It's going to take a lot of apologising before I can forgive that."

"I'm angry with you too, you know," he says. "You're the reason they cancelled the *Firefly* reboot. It was a good show."

"I had nothing to do with that. It's Wingman's show. I was just in the pilot."

"It still hurts."

"That's not going to work, Aman," says Uzma, surprised at how much it stings to say his name. "I'm going to need a lot of grovelling. Knees, flowers, speeches, the works."

"How long do you have?" Aman asks again.

At midnight, Uzma rolls off an utterly exhausted Aman and pronounces him forgiven. He doesn't respond, but from the idiot grin plastered on his face it's clear he's happy about this.

Uzma waves the lights off and curls up next to him, facing away, and he turns instinctively and holds her as he always has. It's ridiculously easy to pretend they've been together all this time. They spend the next ten minutes in perfectly joyous silence, feeling each other breathe, watching the room's curtains flutter in the sea breeze.

"Does Tia know you're here?" asks Uzma, and then winces in the dark, wishing she'd given them both some more afterglow time.

Aman sighs. "She knows," he says.

The silence between them grows uncomfortable. Aman gives in first, waves the lights on, and gets up to drink some water. Uzma sits up and watches him walk about. In a while she realises that she hasn't bothered to draw the sheets up around her as she does with her other lovers.

"We got married last year," says Aman. "She died. The Venezuela thing."

"I'm so sorry," says Uzma. "So… how does that work? Are you still married to her?"

"No," says Aman. "Tia had forty-three husbands around the world the last time I checked. Thirty-nine kids over the last eleven years. And I stopped checking last year. It'll be a while before the law catches up. So no, we're not married. But we obviously still live together, and… you know."

"I don't even want to imagine."

"But she doesn't mind sharing me, she says it's only fair. You know Tia. I manage to wrap my head around the whole situation from time to time."

"But your Tia was yours," says Uzma. "Were you happy, being married? Please tell me you don't have children."

"I don't."

"Wow. Your love life is probably the only one in the world more complicated than mine."

"Yeah. Well, we're both several light years behind Tia, of course. And even Tia says she doesn't remarry her own widowers."

"Conservative. It's age."

"And you? Who's the lucky man now?"

"The usual. Nothing extra interesting."

"Well, you've obviously been practising a lot. I noticed some exciting new tricks."

"You too. But then, Tia. Well played all around."

Aman's idiot grin reestablishes control over his face.

"Are you all right, Aman?" asks Uzma.

"I am," he says, and manages a grin. "I mean, look at you."

"I love you, you know," says Uzma.

He looks at her, smiling and blinking, savouring the moment.

"If you say 'I know' I'll smack you," says Uzma.

"I love you too," says Aman.

The next afternoon, Aman drags a reluctant Uzma to the newly restored Park Guell. They walk through the gardens, watching the milling tourists and musicians with their holo-zithers. Aman still hasn't told Uzma why he insisted they meet in Barcelona, and she's well past impatient; as the slow Spanish hours roll by, she works herself up into a quiet frenzy. But at sunset, when he drags her to the fountain presided over by Gaudi's wonderfully insane salamander mosaic, she understands his reticence. If he'd told her who they were going to meet, she might not have come.

Vir is dressed in classic awkward-Indian-tourist gear,

complete with baseball cap and dangling entry-level DSLR camera. He lacks the belly to really pull it off, but he makes up for this with an exaggerated slouch. Aman greets him warmly and declares him a master of disguise; Uzma and he nod stiffly at each other. Vir's last public appearance was in Barcelona, weeks before he quit the Unit. He had stopped an Algerian supervillain from sandblasting the Sagrada Familia, and then ended up in a huge fight with the Unit's former press agent over official photos. Uzma had had to Talk him out of making a scene. He'd tried out a few other superhero teams – former Unit members were always in demand – but eventually went back to his nomadic stranger-comes-to-town brand of helping people.

Vir is not here to build bridges with Uzma today, in fact he seems wary of talking in front of her at all. They leave the gardens, and walk downhill until they find a cluster of cafes, which both in the quality of coffee available and general atmosphere are opposite in every way to the crowded, generic cafe in Mumbai where Aman and Vir had met for the first time. Aman wonders who has changed the most since those days. He doesn't have to think about this for long: it's Vir.

"We've had these conversations before," says Aman. "Vague threat of the world ending, no one knows where it's coming from, Jai on the loose, other sinister powers at work. But this time there seems to be a general consensus on when it's all going to go belly-up. One week. So. What do we do?"

"I've looked everywhere you asked," says Vir. "The only people on your list who I thought were real suspects – the magicians – have no idea what this particular apocalypse is about. They're trying to build new dimension gateways, but there's nothing there that could destroy the world. They're not planning to let anything in that could."

"I have no idea what you're talking about," says Uzma.

Aman explains that he sent Vir to look at a few far-flung corners of the world where supers were working in isolation: groups of magicians in Tibet, Sri Lanka and Cameroon who'd gone off the grid a long time ago, wary of governments, other supers and Utopic gather-squads. A lot of their work was in the field of imagined sciences: they were trying to build new worlds, new havens for supers, new dimensions in which to practise their magic. None of their powers fit into the structures of the real world.

Aman had met one of the ringleaders, a young woman whose power was to bring her favourite characters from fiction into existence for brief periods of time; he'd found her while she was on the run from Utopic's notoriously trigger-happy copyrights division. Uzma has dealt with magical cases before: at least five different schools along the lines of Hogwarts have been closed down over the last decade, and the Unit was recently involved in shutting down a scam where a Utopic subsidiary had collected vast amounts of money from real estate sales in a Narnia-esque fantasy dimension they said was under construction.

No one really knows the truth about magic, of course: whether it has always existed, or whether each act of magic is merely a super's power in action. Even Wu doesn't know if the spirits she summons are her own creations, or if they have always been there, lying in wait for the right vessel. Aman's always felt it was unfortunate that the First Wave happened at a time when most of the globally popular works of fiction were fantasy in one form or the other, the whole super phenomenon was tough enough to deal with without the occasional outburst of vampire and zombie plagues.

"In any case," says Vir, "they were all perfectly happy to shut down their projects for two weeks, none of them wanted to be accidentally responsible for ending the world."

"Or so they claim," says Uzma.

"Either way, I've sent them all on holiday," says Vir. "Aman's paying."

"Utopic is paying," says Aman. "But if it's not the magic supers, who could it be?"

"Doomsday cult," says Vir. "You can't possibly be sure you've got them all."

"But they've tried before," says Aman. "It never works."

Plenty of supers have already sought to end the world, the universal death wish is a distressingly common super desire. But the mysterious power or natural force behind the super waves has, fortunately, its own system of balance: whenever a super has tried to turn world-ender, the attempt has failed. In 2013, a very depressed failed bank CEO in Australia had just wanted everyone to die; everyone in the world had blacked out for a second, but then normality had been restored. There had been thousands of deaths in that moment, of course, but that had been because of accidents, not the unhappy super's death wish. It happens occasionally, some strong mind, whose sole wish has been to change one particular aspect of the whole world, turns super, and implodes under the weight of its power at work. The 2019 attack of virulent pimples among everyone in the world who happened to be wearing hipster glasses at the time, is still widely discussed in fashion and law circles.

But whatever the balancing power is, the super-apocalypse has always been diffused thus far.

"The only super we know who can actually affect the whole world is Viral," says Uzma. "Could he be used in some way to harm every human?"

"Bloody Viral," says Aman. "But no. I don't see the end of the world coming from relentless advertising. But if you want to hunt him down and kill him, I'm on board."

"Which leaves only one definite suspect," says Vir. "Kalki."

"Then it leaves no known suspects at all," says Aman. "Kalki's fine. Sher keeps him safe."

"How long has it been since you checked?" asks Vir.

"Tia joined Sher's army," says Aman, "and their communications are monitored. But she gets a message through from time to time. Kalki's crazy, but happy, and Sher keeps him well protected and on the move."

"But the question is, what if Kalki's protection is not the issue? What if Kalki himself is the danger?" asks Vir. "His mission as far as we know is to cleanse the world of evil. What if that involves ending it?"

"We have no idea what Kalki's mission is," says Uzma. "Kalki can't speak. He's never threatened anyone. We had a lot of trouble with Utopic over this, when they were going to send in an army to extract him."

"I remember," says Vir. "I also remember agreeing with them. Kalki is dangerous. We've all felt it. There's something deeply wrong with him."

"There's something deeply wrong with all of us," says Aman. "And a lot of people think we deserve to die because of it. In Kalki's case, though, all the fear is completely unfair.

Rumours off the internet based on legends based on what he looks like. We called him Kalki. He's not done anything to deserve this suspicion."

"First Wave," says Vir. "Unique. Superpowers before birth."

"They've tried to replicate it, you know. The Chinese sent up whole planes full of pregnant women," says Aman. "Hasn't worked so far."

"Well, that makes Kalki even stranger," says Vir. "Unquantified powers. Growing every day for eleven years. Insane. I say he's our prime suspect."

"You want to kill Kalki?" asks Uzma. "I thought you'd become some sort of wandering sage."

"I could take him up to one of the space stations," says Vir. "Keep him in orbit for a month. He's a ticking bomb, Uzma."

"You can go and have a word with Sher about it," says Uzma. "An ex-Unit reunion. That should go well."

"They always do, don't they?"

"Children. Behave," says Aman. "What else do we have?"

"We have any number of possible situations," sighs Uzma. "Villain collective. Monsters, like the thing we saw in Tokyo. More magicians. Or some true believer creates a god."

"There's always the old-fashioned nuclear holocaust," says Vir.

"No," says Aman. "I've got that covered. Let's stick to threats we know. I still think the magicians are our likeliest danger. How far have they got with their world building?"

"Not far at all," says Vir. "None of their alternate realities are self-sustaining. We're very far away from the day when we can actually build new worlds that people from here can travel to."

"So, no mirror universes full of our evil alter-egos," says

Aman. "I always dreamt of Evil Dominatrix Uzma with a French beard and everything."

"Save it for later," says Uzma with a grin.

Vir looks at them sharply.

"If you two are done," he says. "Yes, there will come a time when somebody creates an alternate world and people try to move there in large numbers. And yes, I'm sure things will go horribly wrong and people like us will have to step forward and do something. But I'm confident it won't happen next week."

Aman is distracted. A teenaged boy at the table next to theirs is recording their conversation surreptitiously. Aman deletes the video and forwards a set of sexts from the boy's phone to his online public profile. The boy reads his email and runs out of the cafe in terror.

"And then there's Norio," says Aman. "Have you found him yet?"

Uzma has not. Worse, Azusa escaped when Wu and Wingman raced to rescue the rest of the Unit.

"And have you found Sundar?" asks Aman. "Sorry, I know you haven't. We should. There's a doomsday device builder if I ever met one. Norio told me he was his research head. But he isn't on the Hisatomi payroll."

"No one in the company knows anything about Norio's other life," says Uzma. "I've asked. Norio and his gang are missing, and presumably still working on whatever plan Norio has."

"I've been through the list I gave him," says Aman. "Lots of troublemaking potential, given his mind control machine, but nothing that can end the world."

"What is this plan of his?" asks Vir.

"I honestly have no idea, and I've been tracking him for a while," says Aman. "He clearly has a problem with supers, but his attack on all of us can't have been in the works for very long – he got to Rowena through sheer good luck. Killing Jai was something he's wanted to do since his father died. But there's more to it. More to him. To know what he's planning, we have to find out what else Sundar built for him. But I don't see how we can do that."

"You'll find him eventually," says Uzma. "He's only human."

"A human who drives a three-hundred-foot-tall mecha and defends Tokyo from giant monsters, when he's not being a playboy billionaire and flirting with Utopic," says Aman. "If he wants to stay hidden, I might not find him for a while. And in the meantime, we'll have to find someone else to defend Tokyo."

"What about the other members of ARMOR?" asks Uzma. "Can't we get to them?"

"I know who they are," says Aman. "Azusa is one. The other three are Tokyo gamers. They met online. They don't know about Norio's grand plan either. They don't even know who he is."

"Well, like the magicians, he's going to be a problem, but not this week," says Vir. "And if he pops up, we'll get him. In the meantime, you have to find a way to listen to every phone call and read every message in the world."

"On it," says Aman. "And then there's our dear friend Jai."

"Jai doesn't want to end the world," says Vir. "He wants to rule it."

"Who knows what he wants now," says Aman. "But for starters, you should stay away from the Unit for a while, Uzma. Because when he wants revenge, it's you he'll come after."

"Eleven other supers that we know of have powers like Jai's," says Uzma. "It's not like it was when it was just us. He can be beaten."

"Then you need to stay hidden until he is."

"I'd love to skulk around the world with you, Aman," says Uzma, "but I'm needed at the Unit. If I'm gone, it's only a matter of time before I'm manoeuvred out of the team. I'm going to get blamed for this whole Jai problem."

"How are you going to stop that?" Aman asks.

"I can be fairly convincing in person," says Uzma.

Vir sighs. "I don't understand how you can tolerate the nonsense that goes on in the Unit," he says. "But then, it is what you wanted. World's most famous."

"This is nothing even close to what I wanted," Uzma snaps. "But maybe I have a harder time quitting than you. Than either of you."

"Well, you walked into that one," says Aman. "I wonder sometimes whether I should have joined up. It might have gone better."

Uzma looks puzzled. "I thought you were happy," she says. "I thought you were the only one who was actually free."

Aman shrugs. "Well, I wasn't," he says. "But maybe that has nothing to do with all this hero nonsense. Maybe this is what being in your thirties is like for everyone. Life not turning out how you expected it to. Regrets, misses, what-might-have-beens. What really twists the knife in is that we have superpowers. If our lives don't meet our expectations, what's the point?"

"Well," says Uzma. "There's an empty slot in the Unit now. And a suit of armour, I know someone who would fill it quite nicely."

Aman laughs, but stops when he realises she's completely serious.

"It would never work," he says. "I've taken huge sums of money from every government in the world. Most big companies too. Exposed too many powerful people. Utopic alone would ensure I didn't survive my first week."

"Sure," says Uzma. "No one else in the Unit has any enemies at all. Do you have any idea how many assassination attempts I've survived?"

"Yes," says Aman.

Uzma shrugs. "I could use some company," she says. "Someone I trust. That would be an interesting change."

Aman is quiet for a while. He looks from Vir to Uzma and back, trying to think of the right thing to say. He looks around the cafe, at chattering tourists counting souvenirs, and annoyed writers pretending the noise the tourists are making is the only thing preventing their great novels from bursting forth into the world.

"You're serious," Aman says finally. "Join the Unit. Now. After all these years."

"For me," says Uzma. "And, you know, the whole 'world is ending in a week' thing. You could be the new Faceless. What could go wrong?"

Aman breathes deeply and tries to think with any degree of clarity.

"No," he says finally.

"Ah well," says Uzma. "You, Vir? You want to come back? Suit up?"

"Yes," says Vir.

# CHAPTER TWELVE

In the dusty, sweltering heat of Gurgaon, a bright yellow school bus trundles down a narrow road. On either side of the bus are ghost towns, their walls, once white, are now burnt and occasionally blood-streaked. A short way ahead, five pink arches straddle the road, proudly proclaiming, on solar-powered flashing boards bordered with orange flower-shaped lights, "Sunny Luvs Baljeet". Norio asks the driver what this means, and is told it was for a traditional wedding. Though it is also apparently impossible to tell which one the groom is. As the bus passes under the arches, Norio sticks his head out of the window and looks up. There's a dead dog on top of the third arch. Filing it all under Mysteries of India I Don't Need to Solve, Norio leans back in his seat and reaches for his NutriPac. He picks up his phone, and holds it to his chest, tapping his fingers on its warm metal skin. It would be so easy to switch it on, call Azusa, apologise, ask for help. But Aman might be listening. Norio grits his teeth and stuffs his phone back in his pocket.

He'd arrived in India two days ago. It had been tough finding an authorised flight under a false name, but he'd been prepared: there were several apartments in central Tokyo alone where whole identities awaited him, along with enough cash to last him a decade. The only real danger had been Aman watching the biometric scanners as he passed through them, but Utopic board members could always find helpful airport officials. His Indian contacts had proved useless. The Indian head of Hisatomi's software division in Hyderabad had refused to go anywhere north of Mumbai, but had put him in touch with various wheeler-dealer politicians in Delhi. They'd arranged for a police escort to take him from the walled city to Gurgaon, and so he'd set off in a convoy of white SUVs with flashing lights.

A minute after entering Gurgaon, his Delhi Police protectors had tried to kill him. But they were about as efficient at robbery as they were at actual law enforcement. Norio had thrown two policemen out of his car, and with a gun to the driver's head, raced fast and far into Gurgaon. His pursuers had given up as soon as they approached gang territory. He'd ditched his car and its driver, and hired new transport easily enough in a karaoke bar that night.

The school bus is slow, but clearly one of the safest ways to travel in Gurgaon; several gangs have driven by it already, taken a cursory look, and moved on. The air conditioning doesn't work, of course, and Norio's paid extra to make them shut off the endlessly cheerful Bollywood music. This has not endeared him to the rest of his hired crew, three teenaged boys who sit at the back of the bus playing blackjack, and occasionally shooting speculative looks at their new foreign employer.

Norio shuts his eyes, and despite his best efforts, remembers another awkward silence, just a few days ago. But those men and women hadn't been strangers. Norio has never had many friends, something he's considered quite an achievement given his wealth, charm and good looks. But he'd never felt as close to anyone as he had to the ARMOR squad. The former ARMOR squad.

They'd stood around the underwater ARMOR base, awkward as action figures abandoned mid-play. He'd known there would be trouble the moment they entered, something about the way they'd looked at one another in the delivery pod, standing stiffly as cheesy music wafted through the heavy silence. They'd clearly had a conversation about this earlier.

The silence had to end eventually. Oni, always the most dramatic, had jumped in first, demanding to know why they hadn't been summoned when the giant bear rose out of Tokyo Bay. Norio had lied, saying something about communications errors, but the rest of the team knew too much to believe him. They'd all seen the news about the Unit coming to meet him, the Unit battling the monster, and the unexplained goings-on later at Hisatomi Tower.

"We know who you really are, Goryo," Raiju had said. "We've known for a while. But we talked about it, and agreed we should pretend we were all strangers. We liked the rules. But then you broke them."

They'd been unhappy ever since the trip to Aman's island. They'd spoken to Azusa, demanding to know why ARMOR was being used for Norio's personal business instead of protecting Tokyo. She'd defended him: telling them they were hunting the Kaiju King, that they were close. Norio had tried to seize this opportunity. He'd told them he'd learnt the Kaiju King was somewhere in India, that ARMOR had to go there and bring him back. The rest of the team had swallowed that lie, and he'd been on the verge of winning them over, when Azusa had betrayed him.

"We do not know where the Kaiju King is," she'd said. "But Kalki is in India. I think that's who Goryo wants to find."

A bitter argument had exploded: Oni and Baku had threatened to quit right then, saying this had nothing to do with defending Tokyo, that they hadn't signed up to be some billionaire hero-wannabe's hit squad. Norio had told them it was all connected, that finding Kalki would lead to the Kaiju King, and to so much more. He'd given them a fantastic speech: honour and duty and nobility, human endeavour against freaks and monsters, human ingenuity against unfair powers.

When he had finished, he'd taken his helmet off with a flourish, and asked them, hand on heart, to help him fix the world.

Instead, Raiju had asked Norio to stop this madness, or to at least keep ARMOR out of it. He'd found the energy for another speech then – he told them what a perfect team they were, what a symbol of human achievement. He reminded them of their greatest battles, conjuring up vivid pictures – ARMOR driving its sword through the heart of a T-Rex kaiju, their mechas in a five-point formation, cutting through the King's classic floating eyeball kaiju. He reminded them of the fights, the glory, the friendships forged in black kaiju blood. He'd been exhausted when he'd finished. The rest of the team had taken their helmets off while he spoke, and he had seen how inspired they looked. He'd seen the tears in every eye.

"I call for a vote," Raiju had said. "Goryo has forgotten the mission. We need a replacement."

"Well, you can't have one," he'd snapped. He'd immediately regretted his words but had been too angry to stop. "This is *my* team. *My* mecha."

"And your rules," Baku had said. "But they apply to us all."

"They apply to you," he'd said. "Not to Amabie or myself. We are permanent. And if you have a problem with that, you can leave. I can replace you in an hour."

Raiju had turned to walk away.

"Wait," Azusa had said.

He'd looked at her, and seen, for some reason, the face of the little girl she'd been when they'd first met. He'd felt his heart stop as she spoke, her voice loud and clear, her eyes expressionless.

"We should have a vote."

The bus comes to a lurching halt. The boys race up to the driver. Norio gets up and looks around, but sees nothing. The boys seem to be having some kind of argument with the driver. Norio picks up his revolver and stands up.

"Don't worry," calls the driver. "Sit down."

"What's going on?" asks Norio.

The driver indicates the boys. "They are saying big trouble ahead. Saying we are turning around."

"That's what they said on the highway. I thought this road was safe."

"Sher Sena land. Big trouble. Bad people. Tiger boys."

"That's fine," says Norio. "Keep going."

But the boys turn away, and start arguing with the driver

again in Hindi. Norio walks down the aisle, gun held lightly in his right hand.

"You can leave if you want," he says to the boys. "I just need the driver."

One of the boys pats his AK-47. "Security," he says. Norio doesn't like his smile.

In the distance, ahead of them, a song starts playing. It's loud, thumping, a recent K-pop hit. The boys shuffle around and look out of the bus. One swears loudly.

"Call Centre Mafia," he growls.

Norio looks too, half expecting an army of cubicles on trucks, and gangsters with earphones and American accents, but the Call Centre Mafia is just a convoy of white delivery vans, approaching the bus with alarming speed. The lead van's sliding door is open, and a man leans out of it. In his hands is a grenade launcher.

"Out!" screams the driver.

The boys and the driver race towards the door, scramble out, and run into what looks like an abandoned market. Norio simply dives out of the nearest window. He lands on the road and rolls, gun out and pointed at the lead van.

The Call Centre Mafia vans reach the bus. Other van doors are open too, and an array of guns point out of them. The grenade-launcher-toting man in the lead van scans the abandoned school bus, and raises his weapon. Norio dives off the road into the ditch.

The vans pass on. One of the gunmen shoots idly, smashing all the windows of the bus. Norio hears waves of laughter through the music.

Norio stays down until he sees his rag-tag army emerge from

the market and head swiftly towards the bus. He gets up, then, and shakes dirt and glass from his clothes.

"Oye. You. Japan."

Norio looks up. Four rifles point at him.

"Danger boss. Give more money," says the driver.

Norio tosses him his wallet. The driver smiles. The boys file into the bus.

Norio sighs, and takes a step forward.

"Hello? Hero? Where you are going?" asks the driver.

"To the mall," says Norio. "We had an agreement."

The driver laughs.

"First time in India?" he asks.

"I am a powerful man," says Norio. "Cheating me is a very bad idea."

"Bad idea? Good idea if we take gun? Take phone? Take life also?" the driver asks. Norio shakes his head.

"Bye bye Japan. Now tell thank you."

Norio thanks him, and watches as the school bus drives away. He stands alone in the sun, wondering when he'd signed up to be microwaved. He's fired hundreds of people, shot or otherwise injured several others, but never in his life has he felt this unpopular.

Baku, Oni and Raiju hadn't even pretended to think about it, they'd voted him out. He hadn't expected Azusa to reprimand them, as she'd always kept up the pretence of team equality. And then she'd spoken. Voting him out as well. He'd stared at her, blinking in disbelief, all his attention focused on suppressing a squeal of indignation. The rest of the team had been stunned as well.

"Don't you work together in real life? Isn't he your husband or boss or something?" Oni had asked.

"On this team we are equals," she had said. "I believe Goryo has other priorities at this time in any case. We will consider this vote cancelled if he chooses to stand down voluntarily. We already have a replacement lined up."

"Get out," Norio had said, as quietly and firmly as he could. "All of you."

A few extremely tense moments had passed, with Raiju and Baku clearly considering violence. Fortunately for them, they had abandoned the idea and left the base. Azusa had gone with them. Norio had stood alone, staring at the mechas glowing quietly at ARMOR station. He'd walked up to each one, stroked each ghost-machine head. He'd wished, once again, that Sundar had designed a giant mecha capable of being operated by a single pilot, but ARMOR needed at least three people to work. He had considered, for quite some time, the idea of just taking off with the Goryo mecha, of giving its flight capabilities a real challenge, but that was clearly a bad idea, no matter how many angles he considered. An unauthorised flight across China was always fraught with danger, and Goryo did not have the speed or strength to withstand Chinese surface-to-air weapons or, more significantly, Chinese supers. And an underwater and overland voyage would have been too long and complicated. Especially because he had no idea where Kalki was, or even how to find him. A ghost-mecha floating around the wild suburbs of Gurgaon, stopping occasionally to ask the locals for directions to a mad blue horse-headed super-god, might have drawn a certain amount of attention.

Norio had patted the ghost-mecha's head, bade it goodbye, and walked to the delivery pod, waving the lights out as he left, wondering if he would ever see ARMOR again. Behind him, the eyes of mecha-bots glowed defiantly and then dimmed, one by one, into darkness.

Above him, the sun is a blinding, unrelenting ball of light. Norio can feel heat washing over him, can see the edges of the potholes in the road melting and shimmering. Time has lost all meaning: he feels as if he's been walking the streets of Gurgaon for years. His eyes sting with dust. He's tried resting in shadows wherever he finds them, but stillness only makes the heat worse. His NutriPacs are still on the bus, no doubt being consumed with great delight by his former companions. His steps are getting shorter. A few feet behind him, two dogs skulk by a wall, watching, waiting for him to drop, their low growls a constant reminder that he has to keep moving. He's waved his gun at them a couple of times. They've fled, but always returned.

He hears the sound of car engines behind him, and dashes for cover.

This gang evidently believes in style. They're driving smart, well maintained and strangely clean luxury sedans. But these aren't just high-end cars, a gun turret sits on each roof, along with a swivelling chain gun manned by a suit-clad gangster. Norio has no time to worry about how they're dealing with the heat, a volley of bullets carves out deep grooves on the wall in front of him, sending him scurrying back onto the road. More gunshots send gravel flying near Norio's feet. He dives and rolls, pulling his gun out. But before he can fire, three cars surround him, cannons in every direction. He drops his gun and raises his hands.

The gangsters emerge from their vehicles. They're clearly based in one of the local malls: they're all dressed in designer clothes; though the fact that they're also carrying bejewelled ladies' handbags indicates that they're probably not fashion experts. Several men surround Norio, most have guns, and the rest carry exotic bladed weapons that weren't available in malls the last time Norio visited one. The leader, thus designated by what appears to be diamond-studded sunglasses, stands in front of Norio, holding a golden gun to his head.

"Listen to me," says Norio, his voice a hoarse whisper.

"No," says the leader, smiling.

"Are you human?" asks Norio.

The gangsters look puzzled.

"Yes, you are. Then listen. This is the most important thing you'll ever hear."

The gang stands around him, brandishing their weapons, waiting for a signal from their leader.

"Say say," says the leader, looking vaguely interested.

"I'm one of the richest men in the world," says Norio. "And I'm here to change everything. To end all this."

He gestures at the broken buildings around them.

"What ya. Boring," says the leader.

The gang jeers at Norio. Someone prods him with a rifle barrel.

"There's no reason for you to believe me, or trust me," says Norio, finding his voice again. "But if you kill me, all hope ends. Listen. Who is your biggest enemy?"

"Sher," says the leader.

"Yes. Sher. And others like him. All supers. And in time, the supers will take all you have, and you and your children will be their slaves."

"You are stopping Sher?" asks the leader, clearly curious despite himself.

"I have a plan," says Norio. "And you're a part of it. Because you're going to work for me. You'll be powerful. More importantly, you'll be rich."

The gang considers this for a while. They turn to their leader.

"We just take all your money and kill you, no? Then also rich," he says.

"This is your chance to bring humans back into the game," says Norio. "If you miss it, the supers take everything. But you have a choice. Wealth, power, fame on the one hand. Death and destruction on the other."

"Big plan, boss. Full masala. Interesting," says the leader.

Norio extends his hand. "Do we have a deal?"

The leader grasps his hand and grins.

"No," he says.

Norio doesn't know who hit him on the back of the head at this point. Or why he thinks he hears, in the distance, a tiger roaring. But he is knocked out immediately, so there isn't time to get into any of this.

He'd gone to one of his secret Ginza flats very late that night, after a long private sulk in a large central Tokyo beer hall filled with businessmen drowning their sorrows and diving stocks. He'd not planned to spend any time at home, only to stop to pick up his suitcase and head off to his private airport, but he'd found Azusa waiting for him.

They'd circled each other in his fancy living room for a few minutes. He'd poured himself another drink; she'd waited demurely next to the glow-fish aquarium, looking unflinchingly at him.

"You don't need to hand in your resignation," he had said finally. "I understand why you betrayed me. There's nothing else to say."

"Don't go," she'd said. "You took your shot against the supers, and you failed. There's no shame in that. You have your honour."

"This isn't about me, or my family," he'd replied. "Azusa, you've known me longer, and better, than anyone else alive. If you don't see why I must do this, there's nothing left to say."

"Don't go," she'd said again. "I understand your hatred of supers, and I will help you fight them. But not now. Now you need to disappear again. They won't hunt you for long, they have a new crisis coming up every minute. You'll come back with a bigger plan, a better one. But running off to India to find Kalki is not the answer."

"You looked at the lists with me. It's our best shot."

Azusa had sighed. "All the years I've known you," she'd said, "I've never seen you as a person who wanted to do anything but take the world forward. To the future. Yes, the world we lived in before supers was wonderful – for you. Yes, I can see how you'd hate being irrelevant, and want to do something about it. But I don't understand why you want to end it all. Because supers make the world better, Norio. They take it forward. Whether you like them or not."

Norio had stared at her. "What do you think I'm going to do with Kalki?" he'd asked.

"You're going to ask him to remove superpowers from the world," she'd said.

He'd laughed. It had started out fake, and then grown embarrassing, and he'd stopped.

"You don't know me at all," he'd said.

"And you don't know what you're doing," Azusa had snapped. "You think you're going to find Kalki from Aman's list? Sher has him. His army stays on the move. You don't have the slightest idea where to find him."

"I'll ask around."

"You'll get killed."

"Then help me," he'd said, grasping her shoulders. "Not as an employee, or a teammate. Help me as a friend. Find him for me."

"No," she'd said, and drawn away.

He'd shrugged, and tossed a bag over his shoulder.

"Goodbye, then," he'd said. "I might never see you again."

"Goodbye."

He'd turned at the door. "I've been in love with you for a few years now," he'd said. "Just thought you should know."

He'd never seen her cry before.

"I've always loved you too," she'd said, wiping away her tears defiantly. "But you don't. Or you won't when you find out who I really am."

They'd stared at each other across the room for what had seemed like hours.

"Who are you?" he'd asked, wondering whether or not to look for a weapon.

"I'm a super."

It is a while before Norio can speak. "How long have you known?" he asks finally.

"Eight years."

"What's your power?"

"I find people. It's how I always found you."

"And how did you find Aman?"

"I can track people after I meet them. It feels like I can smell them, but that can't be true. Whatever it is, I just know where they are in the world. I tracked you to find Tia in her submarine. Once I met her, I tracked her back to Aman's island. If we'd ever managed to make a kaiju turn around, I could have found the King."

He hadn't known whether to laugh or cry, so he'd settled for making a noise like a soda bottle opening.

"I should go," she'd said.

"Yes, you should. You should come to India, and save the world with me."

She'd shook her head. "Let's not talk about this any more. If this is really the last time we meet, then I'd like to see you smile before you leave."

And he had been smiling, but not because she'd asked. It was because he'd been filled with joy and hope, and he couldn't remember when he'd last felt that way.

He'd told her what his plan was. And he'd seen her eyes light up, and fear and excitement blossom in her eyes.

"Do you think it's possible?" she'd asked. "Can he really do that?"

"According to Aman's files, he can do anything. He grants wishes."

"Then yes. It's the right thing to do. But why didn't you just tell me this at the beginning?"

"Have I ever shared any of my plans with you before?"

She'd smiled, then, and he'd covered the distance between them in a second, and crushed her against him with enough force to set her struggling in a minute or so. But it had been a very good minute.

"Don't go now," she'd said then, and he'd groaned. "This isn't the time. They're looking for you now – you picked the two worst supers in the world to be hunted by. If Jai doesn't find you, Aman will. We'll lie low for a few weeks. And then we'll go together. You can't just rush off like this, alone."

"It's the only way," he'd said. "It has to be now, Azusa. Because they will find me. And my sources at Utopic tell me they're going to be very busy over the next few days."

But Azusa was as stubborn as he was. She'd always been. She'd refused to go, and when he'd refused to stay, she'd given him the co-ordinates of the twenty-seven Tias that had sprung from Tia Prime after they'd met in her submarine. They were all in Gurgaon, in what the internet told him was formerly the biggest mall in the world. She'd warned him that that didn't mean that Kalki was anywhere in the vicinity. But even this had been a treasure-trove compared to what he'd known before, and he'd left right then, practically run off, ignoring her arguments, trying and failing to explain to her that there just wasn't enough time, that he didn't really want her to go anyway, as he didn't want to put her life in danger ever again. He'd promised Azusa he'd return and be with her, and sworn that he'd fix the world and then it would be theirs.

She'd been crying when he left. He'd told himself they were tears of joy, and had decided it was best not to check.

\* \* \*

When Norio wakes up again, it is to the now familiar sensation of a rifle barrel prodding him in the stomach. But when he opens his eyes, he doesn't see a gangster from the stylish mob he's privately named the Fashion Police. Instead, it's a young man in khaki fatigues. His face and arms are covered in tattoos that look like tiger stripes.

"Hello hello," says the man.

Norio looks around. He's lying in the back of a large truck, speeding down the highway. Empty fields on either side, what looks like a factory to the east. In the distance, he can see skyscrapers, twinkling and shimmering as they catch the sunset.

"What's your name?" asks Norio.

"Jai."

"That's nice. I have a close friend named Jai. You're in Sher's army," says Norio.

"Yes, Sher's army," says Jai. "You are Japanese." Perhaps to congratulate Norio on his nationality, he hands him a bottle of water.

"This is true," says Norio. He takes a deep swig, tries to summon the energy for an inspiring speech, considers how well his last few inspiring speeches have gone, and gives up.

"I have come to see Kalki," he says. "Do you know where he is?"

"Yes."

"Please take me to him," says Norio. "It's incredibly important. I need to save the world."

"You are not surprised to be here in my truck?" asks Jai.

"You saved me from that other gang," says Norio. "You found me just as they were going to kill me. Maybe I'm just lucky. Maybe it's destiny. Maybe you saved me for a reason. Because Kalki wanted to see me."

"We have actually been following you since the bar," says Jai. "We were betting to see how far you'd get. I lost my money."

"Please tell me you'll take me to see Kalki," says Norio. "I've come a long way."

"Can't meet Kalki direct. First see Sher," says Jai. "Only if Sher say you okay, you safe, you see Kalki."

Norio sits up. "Do you like money? Really large amounts of money?" he asks.

"Yes," says Jai. "Sher also likes."

"That's good then," says Norio. "But I'd like to give you something extra."

"Extra money? What you want me to do?"

"Just get me to Sher secretly. Don't tell Tia I'm here."

Jai grins. "All right. Secret. I won't tell to Tia."

Norio breathes in and out deeply and shuts his eyes.

"Thank you," he says.

"Too bad I already know," says a voice behind him.

Norio looks around. Two Tias, bodies covered with tiger-stripe tattoos, climb out of the truck's cab through the broken rear window.

"I owe you three bullets in the chest," says one.

Jai tosses her his rifle with a grin.

"I'll apologise profusely later," says Norio. "But this is beyond you and me. This is about—"

"Shut up," says Tia. "You're not seeing Kalki. Or anyone else. And Aman says hi."

She points the rifle at him, and grins.

"You're done," she says.

# CHAPTER **THIRTEEN**

"Are you sure about this?" asks Aman. Wherever he is, the network is weak, his voice sounds hollow and far away in Uzma's earpiece, as if he's going through a tunnel.

Uzma adjusts her earpiece nervously. "Can you hear me?" she asks.

"Yes. You don't have to shout. Vir?"

"Clear," says Vir. "Where are you? I can hear traffic."

"Never mind that. Uzma? Have you heard from the kids? Are they in India yet?"

"No. On their way."

"You do realise Tia's perfectly capable of holding Norio for a week on her own, don't you?" says Aman.

"Yes."

"And that I think sending Jason and Anima to India is a bad idea?"

"Well, if you wanted a vote, you should have joined the Unit."

Uzma climbs the steps to the Unit headquarters and takes a

look around. It's a clear day, the sky is cloudless, and the Upper Bay is a brighter shade of blue than she's ever seen in New York. Vir stands beside her, hair blowing about in the steady breeze. He hasn't been to this Unit building before, but just the approach seems to be stirring up bad memories.

"Are you sure this is a good idea?" he asks again.

"No," says Aman. "But get on with it."

A few minutes later, in a third-floor armoury, amidst lines of shelves stacked with expensive and deadly super-weapons, Vir stands facing the suit of armour recently vacated by Jai. It stares back at him impassively, black and silver and radiating menace.

"Go ahead," says Uzma. "Put it on."

Vir does, picking up one plate at a time and slowly attaching it to his body. Fortunately, the armour doesn't smell of Jai – the Unit's housekeeping has always been excellent, as superhero housekeeping needs to be. Vir puts on the helmet last, his face troubled, and then floats upwards slowly, extending his arms.

"It's heavy," he says. "Isn't it supposed to change to fit to my size?"

"It did for me," says Aman. "I think you have to be online for it to read your thoughts."

"Well, at least he can still fly," says Uzma.

"Then fly to your meeting," says Aman. "You're late."

The moment Uzma enters the central chamber on the top floor, she senses something is amiss. Wingman and Wu sit in their usual places, faces carefully blank; That Guy smiles at her nervously from behind a celebrity holo-mag. But Uzma doesn't even notice them, her attention is fixed on the other occupant of the chamber, who's sitting in her chair. A tall, thin, handsome man in his forties, dressed in an immaculate suit, reading a document on a tablet. He doesn't rise or acknowledge her presence as she storms towards him, and it's only when she stands in front of him and clears her throat loudly that he even looks at her. She seethes as his eyes move past her, and settle on Vir.

"I'm afraid access to that armour goes through me now," he says. "It will have to be returned."

"Where is Ellis, and who the hell are you?" demands Uzma.

The man smiles. "You can call me Agent N," he says. "Think of me as the new Ellis."

"Agent N? Seriously? Never heard of him," whispers Aman. "Give me a second."

N hands Uzma his tablet, she tosses it onto the table and subjects him to a withering glare.

"You should have asked Ellis how things work here," she snaps. "Get out of my chair. I'll deal with you after our meeting."

"I'm afraid that's not how this is going to play out," says N. "I could explain, but it's probably simpler that you read it for yourself." He gestures towards the tablet.

"Don't bother, I got it" says Aman in her ear. "Independent strategic consultant. New team manager, agent, the works. You hate him, don't you? It feels like you hate him."

"Let's get started, shall we? Where are Jason and Anima?" asks N.

"Get. Out," Says Uzma. N smiles at her, and stays in her seat. Uzma notices the transparent bands of AR plastic that cover his eyes and ears.

"He's covered," says Aman. "You could still beat him up, I suspect."

"Jason and Anima. They were supposed to be here," says N. "They're not. Why?"

Uzma takes a deep breath.

"All right," she says. "You have my attention. Why are you here?"

N looks at her and smiles. "The inauguration is in three days. There were performance reviews across the board. Ellis was found wanting."

"He did nothing wrong!" yells Uzma.

"This is true," says N. "He is an unfortunate scapegoat, Uzma. The real fault lies with you."

He stands and looks around the table at the assembled members of the Unit. Uzma turns too, outraged, and notices Wingman smiling.

"The Unit is now under new management," says Agent N. "You have been damaging the reputation of the United Nations and using the world's greatest superhero team for personal errands. I've been sent here to ensure this changes."

Uzma sits in another chair, too furious to speak.

"You need to watch your tone, Agent," says Vir.

"And you need to leave this room," says N, unperturbed. "You are always welcome in the building, as a respected former member of the Unit. But you are not a member of this team until your application is approved. I'll send you the form."

Uzma turns to Wingman and Wu. "You people are all right with this?"

Wingman shrugs. "The Japan debacle was your fault, Uzma," he says. "There were bound to be consequences."

Uzma nods.

"Vir," says Aman, "I think you should leave. And I think you should take Uzma with you."

Vir stays where he is.

"I'm afraid removing me is not that easy," he says.

N nods. "That's your decision," he says. "Though it's one you might have cause to regret."

He waves his hands, and a holo-screen appears over the centre of the table. Another wave, and the screen morphs into a hologram of the globe.

"Nuclear reactor meltdown in Chechnya four days ago," says N, and a glowing red cylinder grows out of the map. "Floods in Bangladesh. Earthquake in Iran. Insect hive in Prague. Forest fire in Brazil. Super-induced tsunami in Chile. Super-combustion in the Arctic Circle. Crocodile-man infestation in Kinshasa. Oil spill in the Gulf. And the punch line, the Black Plague. In western China, Uighur country."

The Unit watches the holo-globe spin in front of them, red spikes sticking out in every direction. N raises his arms, and the globe stops spinning.

"Three million casualties in one month," says N. "Did you even notice?"

He glares around the room, and the Unit glares back.

"Uzma?" asks N. "Do you have any excuses?"

"I don't owe you any explanations," says Uzma. "If we'd known any of these were going to happen, we would have stopped them."

N shakes his head. "Pathetic," he says. "The United Nations has let you live like kings. And what have you given the world in return? Three million corpses."

"All right, that's enough," says Wingman. "Trying to pin the blame on us just makes you look bad, N. Tell us what you want."

"It's not a question of what I want," says N. "It's about what is right for the UN. For the world."

"I've tracked your N," says Aman in Uzma's ear. "Long trail of companies, but bottom line, he's Utopic. Get him out."

"My team has gone through all available Unit records, and we've come to several conclusions," says N. "I suggest you all listen closely."

"We reject your conclusions, and we reject you," says Uzma. She turns to her team. "Tell him."

Wingman stays silent.

"I support Uzma," says Wu.

"And so do Jason and Anima," says Vir. "I do too, of course. You should leave, N. I'd advise you to remember what room you're in."

"But Jason and Anima aren't here," says N.

"This guy's tried to hide his tracks. His funding chain is all over the place," says Aman. "But if you don't fix this, Utopic will take over the Unit."

"Uzma," says N. "Time and again over the last decade, you've put the reputation of the Unit in danger. You've gone against your briefings on several assignments and single-handedly created diplomatic disasters."

"By stopping wars," says Uzma. "I suppose your masters at Utopic lost some money there."

N ignores her. "You've shown on several occasions that fame and celebrity rankings mean more to you than your duties. You've also made several decisions that have called into question your abilities as a leader. Our team of experts has deduced that you have kept this position all these years as a result of your unique abilities, your glamour and your popularity."

"Actually, I kind of like him," says Aman. "He's sweet."

"Your decision to keep Jai Mathur in the Unit, instead of allowing him to be tried for his crimes, has on several occasions proved to be unwise," says N.

"I see," says Uzma.

"Now that you have allowed him to escape, on a mission you undertook against your UN liaison's direct warnings, you have created a situation that might bring the whole UN into disrepute. I'm sorry to have to say this, Uzma Abidi, but you are no longer fit to lead the Unit."

Uzma nods. "And who is, may I ask?"

"Wingman will lead the team. Wu will remain a core member, as per the agreement with China. That Guy is fired, and his presence at this table is no longer permissible. We've decided to let Jason and Anima focus on their entertainment careers. And Uzma, we've decided that since the Faceless is no longer around to ensure your safety, your role will be changed from here on. We're going to use you for covert diplomatic missions. Out in the open, you're too much of a target."

"So it's concern for my safety now?" asks Uzma. "I thought it was because I couldn't get the job done. Hysterical, emotional and all that."

"The record will show that it was our inability to provide adequate security for you that led to your removal from public duty," says N. "We appreciate your many years of service, and will certainly not cause you any public embarrassment."

"Uzma," says Aman, and his voice sounds very different. "A

hoverjet just landed in front of your building. And a speedboat's heading towards the island. Also, and this is a problem to worry about later, I can't track Ellis."

Uzma turns towards Wu and Wingman. "This man is a part of an attempt by Utopic to take over the Unit," she tells them. "Are you Utopic agents?" she Asks.

"No," says Wingman.

Wu shakes her head.

"Then take him down!" Shouts Uzma.

Wu's eyes turn white. Wingman launches himself across the table towards N.

And passes right through him.

A second later, a thunderous punch from Vir meets the same fate, swooshing through N's amused face.

"This is just immature behaviour," says N. "Sit down."

Wingman picks himself up, glaring at Uzma.

"They're getting a message inside the hoverjet. One of the people on board is an assassin. Reload," says Aman. "Utopic's top killer. Regenerates at save points if his missions fail. I'm scanning for the others."

"There's a hoverjet outside our building," says Uzma to N. "Who's in it?"

"How did you find out?"

"Answer the question."

"The rest of the new Unit," says N. "Team meeting."

"He's lying. This is a Utopic attack," says Uzma. "Call a high alert."

"You don't have clearance," says N.

"Someone just ordered a strike on you," says Aman. "Get out of there."

"We have to hold the tower," says Uzma. "Something's coming."

"You'll have to tell us in your special voice," says Wingman. "Otherwise it just looks like you don't like getting fired."

"What should I do?" Uzma asks Aman.

"Get out," says Aman. "Vir. Get her outside now."

Vir turns to Wingman and Wu.

"If the Unit ever meant anything to you," he says, "defend it now."

That Guy disappears.

Uzma wants to think of a suitably powerful line to deliver before she departs, but Vir grabs her, and flies straight out of the nearest window. The glass is reinforced, and Vir's magnificent escape attempt might have ended in tragicomedy, but the armour provides just enough extra weight to smash through. Uzma finds herself airborne, screaming, with the bay below her and the new Statue of Liberty above her.

"Where now?" asks Vir.

"I have you on sat-vid," says Aman. "Head north. And quickly."

"We should get Wingman and Wu," says Vir.

"No," says Uzma. "You heard them. They'll stay."

Below, Uzma can see a large hoverjet on the Unit's lawns, its exhaust sending wide concentric ripples flowing through the squares of grass. To the east, twin white lines in the water trail a small boat as it draws close to Liberty Island.

Vir swoops down for a better look. Six figures, dressed in black, leap out of the hoverjet and towards the Unit's tower. Further out, the boat draws closer. There's just one man on it.

"I've got four out of the six," says Aman. "Supers.

Disappeared. In Utopic zoos I suspect. So they're either Utopic mercenaries or zoo pets. Boat guy could just be a tourist."

Vir and Uzma fly eastwards and dip lower. The man on the boat is wearing a cap and glasses, but they'd know him anywhere. They hear Aman gasp in their earpieces.

Jai takes his sunglasses off. He gives Uzma and Vir a cheerful wave.

"Get out of there," says Aman. "Now."

Vir shoots upwards, Uzma howling in pain as her body flails about in the sudden rush. Far below them, two of the black-clad supers charge towards Jai; the other four rush back to their hoverjet.

To the west, as they climb, Uzma sees Wu and Wingman burst out of the shattered top-floor window. Wu has a spirit in her, a wild red phantom that makes her hair stand straight up and trails tendrils of red plasma as she floats. Wingman gestures frantically at them to stop.

"I don't know him at all," says Aman. "Do you trust him?"

"No," says Uzma.

Vir grimaces and jets upwards. Wingman flies towards them for a few seconds, but Vir is faster. When they clear the statue's shoulder, Wingman turns, facing the intruders.

The hoverjet starts up, tilting to left and right as it wobbles off the ground.

Jai leaps off his speedboat, arms extended, as if he's flying too. It's a mighty leap: he streaks through the air, lands, rolls on the lawn, and comes to a halt on one knee about twenty feet from the hoverjet.

Vir and Uzma fly over the Statue of Liberty's torch. Uzma pats it for good luck as they pass, and wonders if each version of it remembers how the last one fell.

"Right. Now go to Ellis Island, and take a sharp right," says Aman. "Let's see what we're up against."

"If there's going to be a fight, I don't want to take it to the city," says Vir.

"Just trust me," says Aman.

"I do," says Vir. "I'm ditching the armour, it's slowing me down."

"No," says Aman. "Now less thinking, more flying."

On Liberty Island, four flaps open on the hoverjet's left side, and four supers fly out, teetering slightly in mid-air as they burst out of the jet, but correcting their course in seconds. One of them is a flier, he skids over the Hudson's waters in a suit with large flaps that link his arms and legs, but the other three appear to stand in mid-air, hovering, knees slightly bent, as they turn and head northwards, following their flying leader. Aman zooms in, and sees they're strapped to what look like bulky backpacks. Backpacks that vibrate at high speed and leave a shimmer behind them in the air.

"Jetpacks!" yells Aman. "They have jetpacks!"

Vir grits his teeth and hurtles towards Ellis Island.

Aman turns his attention to the scene on Liberty Island, as Jai strides towards the two remaining black-clad Utopic supers. One of them seems larger than he was a second ago. Aman gapes as the super swells, stretching and then shredding his costume; within seconds he turns into a twenty-foot-tall giant. White fur sprouts all over his body, his posture changes as his arms elongate further and his neck and shoulders broaden.

"We might have a yeti," says Aman.

Jai watches impassively as the man beast in front of him roars and pounds his chest. Beside the yeti-man the other Utopic super, a young woman, flows into a t'ai chi low horse stance, perfectly balanced.

The yeti-man charges at Jai, and Jai stands perfectly still as he pounds Jai's head and neck, roaring and snarling. After three strikes, the yeti springs back. Jai appears unharmed, though his clothes have been torn to shreds.

The woman flings her arms forward, and Jai goes flying back. He lands heavily, shakes his head, and springs to his feet. And goes down again as the yeti-man leaps on him.

Vir crosses Ellis Island and turns in a wide arc, aligning himself with the East River. Uzma moans in pain as her body tilts below his, and she scrabbles, trying not to let go of him. She can't hold on much longer. Vir grasps her firmly and twists until she's dangling from his back, arms looped around his shoulders. He flips over, taking her weight, one hand holding both of hers in front of his throat.

"All this is very pretty, guys," says Aman, "but they're gaining on you."

Behind them, the Utopic squad is now in a diamond, with the flying man in the centre, and Reload to his right. Aman watches as Reload pulls something out of his backpack.

"Missiles!" yells Aman.

Two small rockets burst out of Reload's launchers, leaving white streaks behind them as they close steadily on Uzma and Vir. Vir swerves, arcing upwards, but the missiles follow him, closing the gap steadily.

On Liberty Island, Jai makes his move. Not bothering to dodge the yeti-man's strike, he takes the massive paw-swing to his face without faltering, then darts forward, grabs the yeti-man's head, and twists sharply. Aman winces. He can't hear the giant's neck snap, but it's all too clear what happens. Jai tosses the yeti-man's body aside.

Vir dips sharply, trying to dodge the missiles, but they follow him relentlessly. Uzma can hear the missiles now, sizzling and whining as they streak behind her.

Back on the island, the woman flows into another posture and thrusts her arms out, fingers splayed. Jai's body contorts, his neck snaps back, his arms rise. There's something unnatural about his posture. The woman dances slowly, pulling invisible strings. Jai staggers back, his body shaking, his impossibly strong limbs caught in some unnatural web. His face is turned towards the sky. His mouth hangs open.

"Take a deep breath," says Vir.

Uzma tries to breathe in, ignoring the wind howling around her face, but there's no time as Vir dives into the East River. The impact breaks Vir's grip on Uzma. She spins underwater, her body flailing helplessly, too shocked to even register how cold the water is. Vir's dive takes him far below her; he turns, thrashing about, trying to see Uzma through the haze.

Above, the missiles streak into the water and explode. The shockwave knocks Uzma back several feet, and the world spins and fades as she loses consciousness. The last thing she hears as the light dies is the pounding of her own heart.

Vir shakes his head and tries to swim up, his lungs threatening to burst. His armour drags him down. He brings his arms up to his head and tries to pull his helmet off, but it seems fused to the rest of it. He sees, as if from far away, his arms and legs drifting helplessly, as strange lights go off at the corner of his eyes.

And then the world turns red. As if in a dream, red tentacles penetrate the water and curl around him. There's a writhing cluster of darkness above him, and within it he sees Uzma's drifting form. And then he feels a strange, sharp pull, feels the world rushing around him, and he's suddenly out of the water, wrapped in what appears to be a red tentacle. Uzma's body hangs limply on another tentacle just next to his. He can't tell if she's alive.

Wu floats above them, arms extended, squirming, squid-like, her eyes unseeing, the wind whistling sharply all around her. She lets Vir go, and he finds flight again, and speeds towards Uzma. Wu releases Uzma as well, and she falls, but Vir catches her, and almost sobs with relief as he sees she's breathing. Wu cries out, the words are not in any human language Vir has ever heard.

"Welcome back," says Aman's voice in his ear. "Now head for the Brooklyn Bridge, and take a left."

Vir looks around. Above him he hears the sound of battle. Wingman is shooting plasma bolts from his arms at the Utopic supers. Wu calls forth one of her thunder-and-lightning demons, and clouds take shape in the skies above them.

Then Wu cries out in pain: one of the Utopic supers has cannoned into her, his body strangely bloated, his features blurred, and Wu falls into the water in a shower of sparks. The sky growls. Another of the Utopic supers calls out. The bloated man turns towards Vir and Uzma.

"Move," says Aman.

Vir spies the Brooklyn Bridge to his right, and he dashes

towards it. He feels waves of heat through his armour as the cannonball super whizzes past.

"Wu's alive," says Aman. "They want to hire her, not kill her. Don't look back."

But Vir does. To see Wingman and the flying leader locked in a dogfight. The black flaps that joined the leader's arms and legs have disappeared. In their place, batwings have sprouted on his arms. He's trying to close the distance between himself and Wingman. His hands look enormous, long black claws curl and flex and scythe through the air, but Wingman manages to keep his distance. He sends plasma bursts at his opponent, but when they strike the batwings, they fall apart like burnt scraps of paper and regenerate instantly.

Below Vir, the water hisses and fountains as a stream of bullets dances across it. Reload flies towards them, wielding twin chain guns. Vir turns, shielding Uzma, and takes a barrage of bullets to his back. They bounce off his armour, and he streaks forward.

Another speed-burst from the bloated super. Vir dodges, and manages to get a hand on the bloated man's jetpack. Uzma awakens with a jolt as Vir rips the jetpack off, almost dropping her in the process, and the cannonball super falls howling into the river. The fourth super is upon them now, face strangely blue as she charges towards them, but Vir doesn't get to see what her power is. As he darts away, a burst of chain-gun fire from Reload hits her in the stomach, and she flies on, slumped in her harness, bleeding into the river until the waters swallow her up.

His muscles scream for rest and the world is a throbbing band of noise and colour, but Vir pays no attention. He sets off for the bridge again, and Reload follows him. Rivers of pain run through Vir's body again as the assassin strafes his back with chain-gun fire.

Reload is out of ammo, and tosses his chain gun away. Behind him, the batwinged leader and Wingman abandon their dance of death, and the leader flies at full speed behind Reload.

Vir swerves to his left. As he swoops between the cables by the western pillar of the bridge, he hears a loud bang and a series of metallic pings. A shotgun shell hits a cable a foot from his face. Reload flies alongside, above the river, matching Vir for speed. He holds a shotgun in his hands, lining up his next hit. Vir finds the strength to move faster. The cable blurs beside him, and in the distance he sees tilting skyscrapers.

Reload takes a headshot. Vir's helmet saves his life, but the jolt of the shell breaks his flight. He loses his grip on Uzma. She clings on, somehow, one hand grasping Vir's. Below her, she sees a massive pileup as cars spill over lanes and into each other. Above the roar of the wind she hears screams, car horns and crashes.

Then her hand slips and she falls, spinning. Sky and street and river and bridge swirl and blur; she feels like she's suspended in mid-air as the world arcs around her.

Wingman catches her four feet from the ground, and scoops her up. She breathes in huge gulps, eyes glazed, unable to think or feel anything. Wingman smiles his most movie-star smile yet as he sets her down on the ground. Her legs shake violently. She collapses.

"You should have trusted me," says Wingman.

Then Reload shoots him in the head.

As Wingman's body falls, Reload swoops in between the bridge's cables, powers his jetpack down, and lands running on the street. He jogs to a halt.

Behind Uzma, Vir swoops down like a hunting eagle, but the batwinged leader tackles him, claws out, and they roll into the street.

Reload raises his gun and points it at Uzma's face.

"Bang," he says.

Uzma kicks him in the crotch. As he doubles over, firing harmlessly into the air, she leaps up, claws his face, rips off his AR film, and tosses it into the street. She grabs his chin and tilts his face up. She looks into his eyes.

"Shoot yourself," she Says.

He does.

Tossing a cab and its angry Bangladeshi driver aside, Vir staggers up behind Uzma and puts his arms around her. A second later, they're up in the air, shooting over the bridge and into the city. Uzma sees herself and Vir reflected on skyscrapers as they soar through the streets. Vir swerves, soars and dips, turning corners, cutting across alleys, looping around towers, until the world becomes a spinning bowl of shining glass.

"Welcome to Manhattan," says Aman.

The leader is still in pursuit. He's folded in his batwings, and is following them Spidey-style now, sending thin black cables shooting out from his shoulders and smashing into buildings, swinging through the streets like some future-dream Tarzan. Uzma watches him draw close and fall away, and shudders. He seems to have no face, just a blank black mask.

They streak eastwards through Lower Manhattan. They

almost lose their pursuer at the Stock Exchange, but he finds them again at Wall Street Station.

Vir's out of breath. Uzma can hear him moaning and grunting as he flies. He goes through patches of dizziness, blanking out mid-flight, just dropping, and then waking up just before they hit the street. Uzma feels like she's on the world's worst roller coaster. But when Aman tells them their final destination, Vir finds a final burst of energy, and they soar up and away towards the New Twins.

NYPD skybikers race along with them, sirens fill Uzma's head. She and Vir are both familiar faces in New York, the cops are more interested in their pursuer. As Uzma watches, he swings up to a marauding skybike, extends his arm into a long sword, and smashes it through the rider's skull. A second later, he's vaulting off the bike, and grappling on to a tower in a stomach-churning swing that almost brings him right next to Uzma.

And then Uzma's worst fears come true.

At the peak of one swing, the leader sends a black rope arcing their way. Vir screams in agony as the end of the rope transforms into a harpoon and cuts right through the armour into his foot. They're at the New Twin towers now, but Vir falters. Uzma watches in horror as the faceless man pulls himself up and towards them, and Vir loses control, flailing and flapping as they hurtle downwards.

"New plan!" yells Uzma.

"No," says Aman. "The roof. You have to make it."

Vir roars and speeds upwards. Uzma feels her fingers slipping, and hangs on to him with sheer force of will. The leader pulls himself closer.

Windows speed by, horror-stricken office workers' faces

flash past her. She looks down again, into the shapeshifter's empty face. There's a crack where his mouth should be. It looks like a twisted smile.

"Why the roof?" she screams. "What's on it?"

Vir reaches the roof. He throws Uzma forward, and collapses. The harpoon in his foot shrivels away. A sound of flapping wings, and the shapeshifter appears above the roof, batwinged, deadly.

Vir's armour crumbles and falls off him. Through a dizzy, delirious haze, Uzma watches it as if there's nothing else in the world. It folds at incredible speed, and unwraps itself upwards, a high-speed Lego stop-motion tower. It forms a crude human shape. She hears the sound of running feet.

"I am," says Aman.

The armour opens up and folds itself around him mid-leap. A pulse of energy races through the roof. The shapeshifter lands lightly near Uzma. There's a blinding white flash, a shrill scream.

Aman leaps over them, his armour whining and throbbing. He lands and hits the shapeshifter with another plasma blast. As the super's body twists and churns, Aman leaps up to it. He raises his arms and grabs the shifter's head.

Uzma hears a sizzle and smells something horrible burning.

She looks up. Aman stands on the roof. Near his feet is a twitching waist-high blob, wobbling, hissing. Gaps open on its surface, and she hears screams coming out of them as Aman pounds more plasma into the creature. A minute later, it's over, and the shapeshifter is a puddle on the New Twins roof.

Aman races to Uzma. They embrace.

"We're in trouble," he says. "Utopic has Jai."

# CHAPTER **FOURTEEN**

Agent N gives the hoverjet pilots their instructions, and then walks slowly out of the cockpit. His face is grim as he strides through the armoury, and the launching bay. Before entering the holding area, he takes a deep breath and straightens his tie. He mutters a few motivational phrases he picked up that morning from a self-help book. He considers ghosting through the door, giving Jai a bit of a surprise, but instead he counts to ten, mans up and steps forward.

As the door slides open, he sees Jai standing in the middle of his makeshift cell, arms extended unnaturally at his sides, fingers bent into claws, head bowed. Beside him, his young captor holds her tiger stance with grace, though not without effort, great beads of sweat dot her forehead. N clears his throat and rubs his hands together.

"We have several teams combing the planet for you at this very moment," he says. "I've just sent word to them. They'll be relieved. We were all looking forward to meeting you. But I confess we were all terrified of finding you.

"The young lady to your right is someone you've actually met before. May I present the Shadow Puppeteer? You almost caught her last year, when she made the old Statue of Liberty walk. I can see from her face that that was far easier than holding you prisoner."

N considers patting the Puppeteer on the shoulder, but she shoots him an anguished glance and shakes her head, and he decides against it.

"I am known as Agent N," he says. "It's an honour to meet you, Jai. I'm a huge fan. And I have so much to say. I wish we could have just sat down over a drink and discussed it, but I frankly don't dare. But may I start off by saying that we – by which I mean my employers, the board of Utopic, and myself – are your well-wishers, and want to be your friends. And that once I've laid down my proposal to you, we will land the jet and set you free. The only reason we're causing you this discomfort now is that we needed to ensure we had your attention while we explained our intentions."

Jai stands perfectly still.

"Is there any way you could release just enough control to let him shake his head?" N asks the Puppeteer. She rolls her eyes and grimaces. Jai's shoulders twitch, and the Puppeteer groans as she reapplies herself to the task of keeping him still.

"Well, we shall make do," says N.

"Yes," says Jai. "We shall."

He straightens himself up and smiles. The Puppeteer crumples like a paper doll and collapses, moaning. Jai looks at her with interest.

"She's good," he says. "But I've had better."

He thunders towards N, hand outstretched to grip his throat. His hand passes through the agent, and he staggers, but collects his balance immediately.

"Coward," he says.

"Agreed," says N. "Another word for that is smart. Now, Jai, please, before you do anything hasty—"

"I wonder how long it would take me to kill every person on his jet," says Jai.

"A few seconds," says N. "You could also just jump out of the window and make your escape. We're above the Atlantic now, but it wouldn't take you long to swim to wherever you wanted to go. Or you could just take control of the jet."

Jai nods. "But you want me to hear you out before I go," he says.

"Exactly," says N. "Should we get that drink now?"

They sit in the passenger cabin behind the holding area and a crewman brings old-school military Old Monk rum for Jai and a cobalt-coloured cocktail for Agent N. Jai takes a deep swig and sets his glass down with a quiet smile. N doesn't touch his drink.

"Please tell me you didn't just try to poison me," says Jai.

"Of course not. It wouldn't work, would it?"

"No. So you can't eat or drink when you're in this form?"

"No."

"That makes sense. But why aren't you falling through the jet?"

N smiles. "If we were following the laws of physics, Jai, we wouldn't be having this conversation."

"I suppose not," says Jai.

"Finding the limits of our powers is one of the best things

about having them, isn't it? You know, I've spent time in a team whose exclusive mission was figuring out how to kill you."

"Time well spent, clearly. Did you reach a conclusion?"

"Sending you out into orbit was the most popular theory. We thought about dropping you into a volcano—"

"Someone tried that a few years ago. It's not nice. I showed him that. Throwing me into space is the most popular one. Good luck getting me up there, though."

"I see. We also thought the sea floor might work. Put you at the bottom of Mariana Trench and see what happened."

"That's not a bad one, actually. I've never tried that."

N smiles. "Well, hopefully you'll never have to. Of course, capturing you and keeping you unconscious for long enough to put you where we want is the main problem. And we've tried that for a decade now. We've tried to find replacements as well. But the First Wave was something special, wasn't it? Other people have your powers, but you – you stand alone. It's the same problem with that internet supertroll, Aman Sen. We had him killed, but we think he managed to leave this cyber entity behind, a sort of online version of himself. Now all the superhackers we have can't manage to delete it from the internet. It just keeps getting worse. In a way, he's attained immortality."

"Aman Sen is alive," says Jai.

N's eyes widen. "Do you know where he is?" he asks. "He could be very useful."

"He could," says Jai. "But he won't. I should tell you I'm beginning to get a little impatient."

"All right," says N. "Then let's talk work.

"If you had to name the default global villains of the

twenty-first century so far, apart from supervillains, it would be terrorists and big corporations. You could say politicians as well, of course, but there's no point in human history when politicians weren't a central problem. When supers arrived in 2009, that changed. You changed it. Suddenly there were new people, new Alexanders and Genghis Khans, capable of transforming the world singlehanded.

"And then Utopic was formed. Its chief aim: to create a world where humans and supers could live together in harmony. A sustainable world. A noble goal, if we say so ourselves."

"You do. You say so every day, but that doesn't make it true. Your goals and mine were the same, conquest and power, but you lacked the muscle to take my direct approach," says Jai.

"Yes. Which is perhaps why we have succeeded. You could say we were like any other megacorp – worldwide presence, corporate greed, reckless endangerment of powerless humans and natural resources, widespread corruption. And then something changed."

Jai shrugs. "Make your point," he says. "You want me to work with you. What do you want me to do, and what do you want to give me in return?"

"We want you to rule the world."

"Don't be ridiculous."

"Hear me out. It'll all make sense. Look, we're crossing the Atlantic in a fast jet. If you break it and jump into the ocean, you'll have to swim a long way. There's really nothing else particularly productive you can do with this time."

"I suppose not."

"The Utopic board of directors, at this point, is the most powerful collective of people in the world. We own most of the

UN. Most of the US, the EU and South-East Asia. Significant parts of the Arabian Peninsula, and nearly all of Africa. Through subsidiaries, partners, governments and treaties, we run the world. Energy, defence, food, technology, media, entertainment. If there's a pie worth eating, we've got a finger in it. The ultimate comic book evil corporation, yes?"

"Looks like it."

"But then something changed. The board of directors turned super during the early part of the Second Wave. And what a board it was. Businessmen with hearts. Tycoons from across the world, each known for his or her dedication to the sciences, the arts, humanitarian causes, all award-winning leaders of the world."

"Such love. They must pay you very well."

"I can't complain. Six extraordinary individuals who run the world today. There should have been seven, but you killed one of them – the head of the Hisatomi zaibatsu in Japan, one of the founders of the company."

"So I hear. And his son got his spot."

"No. The son was deemed unstable. If you're on the Utopic board and you don't show up for meetings..."

"What powers did they get?"

"Immortality. Each and every one. It makes sense, doesn't it? They were all obsessed with their legacies, and with making the world a sustainable utopia."

"You should have an elevator music soundtrack. I don't need to sit here and listen to you sucking up to your masters, you know."

"Well, they deserve it. I know it seems unlikely, Jai, but they are all good people. Six Immortals – it sounds like something from a legend, doesn't it? Four men, two women. The greatest leaders in the world. From all over the world. And now immortal. That's what changed everything.

"Big business. Megacorps. Ruthless beasts that run on maximising profits and exploiting resources in any way they can. This is their greatest strength, and their biggest problem. But when the world's largest company is headed by immortals, things change. The company starts thinking about the long run. About the world we live in, and how it can be fixed."

"By building zoos for trapping supers. By cutting them up and seeing what's inside," says Jai. "Smart."

"We were only following in your footsteps."

"I was fighting a war. Your zoos are for profit."

"What you call zoos, we call SuperCentres. Most of the revolutionary improvements in the world over the last decade have been thanks to supers trained and employed by Utopic. Look at what we've achieved in the last ten years alone, Jai. Global warming? Solved. Oil crisis? Food crisis? Water crisis? Energy crisis? Avoided. Recession overturned. New technology? Research? Progress? Terraforming? Exponentially accelerated."

"So you claim."

"It's all true. Watch the news."

"Which you own."

"Utopic is going to turn our world into a good place to live for everyone alive on it. We run the world. But we are good people. We make things better."

Jai crosses his arms. "You could put this all in a presentation," he says. "Why have you come to me?"

Agent N licks his lips. "Do you know the world is supposed to end in three days?"

Jai gets up. "Enough," he says.

"Sit down," says N, his voice suddenly harsh. "This is important."

A smile spreads slowly across Jai's face. He returns to his seat.

"Let's talk about nature," says N.

"Let's not," says Jai.

"Indulge me. You, me, the Utopic board, and a few thousand others. We are the next stage. Post-human. In ancient times, we'd have been considered demi-gods. Maybe others like us were. Maybe millennia from now there will be no supers, and our exploits will be legend, and young humans will read about us and think we were works of fiction. Who knows how long this will last? Who knows when it will end? But while we have this chance, we must step forward. We must move the world into a new era."

"Yes, yes. Why are you called Agent N?" asks Jai. "What does it stand for?"

"Nemo."

"Seriously?"

"Nigel," says N. "That's my name. Nigel. Nothing major."

"You're not doing too well, minor Nigel," says Jai. "You're giving me generic publicist-speak for a company I have no interest in. You want to live in a perfect world. Good for you. You want me to set it up for you? Me? Do you even know who I am?"

"You're the apex predator, Jai. You're the last piece in our plan. But I have to explain what the plan is."

"Today?"

"If all this – the super phenomenon – were just as simple as evolution, our goals would have been clearly defined. It would have been supers against humans. We'd have fought them. We'd have won. We'd have emptied the earth from end to end and taken it for ourselves.

"But it's not so simple, because we are not really a new species. Supers don't breed supers. We know. We've tried. Our science cannot tell supers apart from humans at a cellular level. We need humans to survive because, apart from our powers, we are still human. There's no escaping that. Do you read comics?"

"I've read a few," says Jai. "There used to be books lying around the Unit headquarters. I'd been turned into a superhero against my will. I thought I should find out how I was supposed to behave."

"And most supers, at some point or other, have done exactly that. Modelled their behaviour on the spandex brigade. But that doesn't work. Because comics were written for humans. So supers protected the innocent, helped preserve society. Human society. Heroes saved lives, held the earth together. For humans. Or they worked in the shadows, and feared humans. Feared being outcasts. And if they worked against humans, or killed people, they were villains. Megalomaniacs, tyrants, people to be super-punched. If this were one of those stories, Utopic would be an evil corporation."

"Run by immortals. And represented by some smooth-talking, suit-wearing, speech-making idiot," says Jai. "Yes, that would never happen in real life."

"The point, Jai, is that humans and supers must coexist because new supers come from humans, not supers. But that doesn't alter the fact that baseline humans are only relevant now as breeding stock. Raw material. In the new world, they will live lives better than ever before. Most of them will count themselves lucky to be able to experience this age of miracles. And if they are really lucky, they will never even know that mankind's days are done. This end of man that the prophets have been going on about? That's real. That's us."

"I'm confused," says Jai. "You want to coexist with humans. You want to end humans. You want to make the world a better place for humans. Pick one."

"What I'm trying to say is that the systems humans have set up don't work any more. The world that the collective struggles of mankind have led us to has ripened, and has begun to rot. We have to build a new one. A better one. Where humans and supers can live together in peace, each strengthening the other.

"No matter how hard Utopic tries to fix the world, it fails. Corrupt governments. Greedy rival corporations. Man and superman clinging on to the idea that they live in the old world. You know, before all this started, I went to your country once. I had no idea then that the cities I went to would be where the new world began. What impressed me most about your country was the ease with which people ignored the poverty that existed inches from their faces. How you could live your whole lives, every day, in denial, without wondering how long it would be before the poor stopped watching and worshipping you and rose up as one against you? Well, the whole world is doing that now. Supers and humans, pretending nothing has changed. If Utopic were just a company focused on gathering wealth, we'd have been fine with that. But we're not.

"Democracy has failed. It's too easily exploited. Again, India's the best example of that. Even before the warlords took over the north, your country was doomed. Greedy local leaders robbing the illiterate masses while grabbing their votes. A complete breakdown of law and order. Incredibly rich businessmen getting richer, and the poor getting angry. Do you remember?"

"No," says Jai. "But then, I was military. I saw things differently. I believed in India."

"And what did that belief get you?"

"Nothing," says Jai. "I was betrayed."

"The US is even deeper in debt than it was before the First Wave. China works, but it breaks its people in the process. Utopic will not stand for that. The world we build will not have room for poverty, inequality, illiteracy and disease."

"All right, then," says Jai. "I'm sold. You have my vote."

"Before Uzma Abidi enslaved you," says N, "you had a plan. A few of your old followers work for us now. They weren't very clear about what your plan was, exactly, but the essence of it, we understood, was that you would conquer the world. Old school. You would take it over, one country at a time."

Jai grimaces. "It wasn't very well thought out," he says.

"But we liked it," says N. "We think you should do it. We'd like to help."

"This is how you want to make the world better?" asks Jai. "By having me break it apart? You know, before all this started, I spent some time hunting Pakistani terrorists. Young boys, trained to kill and die. To burn the world down so that a new one could be built in its place. They thought they were making the world better too."

"That's not us. We're not anarchists," says N. "We want order and progress above all things. Do you or do you not agree that military rule is the best form of government?"

"It definitely is for businessmen," says Jai. "So that's what all this is about. You want me to be your hired muscle. Don't you have other strongmen?"

"Hundreds," says N. "But that's not what we want you for. We want you to conquer the world for yourself. We want to invest in you. Supply you with the teams you need. And the resources. It's all ready."

"And what do you want in return?"

"We want to heal the world when you're done."

"Own everything."

"We want to build a world where there's no need for money or property. Where everything, and everyone is free. A utopic world. Hence the name on the business cards."

Jai sits back and stares at N in disbelief. N looks right back, his gaze frank and open. It's a whole five minutes before Jai speaks again.

"I don't understand," he says. "Why me?"

"Let me be frank," says N. "Your availability is a lucky coincidence. We didn't know you'd free yourself from Uzma. We thought you'd be our biggest problem. Jai, we don't believe in destiny, or divine providence. We're not a religion. But if we were, finding you would be the best possible proof of the righteousness of our path.

"Why you? Because you're the best man for the job. Because you're stronger than any other leader we could find. The truth is we can do this without you. But we'd rather not. And we've studied you. We know you have no interest in running the world. We know you couldn't care less about material wealth. We know that you once offered Aman Sen the job we're going to do. The difference is that we can get it done. He would have failed.

"And let's face facts. A military ruler isn't going to be popular, no matter how wonderful the world he runs is. People need a leader they can fear and hate. Even in our utopia, there will be criminals. There will be rebellions. There will be many who want the old world back. We need a man strong enough to face them. Are you that man?"

"I could be," says Jai.

"Excellent," says N. "Then we have an agreement?"

"That depends," says Jai. "Are you going to shake my hand?"

Jai holds his arm out. N does too, but Jai's hand passes through his.

Jai keeps his hand out. "That didn't work, did it? You'll have to – how do you describe it? Turn solid again."

"Come on, Jai," says N. "You're the most dangerous person in the world. I... wouldn't feel safe."

"That's a problem, isn't it? No one would feel safe. Let's say I agree. Let's say you give me a super army. How do you know I won't turn on you?"

"It's our army."

"How do you know I'll give you the world once I've won it?"

"What would you do with it?"

"Whatever I want. You'd never trust me. You have no reason to."

Jai draws his arm back. "No, Agent, N," he says. "My answer is no. As your friend in the other room found out, I am no one's puppet."

"That's unfortunate," says N. "But you should know this is happening with or without you."

"And what if I decide to stop it?" asks Jai.

"Then our considerable investment in finding out how to kill you would be money and time well spent," says N.

Jai stands up. "Good luck," he says. "I like you, Nigel. One day I'm going to kill you."

N sighs. "I see I'm going to have to tell you why we're doing this," he says.

"That would be a start, yes."

"Sit?"

Jai rolls his eyes and slumps back into his chair.

"We cannot be stopped," says N. "That isn't big talk. It's just impossible to destroy Utopic now. We're everywhere. There's no one person you can kill. No secret board meeting you can invade. No single apocalypse that one brave band of heroes can team up to stop while people eat popcorn and watch them. We're like a hydra. Like a wiki. This is happening because it needs to.

"Much of our efforts, as a species, have gone into extending our lives. It's a basic human desire. People want to live longer. To live forever if they can. All six of our directors – and these are people who are more intelligent and ambitious than you or I can ever dream of being – became immortals when they became supers. But this is not about them.

"Most of economics is based around an essential problem – limited resources, unlimited wants. The earth can support only so many people before we ruin it. But over the centuries, we've become adept at making people live longer. We fight diseases. We invent prosthetics. We replace organs. And this is before the age of supers even arrived.

"Now with the combined power of human science and super abilities, we're making it possible for people to have longer and richer lives than anyone dreamed possible. Not just by making humans healthier and stronger, or by fixing their problems. We're overcoming everything that killed them. We're making super-nutrients and clean energy. We're taming tsunamis, softening earthquakes, preventing epidemics. We're cleaning water, cutting pollution, controlling the weather. We're using Uzma Abidi and her blundering hippy diplomacy to stop wars before they start. We're living, we're growing older, we're breeding, and we're overrunning our planet.

"Our current population is above eight billion people. Without supers, the world would have been able to sustain two billion. With us, and the improvements we bring, three billion people can live stable, healthy, sustainable, long lives in a clean, happy world. Utopic has been exploring the possibilities of colonising other planets, even building new worlds or opening new dimensions for humans to live in. So far, it hasn't worked. In fact, most of the magicians who could make it work refuse to work for us. They reject our help, our facilities. They run and hide, and live in communities in remote parts of the world. We watch them. We help them secretly. They haven't succeeded yet, and we don't know if they ever will. But let's say we keep an extra billion people on the world in case we need colonists. That's four billion people. That's the population of the world in the 1970s. There is more than double that number in the world right now. This cannot work.

"Over the years, Utopic has secretly sponsored millions of deaths. We've allowed natural disasters to take place. We've started controlled epidemics. We've unleashed monsters. We've allowed super-combat tournaments to take place in populated areas. Sponsored wars. We've done this quietly, off the books, away from the news. But though this was all necessary, we couldn't convince ourselves it was the right thing to do."

Despite himself, Jai gulps. "And why is that?" he asks.

"Because it's not fair. We're not Nazis. We're not religious fundamentalists, or bigots of any kind. We believe all people are born equal, and some are made superior by sheer luck. Every population control exercise we've run has led to serious differences among board members."

"That's horrifying," says Jai. "The Utopic bosses... argue?"

"I can see how it might be amusing from the outside," says N. "But yes. We can meet our population targets in a few years with our current programmes, but none of them are fair. We don't want to run our population control measures in any specific part of the world, against any race or religion. We don't think the prosperous deserve life more than the poor, the clever more than the stupid. We believe in diversity. In freedom. We're not killers."

"Not at all," says Jai. "You're just making the world better."

"It's a burden we must bear. And the board decided that the only clean way to achieve our goals would be war. Everywhere in the world. A carefully controlled war, that ends in lasting peace. A war fought without nuclear or biological weapons. A clean war, fought by supers. The thing is, Jai, these deaths are going to happen anyway. The world simply cannot continue the way it is now. Our only chance to ensure that our kind survives is to take charge of it. And with you as leader, we can build the utopia we've always dreamed of. You're the perfect man for the job. Will you take it?"

"Yes," says Jai.

N picks up his drink, finishes it in one gulp, and holds out his hand.

"I've been authorised to offer you a temporary place on the Utopic board," he says. "Seven Immortals. You cannot believe how happy you've made me, Jai. How happy I am to just be a part of this."

Jai smiles. "I started today thinking I'd meet some old colleagues and straighten things out," he says. "And now it looks like I have to kill exactly half the world as well. How things pile up."

"Think of it this way," says N. "Today morning you didn't know if you belonged in the world. And now you know you're going to rule it."

"And when can I meet the rest of the board?"

"Not yet," says N.

"I suppose not," says Jai. "All right then. When do I start?"

"In three days, we'll announce the formation of the new Unit," says N. "This would seem like an ideal day for your first assault."

"Where?"

"New York seems logical," says N. "Traditional, even."

"Perfect," says Jai.

# CHAPTER **FIFTEEN**

"As prisons go, I suppose things could be worse," says Norio. "I guess you set standards really high with that nuclear submarine."

"Would you like some wine?" asks Tia.

"Yes, please."

Tia pours out a glass. "Well, you can't have any," she says, and takes a sip.

They're in a penthouse in Atlantis Apartments, a sprawling luxury complex in central Gurgaon. Sher's troops occupied it two years ago, and converted it into a fortress, but like all high-end Indian concrete jungles it had sealed itself off from the harsh world outside from its very beginning. It is self-sufficient in every way. Norio sits on a massive sofa in the living room, his arms tied behind his back. At the other end of the sofa, a curled-up Tia cradles a rifle. A giant floating screen plays reruns of a marital-discord Bengali soap opera. To Norio's right, bright Gurgaon sunlight does its best to break through the screen that covers the sliding glass doors leading to the balcony. Norio has been outside once, and has no desire to return to the balcony with its depressing view of other residential towers, flyovers and yet more concrete. The room is full of fake Italian marble, fake flowers, ugly statues and large gilt-framed pictures of colourful Indian gods. The previous residents' tastes hadn't been very Japanese. The sound of splashing water and another Tia singing loudly in the jacuzzi float out from a nearby bathroom.

A holo-screen pops up in front of Tia; it's another Tia.

"They're here," she says.

Tia nods, and shuts off the soap opera with a wave.

"A few hours ago, your friends at Utopic tried to kill Uzma," she says. "Like you, they failed."

"Good," says Norio. "I didn't really have any interest in Uzma. I wanted Jai."

"Well, he was there too," says Tia. "Now what I need from you is a way to find the Utopic board."

Norio shrugs. "They don't keep me up to date, you know," he says. "I stopped attending meetings a long time ago. If they're after the Unit openly now, it's a big move. But I don't know what their game is."

"That's good to know," says Tia. "And since you never tell lies, I might as well stop asking."

"You're not going to torture me," says Norio. "If you want me to tell you everything I know, you know my price. Take me to Kalki."

Tia chuckles. "Whatever else you are, you're no quitter," she says. "No. You're not getting anywhere near Kalki. You're not getting anything you want."

"I know your last stint as my jailer didn't go too well," says

Norio. "But let's move past that. This time it's important, Tia. This isn't about revenge. It's about saving the world."

"I'm sure your master plan is a good one," says Tia. "But you have to understand, it's over. We know what you're like, and we're not taking any more chances."

"I need to see Kalki," says Norio. "Please, Tia. When this is done, you'll see I was right."

"Yeah, well, no," says Tia. "Trust me, I'm doing you a favour. He's crazy. He wouldn't understand what you asked for, he'd just do any random thing he felt like."

The doorbell rings and they both jump: it's a screechy Hindu invocation. Tia swears and covers her ears.

"Who do you think that might be?" she asks. "Your detective girlfriend? Why didn't she come with you?"

Norio has nothing to say. A Tia blossoms out of the one on the couch and gets the door. It's Jason and Anima.

Norio waves at them cheerily as they walk to the living room, looking around at the apartment. Tia speaks, but Norio cannot hear her above the sound of a large plane outside.

"This is pretty stylish," says Jason. "Tia, I know we're all about ethical treatment of prisoners, but this is a bit relaxed even for you."

"I'd tied him up," says Tia, glaring at Norio, whose wrists are noticeably rope-free. "What did you expect, a dungeon?"

"Hi Anima," says Norio, yelling slightly. The plane outside is very large… "You know, a lot of Japanese girls grew anime powers in the Second Wave. They all hate you."

Anima giggles. "Not to my face they don't," she says.

"You're quite popular, strangely enough," says Norio to Jason. "But I keep forgetting your name."

"I'm shattered," says Jason. He turns to Tia. "Want to come along?" he asks.

"There are about fifteen of me in New York," says Tia. "Plus I've really had enough of dear Norio here. Enjoy him. You want to get some rest before you leave? How long is that bloody plane going to take to cross?"

Tia's phone rings. Then above the sound of the jet outside, a shrill alarm rings out: a siren. Anima covers her eyes and sparks fly out of her fingers as she yells.

And then there's a massive crash. The building shudders. Every glass surface in the room shatters. The walls crack. A dagger-sized piece of glass flies across the room from the balcony and Norio dives for the floor. It nicks him on the ear instead of slicing into his neck.

The electricity goes and, suddenly, the sunlight is cut off. The apartment falls into darkness. Anima flares up, green orbs appearing, sizzling on her hands, as Tia races through a cloud of dust to the balcony, and pulls the screen up.

Her eyes meet ARMOR's. The giant mecha's empty diamond gaze sweeps the apartment.

Behind Tia, Jason swings into action: small objects, glass and chunks of plaster gather in a swarm. ARMOR's head snaps back, and the apartment is flooded with sunlight again.

They watch ARMOR's right arm clench into a fist, and hurtle towards the balcony. Jason sends his glass-cloud smashing into the mecha's face, but ARMOR shows no sign of noticing it. Anima's light-spears spark and sizzle, leaving burnt streaks on ARMOR's neck.

ARMOR's fist smashes into the balcony. The walls crumple like paper as the metal battering-ram thunders into the room, and stops a few feet short of Norio. Tia falls in a haze of glass and concrete.

ARMOR withdraws its arm, and the floor caves.

Norio scrabbles desperately, but there's nothing to hold on to, the world's tilting and breaking around him. The sunlight blinds him as he falls, empty apartments flash by in a blur as he hurtles towards the ground far below. ARMOR's roar has faded into the distance. The world is a solid wall of whistling wind.

Ignoring Anima, Jason, and three rifle-toting Tias, ignoring the slide of plaster and metal, ARMOR bends smoothly and catches Norio a few feet from the ground.

Anima leaps out of the gaping hole in the penthouse, a ball of green light exploding out of rubble.

ARMOR's lower jaw slides down, it tosses Norio inside, and shuts its mouth. It squats. Plates on its back and legs slide lower, broadening and fanning out. The giant mecha shuffles, moving its legs further apart.

Anima lands on its shoulders. Green katanas grow out of her hands.

Jason leaps out of the building as well, on a metal skateboard torn from a pipe.

Holsters carrying rockets pop out of ARMOR's calves. With a roll of thunder and a billowing cloud of orange smoke, the mecha jets off, straightening up and thrusting its right arm skywards as it streaks past Atlantis Apartments and into the sky.

Anima digs her katanas into ARMOR's shoulders. There's a sizzle and a shower of sparks, but the swords scrape and fizzle as Anima loses her balance, and falls.

Jason, all attention set on building a grappling hook out of concrete in mid-air, doesn't even see the torrents of flame shooting at him. A second before he's burnt to a crisp in ARMOR's jet stream, a lasso of green light curls around his foot. Anima hangs on to ARMOR's thigh with claws of power, and Jason roars in pain as she draws the noose tight, sending him flailing as he flies, higher and higher, columns of rocket-fire a few feet from his bobbing face.

Norio slides through the delivery tube down to ARMOR's stomach. There are spare uniforms in the backup pod, but he doesn't bother putting one on. Still unsteady on his feet, he clambers up to the central control chamber and gestures the passcode, wondering whom Azusa had brought along with her.

The door slides open, and Norio feels tears sting his eyes.

They're all there. Standing on their control pods, display screens floating around them, combat-control holograms shadowing their every movement. Raiju, smiling grimly; Oni and Baku, shaking their heads and grinning. Norio looks at Azusa, but she's too focused on the controls to meet his gaze. Her face is as serene and serious as it is in his guiltiest thoughts, and he can't remember when he last felt this good. He steps up to his control pod, lets ARMOR's scanners run over him, holds his arms out, watches the holograms cover his body, and breathes deeply. He'd thought he'd never get to do this again.

"Thank you," says Norio.

"Save your thanks for Amabie," says Baku. "She is our leader, just to be clear."

"Of course," says Norio. "What's the mission?"

"We know what we're here for, Norio," says Raiju. "Amabie told us. And we're only here because we think you're doing the right thing."

"And you should have just told us," says Oni.

"Can he really make it happen?" asks Baku. "Can he make us all equal?"

"I believe he can," says Norio.

"Then I'm glad I came," says Raiju.

"How did you do that?"

"Flew."

"And no one stopped you?"

"Phones were on silent."

"Over China?"

"Told them we were going to make a lot of trouble in India."

"And they just let you pass?"

"Yes. If I met a three-hundred-foot mecha and it wanted to go somewhere else, would I try and stop it?"

"Well," says Norio, "thank you."

"Look at us," says Baku. "Team unity for humans and everything."

"Should we do one of the group fist-pump things from the anime?" asks Oni. The others laugh.

"Do you know where Kalki is?" asks Azusa.

"No," says Norio. "Do you have the coordinates of the mall where he was supposed to be?"

"Of course," says Azusa. "So we go there and hunt him down?"

"One child. One three-hundred-foot mecha," says Baku. "Shouldn't be too difficult."

"Unless he's fighting against us," says Norio. "He's supposed to be a god. Amabie, is there any way of locating him as you did me?"

"No."

"How many humans in the mall?"

"Unknown. The bulk of Sher's army is there, but I don't know if the surveillance footage I found is reliable. Aman might be tampering with it."

"In that case, we need to smoke Kalki out," says Norio. "How far away is this mall?"

"We'll be there in ten minutes," says Azusa.

"Let's show them it would be a bad idea to stay indoors," says Norio.

"Right," says Azusa. "Time to turn around, then."

ARMOR stands in the sky above the gaping ruin of Atlantis Apartments, shining in the sunlight, the vertical boosters on its lower back humming and pulsing blue as they keep the mecha-bot in mid-air. It raises its wrists and launch tunnels slide out of its arms. One by one, missiles slide into place.

Anima flies out from below ARMOR's waist. A beam of light slices through the air, stopping a hundred feet in front of the giant mecha. Anima turns, crouched in warrior-stance on a disc of light. The anime princess and Tokyo's defender face each other, Anima's round cartoon eyes never leaving ARMOR's blank, sparkling diamonds. If Anima feels any fear at the sight of the tower-sized death-engine floating in front of her, she does not show it.

Seven missiles fly towards Anima.

But another figure, rushing up from below ARMOR, flies faster. Jason sits astride a spinning board of metal he's ripped off a rooftop water tank. He extends his arms and kneels on his board as he flies towards Anima. The missiles swerve and stand in mid-air, shaking and hissing. Jason crosses them and stands up, and the missiles turn again, their noses pointing straight back at the mecha-giant.

Anima hurls her spear. It streaks towards ARMOR's head, and the missiles follow it, smoke streaming in their wake.

ARMOR crosses its arms across its chest. A panel opens on its forehead, and blue rings of light emerge, barely visible in the bright sunlight.

The missiles snap out of their trajectories and fall spinning to earth. Anima and Jason watch helplessly as they land on the buildings below them. Seven fireballs blossom across the complex.

ARMOR spins through a sequence of attack katas, and launches another barrage of missiles that scatter across the development. Jason diverts some of them, but at least twenty escape him, and Atlantis burns.

Twin jets of fire stream out from ARMOR's hands.

Jason builds a wall in mid-air and stops them, but a second later ARMOR charges, covering the short distance in an instant, smashing right through the wall, and Jason and Anima, swatted like flies, fall into the burning cloud.

As more explosions shake the complex, and burning towers fall like dominoes, ARMOR rises again, and heads east.

None of the mecha-pilots in the control sphere in ARMOR's heart notice a lasso of light spin out of the inferno and loop itself around the mecha-giant's left foot. Or the green ball of light at the other end of the lasso that rises behind ARMOR, bouncing about crazily through the crumbling towers, carrying Jason and Anima within it.

* * *

"This isn't right, Amabie," says Baku. "We killed a lot of innocent people."

"They were soldiers," says Azusa. "They knew what they were getting into."

"ARMOR *protects* cities," says Raiju. "This isn't what we do."

"You know what we're trying to accomplish," says Azusa. "This is a war. Lives will be lost."

Baku disconnects from ARMOR's controls.

"Not thanks to me," he says. "I'm out."

"Then get out," snarls Azusa.

The others watch in silence as Baku storms towards the exit, stops, growls, and walks slowly back to his control pod. Azusa waves in adjustments, and ARMOR switches to five-man controls again.

"Tell me what you sense," says Norio to Azusa. "Where are the Tias?"

"Large group at the mall," says Azusa. "All moving."

"Kalki will be with Sher," says Norio. "Tias will run the defence while they make their escape. There should be at least one Tia with Sher when he leaves the mall. So watch out for Tias heading out."

Azusa nods, and closes her eyes. A trickle of blood runs out of her left ear.

"Are you hurt?" Raiju asks.

"No," says Azusa. "Now let me focus."

"Raiju," says Norio. "Give me a visual on the mall. Internal scans, too. Fill the room."

Raiju waves her surveillance panels open. A floating model of the mall appears in the centre of the control sphere, but as the image begins to sharpen, it turns grainy and disappears.

"Lost the satellite," says Raiju.

"Aman's watching," says Norio. "Turn off anything that connects to an external network. And I mean *everything*."

The mall is visible on the main viewer now, and far below them Norio sees the ant-like figures of Sher's soldiers on the roof. Sensors flash red: artillery posts are firing surface-to-air missiles at them, though nothing strong enough to breach ARMOR's hide. The mall courtyard is a flurry of activity: cars, SUVs, motorbikes and armoured auto-rickshaws stream out of the parking lots and out on the street.

The alarms sound again as ARMOR makes its first sweep over the mall: to the south, an attack helicopter approaches, firing missiles. ARMOR's shoulder-pads slide apart to reveal plasma cannons.

One burst, and the helicopter's crew are the first casualties of the battle at the MegaMall.

Suddenly all the lights inside the control chamber turn red, and a hologram of ARMOR appears in the middle of the sphere, its left leg red and blinking.

"Hull breach," says Azusa.


Anima's out of breath, but her strength and stamina are unrelenting as she smashes the point of her power-lance into the joint behind ARMOR's knee. It has taken a while: the mecha's left leg is covered in dents and burns, but she's finally managed to pierce ARMOR's skin. She falls back, screeching in triumph.

A few feet below her, Jason yells too, and slides his metal harness upwards. His face contorts with strain as he reaches up, and thrusts his hand into the metal gash. The crack in ARMOR's hide widens, and Jason peels the mecha's knee skin like a piece of fruit. In a few seconds several square metres of complex circuitry and wiring are revealed. ARMOR's innards are laid bare. Jason's lips curl upwards; Anima is less restrained, howling as she flies forward, katanas raised.

They go to work.

ARMOR twists and turns in the sky above the MegaMall, ignoring the missiles fired from below. For a giant mecha, ARMOR is remarkably flexible, but no kaiju has ever required it to touch the back of its legs. It shakes its leg about, but Jason hangs on grimly, and Anima is too quick.

"We're going to lose the leg," says Baku. "We need to split up."

"No," says Azusa. "Our communications might be jammed."

"Crash down into the building, then," says Raiju. "That'll shake them off."

"Too many casualties," says Norio "If we destroy the mall and the kid hasn't left, all this will be for nothing."

"Focus on the mission," says Azusa. "This is a distraction."

"Tell me," Norio says to her. "Where is Kalki?"

In response, Azusa brings up three screens. One shows a convoy of orange and black SUVs pulling out of the mall's driveway. Another shows three armoured rickshaws, heading west, about a kilometre from the mall's gates.

The third visual is of a single vehicle leaving the mall through the rear entrance.

"No Tias in that one," says Azusa. "But I think it's our prime suspect."

It's obvious why. The vehicle is a tank.

"We hunt them down, one by one," says Azusa. "Let's start with the tank."

"No," says Norio. "The tank seems obvious. They know we're watching. Both the other possibilities are convoys. With Tias splitting up in a hundred directions we could be looking forever."

"What then?" asks Raiju. "We've almost lost a leg."

"I have a plan," says Norio.

"Not you," says Baku. "Amabie. What do we do?"

Azusa walks up to Norio. She grabs his head and kisses him. Oni breaks into applause. Baku and Raiju look away. When Azusa lets Norio go, they're both smiling.

"Here's what we do," says Azusa.

Anima pulls Jason away just in time.

ARMOR's leg snaps backward, plates sliding and interlocking, three blades bursting out of the space where Jason's body was a second ago. The gaping hole they've created in ARMOR's leg disappears in a melee of moving parts as ARMOR transforms.

Anima and Jason keep attacking: she sends light-shuriken sizzling into every undefended gap she sees, and he sends parts of ARMOR spinning out of the whirl of machinery, building a sphere of metal parts around himself. But, despite their efforts, two minutes later, five complete demon-mechas hover above the MegaMall.

\* \* \*

Oni and Baku engage Anima and Jason immediately.

A sonic blast from Baku sends Anima spinning downwards; while Oni goes straight for the kill, sending a horn-missile bursting through Jason's defences.

Jason dodges and the ridged rocket misses him by a whisker, but, in the process, Jason loses control of his whirling metal shield, and falls helplessly towards the mall.

Baku and Oni's demon-mechas follow their opponents down into the combat zone, bullets from machine-gun fire on the roof pinging off their hides like endless rain.

Baku looks down at the column of tanks and artillery vehicles crawling out of the mall's parking lot, and swears as he steers his mecha away, lining up his weapons for a bombing run.

Raiju heads west after the armoured autos. Goryo speeds off east after the SUVs. The tank, to the south, is Amabie's.

The lightning wolf makes the first strike. Raiju's wolf-mecha lands heavily on the road in front of the autos. The first few are thrown off the road by the sheer impact. Tiger-tattooed Tias roll out of the vehicles, bathing the red wolf in gunfire. More Tias leap from the other autos, carrying rocket launchers.

Suddenly, Raiju faces a mob.

But the mecha strides on, its fangs crunching through one auto after another, methodically checking for any signs of Kalki, alive or dead, and shuddering under the impact of rockets and grenades. When Raiju's sensors show critical damage levels, the wolf squats on its haunches. A cannon emerges from its mouth.

The Tias crumble into dust as Raiju bathes them in chain

lightning. The wolf-mecha looks down the road, where four more autos roll resolutely westwards.

Raiju leaps forward in pursuit.

Goryo's ghost-mecha flies over the SUV convoy as it speeds up a flyover. Inside his control chamber, Norio feels as if his body is on fire; every nerve is tingling, time has slowed down. He's never been more in control.

Skylights flip open on the SUVs. Tias emerge, wielding heavy rail guns.

Goryo strafes from left to right, minimising the damage to his bodywork. The mecha's black skull slides forward with an eerie moan as it falls back. Its teeth lengthen and start to spin as it moves lower, and lower still, a line of fifteen razor-sharp spinning blades.

Goryo darts forward, he's just a few feet behind the last SUV. One plasma-burst destroys a Tia. Goryo moves lower. The blades shred through the SUV's roof in a second, like the world's deadliest can opener. Even from inside his demon-mecha, Norio can hear the squeal of anguished metal, see the shower of sparks. He rises swiftly, and scans the SUV. No Kalki. A plasma burst melts a huge circle on the road, and sends the SUV spinning, leaping, tumbling off the flyover.

Norio steers his mecha forward again.

As he mows his way across the mall's roof, dotting it with machine-gun fire, Baku remembers the first time he'd played a First-Person Shooter. It had been a World War II simulation, and he'd been amazing at it. If he'd stuck to it, just played the tournaments, never ventured into online quests, he'd never have met the ARMOR squadron. If he hadn't been so good at the shooters, he'd have killed fewer people on the roof. Sher's soldiers die screaming as he chases Jason across the roof; Baku tries not to imagine their families.

The telekinetic moves fast, pulling himself close to any heavy object he can find, darting from corner to corner as Sher's men die around him. When he finds a heap of moulded aluminium sheets, he stops. As Baku streams ahead, Jason sends them flying after the mecha. The sheets curve and wrap themselves over the metal demon. One cam-feed after another disappears. In one remaining side-cam, Baku watches Anima and Oni battle above the courtyard. The teen princess shields herself well from Oni's attacks. She doesn't know Oni could out-princess her in five seconds anywhere else in the world. Baku smiles grimly.

And then a volley from the tanks below finds its mark. Oni's mecha shudders and lurches. Anima hurls a volley of light-arrows. And Baku watches helplessly as Oni explodes.

Baku tries his communicator again but it doesn't work. He hears his own voice in his head, telling himself calmly to get out while he still can, to turn back time, to fight monsters again, not superheroes.

But he sees his hands waving a change in his flight path. As if from far away, he hears himself screaming in rage as he turns his mecha and races towards Anima.

The tank had left the road a while ago. It's ploughing through an abandoned construction site now, trundling steadily over any obstacle in its path. The gunner is good: the tank's turret swivels with remarkable speed, the main gun firing shells at Amabie with fearsome accuracy as she hovers above it. There's a fast machine-gun on the tank's hatch, sending a steady stream of bullets pounding into the mermaid's body. Azusa ignores it. Only the main gun has the capacity to pierce her scales, and Azusa's reflexes have always been the best in her squad: even Norio could only defeat her half the time. She times her sideways darts perfectly, waiting for the right moment to strike. She's beginning to enjoy herself, to find patterns in the gunner's behaviour. It's only when her tail-cam picks up the mid-air explosion in the distance above the mall that she remembers her teammates need her help.

The golden mermaid's tail curves forward, and a ball of goo speeds towards the tank. The first one hits a crane that comes in the way; the second is on target. The main and co-axial guns are immediately disabled. A third ball takes out the machine-gun. Blind and weaponless, the tank lurches to the right, mowing through half-built walls, and disappearing in a cloud of dust.

Amabie flies low above it. Twin spikes emerge from the mermaid's arms. With the precision of a sushi chef, Azusa slices the tank's hatch open. She runs a scan.

As the tank stumbles into a ditch, Sher leaps out of the hatch. Azusa spots a bright blue bundle cradled in his right arm. She zooms in from her tail-cam. A horse's head bobs wildly as Sher leaps into the dust-cloud, two blue arms wrapped around his neck.

It's Kalki.

There's a fork in the flyover, one branch heading east, another north. Norio spots it too late: he cannot launch missiles in time to break either branch without destroying the SUVs speeding towards it. The convoy divides into two: four cars head east, four others go north. Norio picks the eastern branch, changes his mind, curses, and veers northward.

Clenching his fists, he slows down, and opens distance-cam panels. He can't see Oni. Raiju's heading back towards the mall. Baku's on fire above it. And then he spots Amabie, racing through a construction site. Even at maximum zoom, he cannot see what she's chasing.

Hoping for a miracle, Azusa opens her com-link, but the line is blocked. Cursing the day Aman Sen was born, she chases Sher.

She's amazed at the tiger-man's grace as he races through the construction site, free-running over walls, body almost horizontal, slowing down only to execute incredible leaps over rubble. But he cannot match the mecha for speed. Her attack controls blink and flash; she has him in her sights. One well-placed plasma-burst from the mermaid's shoulder-cannons would kill him. But it would also kill Kalki.

Azusa pops the remote control section on her sphere open. She puts on her AR goggles and remote gauntlets swiftly, watching as they generate holograms that climb up her wrists and around her head. Sher has reached open ground now. He's heading for cover, racing towards the skeleton of a tall building a short distance ahead. Azusa opens up her control sphere and the entrance hatch. The sound of the wind roaring shuts out everything else. She slides out of the sphere, wondering why she hasn't bothered to put on her armour. Her fingers move swiftly, touching spots on the holo-spheres around her hands.

The mermaid-mecha darts ahead of Sher, and sends a burst of gunfire skidding into the ground in front of him. The warning shots sting the earth. Clouds of dust rise in front of Sher. He slows down.

Azusa stands inside the entrance hatch on the mermaid's stomach. She blinks as the dust-cloud covers her, and raises her hand. Sher stops. Hovering twenty feet in front of him, Azusa meets his eyes, and some ancient part of her shivers.

"You've lost," she calls. "Hand him over."

"Never," roars Sher.

"Kalki!" calls Azusa. "Make him put you down!"

The blue boy giggles and shakes his head.

"You'll have to go through me," says Sher.

Azusa nods. She waves, and her mecha descends. Sher sets Kalki down on the ground, and moves forward, keeping himself between the boy-god and Azusa. Azusa jumps down, wincing as she lands on her feet.

"Who are you?" roars Sher. "Why do you want him?"

"It doesn't matter," says Azusa.

Her thumb twitches slightly.

Sher crouches, and charges.

Azusa flexes her thumb. And a plasma-blast from Amabie's cannon hits the tiger-man in the chest. The impact knocks Sher back at least ten feet. His body tumbles, stops, twitches, and is still.

Azusa runs up to Kalki. He seems perfectly happy to see her. The horrible smell of burnt flesh and hair doesn't appear to affect him at all. She gathers him up and races back to her mecha, her heart pounding. She leaps into her control sphere, and sets Kalki down. The boy is fascinated by the displays around him. Something about his large black eyes fills her with terror.

As she takes off, the mecha lurches, knocking Azusa off balance. She regains control quickly, and Amabie rises into the sky. Then the mecha lurches again. Azusa loads her cam-feeds quickly, checking in every direction.

Sher's body is gone.

Something pounds on the mecha's hull, sending loud echoes rippling through the control sphere. Her tail-cam sees it first. It's Sher, scrabbling at the entrance hatch. Azusa watches in horror as he pounds it again, and the metal dents under the force of his paws.

Amabie rises higher, and spikes emerge from her hands. They swivel and swing through the air, but Sher's too close to cut. He's a wreck: his fur is burnt or gone, large patches of pink skin exposed to the swirling dust. Kalki points at the cam-screen, and neighs in triumph.

Azusa gestures wildly, and her demon responds. The mecha twists and turns, tilting as far as it can, but Sher cannot be thrown off – he seems to be clinging on through sheer willpower. They're far above the ground now. All Azusa has to do is knock Sher off balance – his wounds and gravity will take care of the rest.

Sher claws open the corner of the entrance hatch. He sticks one paw inside, and pulls.

Azusa considers leaving the control sphere and trying to push him off. She can hear him roaring now.

Her tail-cam shows a monstrous black shape racing towards her. Azusa gasps.

Goryo.

Sher rips the entrance hatch open. He tosses the door aside, just as Amabie darts forward. Sher loses his balance. He's alone in mid-air for a moment, but gets one of his paws to Amabie's tail as he falls, claws cutting grooves on the mermaid's body. Azusa tilts her mecha again, but in the wrong direction. She groans as Sher leaps off the tail, landing perfectly on the open hatch. She glances at her tail-cam, and catches her breath.

Norio is here. Sher is in his sights.

He flies up next to Amabie, matching her speed with uncanny precision. He takes aim, and hits the tiger-man with a sonic blast.

Sher's body wilts, but does not crumble. He leaps inside Azusa's mecha, looks up, and sees the control sphere.

Goryo fires a plasma burst into Amabie's open hatch.

All Azusa's alarms ring out at once. Several of her control screens flicker and die as the plasma burst rips through the mermaid-mecha's insides. The mecha's out of control now: it spins and darts from side to side, spewing smoke and fire. Azusa and Kalki roll and tumble inside the control sphere, Kalki shrieking with laughter. Azusa hears Sher pounding on the control sphere's door. His strength is beyond belief: three strikes, and the door crumbles.

Sher falls into the chamber.

For a second, Azusa and Sher's eyes meet, and then they're both thrown against the sphere's walls as Amabie rolls through the air. Azusa grabs Kalki. As the gaping hole in the sphere where the door recently met Sher rolls towards her, she closes her eyes, takes a deep breath, and leaps.

She feels a sharp pain in her side as she hits the mecha's crumbling outer wall. The entrance hatch is nearby. A patch of sunlight darts around her, she feels as if she's inside a bowling ball. She holds Kalki close to her, and turns her body.

A blood-curdling roar, and she sees Sher pulling himself out of the control sphere, eyes locked on Kalki. He smells of fire and blood and death.

Azusa leaps for the outer hatch.

And then she's falling through the sky, the earth rushing up towards her. Kalki clings on to her hand, his mane billowing in the rushing wind as time freezes around her.

A horrifying crash. They land on the ghost-mecha's head. Norio pulls back sharply as the mermaid-mecha hurtles downward, past Goryo. It spins like a top, sending spirals of black smoke in its wake. Azusa's body slides towards the edge of Goryo's head, she has nothing to hold on to, but Norio tilts Goryo slightly, and she regains her balance. Kalki pulls his hand away from hers. She panics, but he seems perfectly balanced. He pats the demon-mecha's head and wriggles in glee.

She hears a thump, somewhere near. She smells Sher before she sees him. She turns her head and sees him clawing desperately at the mecha's skull-face as he pulls himself up. His paw is burnt and bleeding, it scratches the black demon-mecha's head.

The tiger-man's weight throws Goryo off balance. Azusa feels the mecha tilting slowly to the side, and feels her body begin to slide towards Sher. Everything hurts. She scrambles to her right. Kalki's sliding too, towards Sher, but still out of his reach.

A hatch opens near her head. Norio leaps out, tottering as the mecha tilts. He holds on to the door with one hand. The world tilts crazily, but he has a free hand, and he can save the world with it.

Sher moves closer to Kalki. He roars, a horrible sound full of fear and anger. The mecha tilts further, and Azusa cannot hold on any more. She slides down, and sees Kalki sliding as well. A few seconds, and he'll be off the edge.

She sees Norio, looking at her, looking at Kalki.

She realises he cannot save them both.

She sees Sher, crouching, preparing to leap at Kalki. She sees Norio, turning away from Kalki, facing her, drawing a deep breath.

He's chosen her.

All the world to save, and he's chosen her. She looks into his eyes, and smiles.

Gathering all her strength, Azusa lunges at Sher. She wraps her arms around his neck. His claws screech, and then lose their grip.

They fall over the edge.

Norio lunges at Azusa, but she's gone.

He grabs Kalki instead, and pulls him into the hatch. He shuts the door and staggers into his control sphere. He searches for the other mechas. He cannot see them.

Norio turns his mecha's face eastwards and upwards. He sets it on autopilot and sits on the floor, eyes wide open, too numb to even think.

# CHAPTER SIXTEEN

After the Doom-Dunker had levelled the fourth Madison Square Garden in a fit of pique after being banned from the NBA All-Star Night 2017, SuperPrez Sara Rhodes had personally given a team of super-architects the task of building a new indoor arena on the historical Penn Station site. Her only instruction – it should be the best venue of its kind in the world. Granted, the Lennon Colosseum isn't anywhere near as large as other several other indoor stadia – Shanghai alone has ten larger – but there isn't a more high-prestige venue for a rock concert, super-fight, theatre performance or basketball game. Anywhere in the world. And the acoustics put the Vatican's to shame. A year ago, when the Pre-School Prima Donna Amber-Z sang for a capacity audience of 25,000, she hadn't even needed a mike.

Jai has been to the Lennon Colosseum once before, for an awards ceremony. He hadn't done the grand tour then, hadn't been anywhere near where he is now: under the central court, waiting to take the ramp leading up, waiting for a trapdoor in the court to swing open, for the roar of the audience, now just a muffled buzz filtering through to the basement, to hit him at full strength. He shifts his weight and breathes quick and shallow, like a nervous boxer. It's been years since he last made a speech.

"Relax," says N. "You have a few minutes."

Jai casts a sharp glance at him. The Utopic exec looks even more nervous than he is, ghosting compulsively through posters of star athletes.

Utopic has booked the Lennon Colosseum for the night. The event is supposed to be an invitation-only audition to join the new Unit. They'd planned to call it a reality-show finale earlier, but the deaths of their supers at the hands of Uzma and her acolytes had proved oddly convenient. They haven't bothered with setting up a grand stage inside the arena; it's not like they've invited the press. The assembled supers sit around a basketball court, sizing one another up, waiting for some leader to appear and tell them what to do next.

Jai looks at the page of notes he's scribbled and has trouble reading his own handwriting; his hands had been shaking when he wrote it. He wonders whether Caesar felt like this on the eve of a battle. A small holo-screen floats near his shoulder, showing him the stage, and the slowly growing crowd of mostly human-looking figures jostling for seats around it.

Supers have been filing in for a few hours now. N has told Jai there's no possibility of conflict tonight: all of New York's official defender squads have been notified about the superhuman influx. And at least one member of every super-squad is secretly or openly a Utopic employee. They've been given very specific instructions not to make a mess at the Lennon Colosseum tonight. They're there, though, hovering in the area, to make sure nothing goes seriously wrong. Superteams are perched on top of the Empire State building, and others are on alert in Koreatown and Herald Square.

A huge police cordon has been set up outside the Colosseum, keeping groupies at bay. Journalists with mikes scurry up and down the street: traffic has been closed off. Every newsfeed buzzes with speculation, and hordes of paparazzi take photos of the unknown supers at the front entrance as the nine-foot-tall granite-skinned super-bouncers from Brooklyn, known as the Twin Towers, check their passes. An incredible assortment of odd-looking people have already entered the arena, and more trickle in even now.

An Indonesian girl causes considerable commotion on the street as she swoops down from the sky perched on a gigantic pterodactyl.

One of the Twin Towers checks her invite. She's on the list – the Komodo Kween, reptile controller.

"The bird stays here," the bouncer growls.

"He doesn't like being alone," she says. "And he's not a bird."

The pterodactyl snaps at the Tower, and he flinches, a first.

"Where the hell did you find him?" he asks.

"Tonga," she says. "Why?"

"Never mind," growls the other Tower, ushering her in. "Just make sure he doesn't eat anyone."

\* \* \*

"We're expecting communications trouble," says N. "Aman Sen is in New York."

"Everyone's instructions are very clear," says Jai. "And don't worry too much about Aman. Uzma saw me the other day, before she managed to escape from your clowns. They're probably far away by now."

"I was honestly surprised to find him alive," says N. "His online ghost has caused us a lot of trouble over the years, but we've always found ways to beat it. I'd have thought his powers would have grown if he were alive – he's probably just given up. Maybe our online security's just too strong for him."

"We'll have to ask him when we see him," says Jai. "I suspect his powers don't work any more. I've seen those stories you've put out all over the internet, discrediting the old Unit, and those filthy rumours about Uzma and me. He'd have stopped those."

"Yes, those were quite juicy, weren't they?" N rubs his hands together and grins. "Have you read the works of Jacqueline Flowers? Forget I asked, you haven't. Super-novelist from Omaha. Top ten bestselling books in the world. Writes a novel every day. She's already done one about you and Uzma and your kinky super-exploits. Do you want to know the title?"

"No," says Jai. "Forget Aman. This is all happening in the real world, and he's no threat there. As long as he has no access to your zoos and the people inside them."

"Our zoos, Jai."

"Yes. Who else knows where these – our facilities are?"

"The board, us, and about ten other supers. Continent coordinators."

"Anyone Uzma knows? Anyone she might find?"

"No. In any case, they'll be wearing protective AR at all times."

"Good. These ten continent heads – will they be part of the first assault?"

"No."

"Then we have nothing to worry about from Aman or Uzma. What about that Chinese girl? Wu?"

"In our custody. Sedated. The only missing ones are Jason and Anima, but they're somewhere in India, off the grid."

"Let's get started, then."

Movement to his right. Jai lunges before even looking, and finds himself on the floor, on top of a mewling That Guy.

"What do you want?" roars Jai.

That Guy indicates through sobs that he cannot answer this question while Jai maintains his iron grip on his throat. Jai releases him, and That Guy lies on the floor, breathing in huge gulps.

"Well?" asks Jai.

"I'm sorry," says That Guy. "This is just the most important place in the world to be right now. I usually manage to avoid the more dangerous occasions, but I wasn't paying attention. There's this new series on—"

"Give me a reason not to kill you right now," says Jai.

"Because I'd teleport somewhere else in self-defence and if you were touching me you'd come with me and then you'd miss your meeting," whimpers That Guy.

Jai gets off him quickly.

"Get out," he says.

That Guy vanishes.

"Let's do this," says Jai.

\* \* \*

One of the Twin Towers disconnects his phone and signals to his brother. They turn and enter the building. Just as they're about to close the door, a young woman in a red cape and hood slips out of the crowd and runs towards them, waving.

"Who're you?" asks a Tower.

"Are you wearing AR glasses, or contacts?" she asks.

"We're closed," says the Tower. "Try later."

"Let me in, and forget you saw me," Says Uzma.

Jai rises into the court and is greeted with a roar of applause.

In her seat in the last row, in the darkest spot she could find, Uzma is amazed at the sheer enthusiasm all around her – the supers give Jai a standing ovation, banging palms and claws and other diverse limbs as Jai smiles and waves as if he'd been an emperor for years. Jai waits for the applause to die down, and beckons at someone below.

Agent N walks out into the court, his ghost-steps sinking slightly into the ground. If he had been expecting cheers as well, he is disappointed: his arrival casts the whole stadium into silence.

Around two thousand supers occupy the arena, around a tenth of its capacity. They're mostly seated in a ring around the court, filling up the front rows, or scattered towards the rear, at a relatively safe distance from Jai. N looks around the crowd, and whispers in Jai's ear.

"It doesn't matter," says Jai, and his voice carries clearly through the Colosseum.

N whispers in his ear again, and Jai steps away, irritated. He turns to the crowd.

"So," he says. "You're my army."

He subjects his army to a glare. Several supers flinch and look at their feet.

"My name is Jai Mathur," he says, "and if we have met before, it was while I was enslaved. Held prisoner in my own body by Uzma Abidi, a spectator and a mindless soldier while she ran the Unit. But all of this you already know. This is our first meeting, then. Hello."

He walks around the court, looking the supers in the eye, one by one. They try their best to look back without blinking. Most fail.

"Eleven years ago, I tried to take over the world," says Jai. "I did not get very far. I lost my country, I lost my troops, I lost my family. And then the supers who formed the first Unit came after me, and for a long time, I lost everything.

"Today I stand in front of you a free man. And our friends in Utopic – my new friends – tell me I have been chosen to rule the world. To wipe out corrupt governments, overcome armies, erase borders; to cut out a new world with blood and strength. Utopic gave a man who had nothing a second chance. And I am grateful.

"I don't know how they found you. I heard they picked up people, threw them into camps and brainwashed them for years. I heard they cut you up to try and understand what made you work. But I was working for Utopic's enemies. And when you deal with power on that scale, there are always dark rumours. You'll hear similar stories, and worse, about me.

"In my case, everything you've heard is true. But I don't know anything about you. Or why you're here. And to be honest, I don't want to know.

"Tomorrow, after the new Unit has been sworn in, I will

walk out into the open and run all the way to the White House. I will replace Sara Rhodes as the President, and kill anyone who tries to stop me. And what will you do?"

He looks at a young man in the front row, he's green with insect eyes and two long antennae on his head.

"Destroy New York," says the man.

"No," says Jai. "I like New York. I'm going to keep it. You will all be given specific areas, and specific targets. You will travel across the country, in groups that have been picked out for you. You will spread out in every direction, killing as you go. You will be assigned opponents, and have grand battles that destroy entire cities. When your missions are complete, you will return to your bases and await further instructions. This is no movie climax with superteams matching wits on top of New York skyscrapers. This is a simultaneous assault, too broad and too well organised to defeat. Other Utopic teams will lead similar assaults in ten other parts of the world. When we are done with one country, we will start with the next. The plans are all ready. I have seen them. I am impressed."

Jai strides back to the centre of the court and stands, feet apart, directly under the largest spotlight.

"When I started out as a super – villain, I suppose – I was full of grand ideas. I believed in many things. But I was still young then. I wanted to start wars, burn cities, plant my flag all over the earth. And I had my reasons, most of which would sound quite good if I told them to you today. Millions, perhaps billions, would have died in the wars I started.

"But I am no longer young, and everything else has changed. I had no desire to make the world better then. Now, it seems our actions will. I had dreams and ideals then. They are gone.

Now we are assembled here to conquer the world, but our real goal is the least inspiring thing I have ever heard."

N, concerned, walks towards Jai quickly. But Jai cannot be stopped.

"We have to kill half the world's people," says Jai.

A loud murmur runs through the crowd.

"Four billion deaths," says Jai. "That's what we're here to achieve. Four billion corpses. That's what you're getting paid for. That's your job now. Meet your death quota, stop, collect your money, get your next assignment. So if you're expecting stirring words from me, don't. Starting tomorrow, we are going to go out and kill people for money, and keep doing it until the earth is empty enough for people like us, and everyone we allow to survive, to live in comfort. That's all there is to it. And if any of you have a problem with it, stand up now and leave this place. No one will hurt you. But this is your last chance."

He stands statue-still for a whole minute. No one moves or speaks.

Jai cracks his knuckles. Gunshot-like echoes fill the stadium.

"You're afraid of me," he says. "And you should be. But you are going to work for me, and fear alone won't get the job done. You think you know what you're about to get into? You think you can actually walk out with a smile on your face and kill humans until you meet your numbers? You can't. You're just supers, not soldiers. And even soldiers falter. You can't run a mission like this on fear alone. You need more."

Jai turns to N and smiles. "You need trust," he says.

"This is Agent N. He passes through things. A silly power, but a useful one for negotiations with people like me. We were on a plane together a few days ago, and for most of that journey

I thought that I was going to kill him. But he was honest with me, and he made me a very good offer. I like him. And he was brave enough to become flesh in my presence, to offer me his hand to make the deal. He is a braver man than any of you. It wasn't the right time then. It is now."

Jai extends his hand. "I'm a man of my word," he says. "A man of honour. A leader you can trust. This will be a journey that ends in blood and fire. But it will start with a handshake."

N unghosts. He shakes Jai's hand. The crowd cheers. Jai puts his other hand on N's shoulder. They embrace.

Then Jai snaps N's neck.

As N's body falls, screams and yells ring out over the stadium. Chaos erupts. A foolhardy super shoots a poisoned dart at Jai. It sticks in his neck, but Jai seems unaffected. Many supers burst out of their seats and race towards the exits.

"Sit down!" roars Jai.

The stadium plunges into silence. Every eye follows Jai's hand as it rises to his neck and pulls the dart out.

"You sat through the boring bit," says Jai. "Now you might as well keep watching, because it's going to get interesting."

Several supers actually return to their seats. Others stand and stare at Jai in disbelief, casting glances at the nearest exit, clearly wondering how long it would take to get out, and how much longer it would take for Jai to catch them.

"I will not harm any of you unless you attack me," says Jai. "Sit down."

He waits, arms crossed, tapping a foot, as the supers shuffle around the stadium finding seats. The back rows are considerably fuller than they were before.

"As you might have guessed," says Jai, "this grand Utopic

conquest is not going to happen. I am going to stop it. Do I have to explain why?"

He gives them three seconds to speak up. No one does. Jai smirks.

"It is said there is a thin line between genius and insanity," he says. "I wouldn't know. I am neither. I can understand completely that the idea of killing half the world is appealing. But actually going out and doing it? That is insane. And I find it insulting that they thought I would do it.

"Eleven years ago, I decided taking over the world was a good idea. I spent a few months trying, and I failed, and I was cast into slavery for eleven years. It wasn't like I got an eleven-year sentence from some sort of justice system. A super decided, on her own, that I was her slave. As far as she was concerned, I would serve her for the rest of my life. When I was freed, it was an accident.

"I spent these years being a superhero. Saving lives. Stopping wars. Killing criminals, human and super. I have saved the world six times. I have been feared and loved by billions of people.

"But because of those first few months, when I was free again, everyone assumed that I would be the same person that Uzma Abidi trapped in London in the summer of 2009. In the case of Utopic, I am not surprised. I am just a file to them. But my teammates? The people I'd fought beside for years, saved from countless deaths, shared meetings, quarters, meals? Every time they met me, they attacked me. Without question. Without even a pause. I tried to speak to them, but they didn't listen.

"So listen closely. I have changed. If you come to me now

and tell me to kill half the world, I will not do it. And I will kill everyone who tries."

Jai gives his audience a dazzling smile.

"So would you like to try?" he asks.

He walks up to another young man in the front row.

"What's your name?" he asks.

"Invinciblo," says the young man with some effort.

"Really?"

"Alexander," says Invinciblo.

"Really?"

"Yes. Well, Alex, really."

"Well, Alexander, would you like to help me stop Utopic?"

Alexander looks as if his dearest wish at this point is to teleport anywhere else, but this is not his superpower.

"Yes," he says.

"But when I asked anyone who had a problem with what Utopic is doing to leave, you stayed. Why?"

"I'm sorry."

"Why?"

"Because I'm afraid of you?"

"Thank you, Alexander," says Jai. He strides back to the centre of the court.

"I have a habit of scaring people," he says. Nervous laughter and headnodding breaks out in every corner of the court. "And I realised that even I could not stop Utopic alone – I hear they've spent a lot of time and money trying to find a way to kill me. And I know a few other people with interesting powers, and I thought they might be feeling a little shy, a little scared. So I thought I'd give them yet another chance. A last chance.

"So to save the world, I sent an email. Let's see if it worked."

He looks around the stadium.

"Uzma!" he calls. "Are you here?"

"Yes," calls a voice from a seat as far away from Jai as possible.

Two thousand heads turn towards Uzma as she throws back her red hood.

Jai waits for the gasping, creaking and shuffling to subside.

"Come on down," he says.

"Nobody move!" Shouts Uzma.

She walks down the steps and into the court.

"Perhaps this scene would play better if the audience weren't looking at an empty seat," suggests Jai.

"Turn and look at us, and then stay still!" Shouts Uzma.

"Precise, as always," says Jai. "Now tell Aman to come up. I heard him shuffling around in the tunnel a while ago."

"Aman, come up," Calls Uzma.

Aman does so. Inside his helmet, he looks extremely sheepish.

Jai waits patiently as Aman approaches, and stands beside Uzma.

"Hi," says Jai.

Uzma and Aman have nothing to say.

"So, how do we do this?" asks Jai. He extends his arm. "Should we start with a handshake?"

"I'd really rather not," says Aman.

"Uzma?"

Uzma reaches out. In the utter silence that follows, Jai shakes her hand solemnly and lets it go.

Two thousand supers remember to breathe again.

"You've become a real drama queen," says Aman. "That's new."

Jai throws his head back and laughs out loud. His laughter fills the hall. No one even smiles in response.

"To business, then," says Jai. "The passwords I sent you. Were they useful?"

"Yes," says Aman.

"What did you do?"

"Well, I deleted the stories about you and Uzma a few minutes ago, for a start. I didn't like those."

"I thought they were very well done," says Jai.

"Well, I didn't. So I shut down all Utopic sites. And their TV feeds. I liked that. So I went to lots of banks and emptied their accounts. You let me into their communications database. I rooted around in there like a big fat pig."

Aman looks around the audience.

"All of you are broke now, I'm afraid," he says. "Utopic is bankrupt. I can give you jobs, though, if you need money."

"I'm surprised you didn't do this years ago," says Jai.

"Well, they hadn't mentioned their world-killing plan in their emails, you know," says Aman. "And they did have a rather strong security system. Everything was disguised. Super-programmers. I didn't need your passwords to break in; I needed them to tell me where to look."

"Excuses," says Jai. "What else did you do?"

"Scrambled their communications, mostly. There should have been a few thousand more supers here tonight, for a start. But I've found their prisons. They're getting a lot of very confusing instructions right about now. With any luck, thousands more might be set free tonight. They know they're under attack now, but they don't know we're behind it. Seventeen people here have tried to tell them what you just did, but obviously all communication out of here is jammed."

"Good. What else?"

"Well, I might have sent a fairly detailed description of everything I found to every government official in the world. I think about twelve of them might not be Utopic servants. Anyway, and to every judge, military chief, police officer and superteam everywhere. Big mailing list. Miraculously immune to spam filters. So, you know, war, death, chaos, scandal. When I have some time, I'll make the news."

"Right," says Jai. "What do we want to do with this lot?"

"We?" asks Uzma.

"Yes," says Jai. "We work together now. And there's a lot of work to do."

Uzma and Aman look at each other.

"Are you sure?" asks Aman.

Jai laughs. "Yes, I'm sure," he says. "Believe me, I've thought about it. Do you trust me?"

"Not at all," says Aman with feeling.

"Well, I don't trust you either," says Jai. "But I've been in love with Uzma for eleven years."

He looks at Uzma's flabbergasted face and grins.

"Do you remember what your powers are?" he asks.

Uzma's mouth opens and closes.

"Will you marry me?" asks Jai.

"No," says Aman.

"Uzma?"

"No," says Uzma.

"All right," says Jai. He winks at them.

"I'll ask again later," he says.

"Can we please talk about something else?" asks Aman.

"Yes, yes," says Jai. "What's the plan?"

"I honestly don't know," says Aman.

"I do," says Uzma. She waves her hand at the assembled supers. "You work for me now," she Says. "We're going to go to the Unit headquarters and take it over. Then we're going to make the world better. It's going to be complicated. Applause."

The stadium shakes as the super-army hoots, whistles and cheers. Uzma raises her hand, and silence is restored.

"Are you really planning to keep them all under your control?" asks Aman.

"I'll think about it," says Uzma.

"Right," says Jai. "So, we take our building back, and then we spend tomorrow drawing up plans."

"No," says Aman. "We really need to go to Japan."

"I don't like Japan," says Jai.

"Well, I need to," says Aman. "Norio Hisatomi has kidnapped Kalki. I think he's going to make Kalki take everyone's superpowers away."

"That could be a problem," says Jai. "Where is he, and how quickly can we get there?"

"I don't know," says Aman.

"You're useless," says Jai.

He turns to the crowd.

"Time to save the world!" he calls. "What are you waiting for?"

# CHAPTER **SEVENTEEN**

The sounds of explosions and screaming have died down, and Aman has deflected another missile attack. It is time for coffee.

Uzma, Vir and Aman sit in the Unit's control room. Uzma and Vir watch with rapidly diminishing interest as Aman juggles a swift-moving whirl of holo-screens in a sphere of light around him, manipulating news, closing bank accounts, cutting off communications and monitoring super-fights across the globe.

The Unit's tower is full of supers. There have been seven waves of attacks since the previous night, some from Utopic, others from government agencies, still others who did not survive long enough to declare their affiliations. The world is churning. Already seventeen governments have fallen, thousands of Utopic subsidiaries have closed down, twelve Utopic super-containment facilities have been transformed into government super-prisons. Riots have broken out in twenty-two capitals.

None of the supers in the room seem particularly impressed

by any of this. The smile that lights up Uzma's face as Jai enters the room, covered in blood, and sets a tray with five coffee mugs on it down on the table is the first sign of emotion she's displayed in hours.

"I just killed Reload again," says Jai.

Uzma shakes her head, tries to suppress a grin and fails. Reload had unfortunately (for him) shifted his save point, base of regeneration, to the Unit's tower just a few minutes before Jai had led a swarm of supers into the building. The assassin is now in a cage in the barracks, seriously reconsidering his life decisions, and getting killed every now and then by every super in the tower who wants to de-stress.

Aman opens his eyes. "Norio's not in any of the bases I've managed to track," he says. "He's off the grid."

"Rowena?" asks Uzma.

"Tia has her, back at my old island. We have a few Tias coming here soon, by the way."

"Sundar?"

"No. Which means we're stuck with nothing. Norio has been back in Tokyo for hours. He's probably got Kalki in that mind control device of his right now."

"Well, the world hasn't ended," says Uzma. "It's almost midnight in Tokyo, thirteen hours ahead. And humans seem to be doing fine. That's a good sign."

"Wu said the world was ending today," says Aman. "She didn't say what time. Or time zone. Is she awake yet?"

"No," says Vir. "Aman, a few minutes ago. Viral's broadcast. New second-hand megastore. It said 'End of the World Discounts'. Could that be what Wu sensed? Everyone in the world thought it for a second."

"Well, until we separate the all-powerful child god from the anti-super billionaire nut we really can't bet on that," says Aman. "I have a hundred Tias going door-to-door in Tokyo. Every Japanese super-squad is out looking for Norio. I have face recognition running on every street-cam. Tokyo's the most well-mapped place on earth. Nothing so far."

"No teleporters among the new lot?" asks Vir.

"There is one," says Aman. "But there's no way of telling her where to go."

"Tokyo," says Uzma.

"But where in Tokyo?"

"Wherever it is, we'll be closer, won't we?"

Aman shrugs. "That does make sense. I've asked the magicians if they can track him, but it's pretty obvious what they said."

"Just relax and drink your coffee," says Jai, and sits. "The solution's been right in front of you all along."

Everyone stares at him in silence as he takes a sip of cappuccino and wipes foam from his mouth.

"I'm surprised none of you ever saw it," says Jai. "I knew it all along: you just wanted me for my body."

"Jai, if you know how to find Norio, please tell us," says Aman, as evenly as he can.

"I have a question first," says Vir. "You say this Norio is going to get Kalki to remove everyone's superpowers. Now I love my powers – but look at the world. Are we sure we should stop Norio?"

"Yes," says Aman.

"That's good. Now, my question. If Norio does get Kalki to remove everyone's powers as you say he will, how is that the end of humanity? Doesn't that put humanity back on top?"

"Well, if we lose our powers we'll get killed in a few minutes. So I for one really don't want to put ordinary humans back on top," says Uzma.

"Yes, Vir," says Aman. "But the real danger is that Kalki's insane. Tia said he takes requests, and then does whatever he wants."

"But you said Norio has a mind control machine," says Uzma.

"Is it stronger than Kalki?" asks Aman. "What if it just makes him mad? I'd rather not find out on a day when the world's supposed to end."

Uzma blinks, and shakes her head. "Sure. Do any of the rest of you have a problem with the words that come out of your mouths sometimes?"

"Yes," says Aman. "So, Jai. What's the answer?"

"He is," says Jai, pointing at an empty seat. The others look at it.

"All right," says Aman after a while. "He's lost his mind. Back to work, people."

That Guy appears in the seat.

Jai smiles.

"I wasn't sure that would work," he says.

"I didn't mean to intrude," says That Guy. "I'll be—"

"Relax" says Jai. He walks around the table, sits next to That Guy, and holds his hand. That Guy is trembling visibly.

"Do you know you're going to be the greatest hero of us all?" asks Jai.

"No," says That Guy. "I'm sorry, I'll—"

Jai squeezes his hand fondly and That Guy's face turns blue, then white. Jai looks around the table.

"All these years and everyone was too busy to notice," he says. "I suppose I was the only one who was still able to think clearly. That Guy teleports to wherever the most significant events in the world are. He even gets to know how dangerous they'll be before he goes, and gets to choose. Whatever Norio's doing with Kalki, it must be more important than anything else in the world, right? That Guy's going to be there. And so will I."

"That actually... why are you holding his hand?" asks Aman.

"Because we don't know when Norio's going to start, and it wouldn't really help if he went to stop Norio by himself, would it?" asks Jai.

"True," says Aman. He solemnly walks to That Guy and takes his other hand.

Uzma holds her face in her hands. "You've all gone completely mad," she says. "We've solved a dozen massive problems. He was never there."

"I was," says That Guy. "If it's important enough, I always land up for at least a bit."

"You weren't there in Prague," says Uzma.

"I was," says That Guy.

"In Tokyo last time."

"I was," he says. "Sometimes I'm not in the same room. I always leave immediately when it's dangerous. Sometimes I manage to go somewhere else, if it's important, like a movie premiere or a press conference. There's always a lot happening."

Alarm screens pop up. Two hoverjets approach Liberty Island.

"Here we go again. Battle stations," says Uzma.

"The others will take care of it," says Jai. "We're spending the rest of today holding on to our friend. It's the only way to reach Norio and Kalki. And we'll only get one chance."

"Why did you never tell us you could do this?" screams Uzma.

"You never wanted to talk to me!" That Guy starts to cry.

Vir watches the hoverjets as they launch missiles at the tower. A man in blue appears in the sky in front of them, and waves his arms. After a second, the missiles explode in mid-air.

"Someone will take care of it," says Jai. "You must learn how to delegate better."

"I don't like this plan," says Vir. "We don't understand how That Guy's powers really work."

"We have at least a thousand supers in the building," says Jai. "Get over here now."

"I am not spending the whole day touching That Guy," says Uzma. "If he gets a warning, he can tell us, and—"

That Guy, Jai and Aman disappear.


Aman recognises the room at once. He's been here before. Large hall, closed windows. Empty chairs.

On a chair by a window sits Kalki. His many arms are tied, each arm to the other on the same side. On his head is a tinfoil helment, stuck on awkwardly with tape. Two wires connect the chips on top of the helmet to Sundar's computer on its bulky trolley. Aman is too far away from the monitor to see what's on it. Kalki's eyes are open and glowing.

Norio stands in front of the trolley, typing on the ancient keyboard.

Aman, Jai and That Guy stand in silence for a second.

Norio shows no sign of having realised they're in the room.

"Ahem," says Jai.

Norio turns and smiles.

"Of course you're here," he says. "I was wondering when you'd show up."

"Step away from Kalki," says Aman.

Norio looks from Aman to Jai.

"Is that Aman in the armour? Aman and Jai teaming up? Classic!" He laughs, his voice is strained and ragged. His eyes are bloodshot, his clothes stained, he's twitching: he clearly hasn't slept or bathed in a while.

That Guy disappears.

"I knew you'd find a way to get here," says Norio. "You wouldn't want to miss this."

"Surrender," says Jai.

"Kalki's been having fun in Tokyo," says Norio. "He hasn't seen much, of course, but he loves wasabi. Not with anything else, though. Just lots and lots of wasabi. We went to see his Uncle Sundar today. That was fun, wasn't it?"

Aman raises his arm. He takes aim at the computer.

"Just wait a minute," says Norio. "It hasn't even started. He's not in any pain, he's having fun. You know, I think he wanted to be here? He's a good kid."

"Let him go," says Aman.

"In a bit. You know, I really hoped Sundar would have made something new for me. Some armour like yours, or something to beat Jai with. But Sundar doesn't do requests, does he? If you went and told him you were going to fight a giant bear, would he give you a giant bear-fighting device? No. He'd show you something he'd made to make burgers healthy."

Jai starts walking towards Norio. Norio whips out a gun.

"Really?" says Jai.

"But I hunted around in a heap of junk in his lab," says Norio, "and I found something nice."

Aman looks closely at the gun, and quickly recognises it. He'd seen it last in a video eleven years ago. He'd been racing up a Versova street in an auto, had seen their enemies advancing on Sundar, had seen Sher preparing to jump, and then a flash of white light. He remembers what Sundar's ray-gun does...

"Dive!" he screams. Norio fires.

A flash of light, and Jai disappears.

Aman stares at the empty space where Jai had been a moment ago, too shocked by the sheer absence of Jai to process the danger he is in.

Norio turns towards Aman – and goes flying backwards as the armour launches a pulse-blast at the ray-gun. The gun flies further, bounces on the floor and comes to rest, a twisted mass of metal, plastic and wire.

Norio's right hand and arm are broken, twisted, but he leaps to his feet, his face contorted with rage. He races towards the computer, but Aman fires another blast, and Norio goes flying across the hall, rolling on the floor.

Aman walks up to the computer as Norio struggles to find his feet.

"You're done," says Aman. "Stay down."

Norio shakes his left hand. Holograms spring up around it.

Aman hears a loud whine above him. The ceiling shakes as, on the floor above, the Goryo ghost-mecha springs to life.

"No," says Aman.

The whine stops.

"Remote control," says Aman. "Bad idea."

Norio staggers, moaning in pain, and stands up. He smiles.

"I'm glad you're here," he says.

"Stay away from the computer," says Aman.

"All right, all right," says Norio. "Supers beat humans. I get it."

"I am human," says Aman. "I was never your enemy."

"Then step out of that armour and fight me like a human." Norio can barely stand, but he manages to raise his arms, and take a slow step towards Aman.

"Don't be ridiculous," says Aman.

Aman's eyes are still swimming from the ray-gun and pulse-blast in the closed room. The monochrome letters on the old computer screen are solid blobs, slowly shaping themselves into letters.

"I couldn't do it," says Norio. "All this time, all this planning, and I was too slow."

Aman looks at the single line on the computer screen as the letters finally sharpen into place. He looks again, unable to believe it. He looks at Norio, at the screen again, at Kalki.

"Why?" he asks.

"I told you I was on the right side," says Norio. "I told you I was trying to save the world."

Aman looks at the screen again.

GIVE EVERYONE SUPERPOWERS, it says.

On the monochrome monitor the long cursor blinks beside the single line, mocking Aman. He blinks.

"You thought I was trying to take your powers away," says Norio. "I just wanted to make everything fair. To change the world. To give everyone a chance."

"Then why didn't you hit 'Enter'?" asks Aman.

"Because I was a fool. And I wanted to defeat you before my

moment of victory," says Norio. "I wanted to look you and Jai in the eyes as I took my revenge."

"Revenge? Me?"

"I blame you for Azusa's death, Aman. I could have saved her." He takes another step towards Aman.

"Why didn't you just tell me what you planned to do?" asks Aman. "Why didn't you just tell everyone?"

"It's obvious. Because you would have tried to stop me. As you have. My mistake was in not trusting my team, my humans, before it was too late. They'd given up on me. But they learned what I was trying to do, and they came back for me. Azusa did too, you know? She was a super. But she was different. She knew what was right."

Aman looks at the screen again, and at Kalki behind it. The boy-god twitches.

"But you can do it for me, Aman," says Norio. "You don't want the world to turn into a comic book. You want everyone to do the best they can. You think supers can help the world get better. The machine works once. After you kill me, and take Kalki back, you'll never get this chance again. Press the button."

"No," says Aman. "The world's in enough trouble as it is."

"You may be right," says Norio. "Everyone you trust will tell you you're right. I'm a criminal. I'm a murderer. What do I know? Press the button. Change the world."

Aman finds the backspace key. He presses it.

"You know it's the right thing to do," says Norio. "But you're too scared to do it. You've grown old. You're like every other person with power in the end, aren't you? Holding on to what you have. Your advantage. When you started out, you wanted to change the world, but you don't really, do you? You'd be ordinary again."

Aman presses "Backspace" again.

"You're a superhero now," says Norio. "You've protected the world from the villain. You've held on to your turf. You've won. I hoped you'd be different, you know. I'd really wanted to just come to you and tell you what I wanted for the world. But I knew I couldn't get anything out of you without using the machine. Because whatever you say, I know what you're all like. Supers and humans are enemies. They can't help it. The powerful and powerless always are."

He lunges at Aman.

But the armour is faster. It blocks Norio's swing and pushes him away. He lands on the floor and groans.

"I didn't want to be a super unless everyone else could be one too," says Norio. "I guess that's the difference between us."

He tries to get up, and fails.

"Stay down," says Aman. "I don't want to hurt you."

"But you do," says Norio. "And I won't."

He moans in pain, and staggers to his feet.

"You know nothing about me," says Aman. "All I've ever wanted is to use my powers to make the world better. To help the weak and the needy. To *stop* supers from controlling the world."

"Then press the button."

"It's wrong. This mind control machine is wrong. I know how it feels."

Norio manages a laugh.

"Look at your powers," he says. "Look at Uzma's. Your powers are terrible. Everything you do with them is wrong.

You're lying to me, Aman. Or maybe you don't see it yourself. But you're going to end up like Jai. You're going to run the world exactly as you see fit. Stop anyone in your way. Do whatever you feel like. And the only thing that can stop you is that boy in front of you. And he won't listen to you unless you make him. So ask yourself this: do you want to move forward, to the future, or just hold on to what you have? Press the button."

Norio's reached the computer now. He moves Aman's hand away, almost gently. He types the letters in again.

He steps back.

"What gives you the right to take this big a decision?" asks Aman. "I tried to fix the world by myself once. It didn't work. I ruined people's lives. People died. I just stopped your Utopic board from trying to kill four billion people. I'll probably have to spend the rest of my life fighting people like them."

"Well, if you want people to talk you out of it, just give anyone you trust a call. Get Uzma to make you stop. Tell yourself people don't deserve to have superpowers thrust upon them, and walk away. There isn't a perfect way to do it," says Norio. "Look at me. Look at the mess I made. But it's the right thing to do. Are you going to do it?"

"Yes," says Aman.

He takes a deep breath, and looks at the computer.

GIVE EVERYONE SUPERPOWERS, it says.

He hits Enter.

Kalki screams, and world turns white.

# CHAPTER **EIGHTEEN**

The car pulls up in a quiet Versova lane, and Uzma steps out. She looks around, remembering the first time she came to this house, trying to remember who she'd been then. The house is freshly painted. Tias have been living there from the very beginning. There's a watchman at the gate, but he's asleep in his chair, and doesn't wake up as Uzma walks to the front door and rings the bell.

Tia opens the door and greets Uzma with a huge hug. Uzma steps in, takes in the living room, the kitchen. Every part of the room is crowded with old ghosts: Sher, Jai, Bob, little Anima, Sundar. She's been all around the world since she first entered this house, but there's no place she remembers more clearly.

"He's in the loo," says Tia. "Woke up a few minutes ago."

"Right," says Uzma. "But he's fine, yes?"

"You'll have to check," says Tia, grinning.

Uzma looks at her sheepishly.

"How are things?" asks Tia.

Uzma collapses on a sofa, pulls off her shoes and wiggles her toes in delight as cold air from the mammoth air conditioner hits them.

"Messy," she says. "I was actually looking forward to flying halfway across the world just to avoid taking decisions. But we're holding the tower against all comers. Vir's in charge. Some ex-Utopic fool declared independence this morning. Liberty Island is a new country now."

"That sounds... not very smart," says Tia.

"Yes. Somebody else declared war on all humans. Some more escaped supers have built an emerald city, or a city that looks like some other gem, in Eritrea. I guess that's what happens when you set hundreds of repressed superhumans free."

"I heard an interesting thing while I was leaving Japan," says Tia. "The Harmony Warrior Squadron might have taken over the Chinese government. You'll have to look into that as well. Okay, this is less important, but I can't get it off my mind. Why do you have so much makeup on?"

"Was in a shoot. Wingman memorial. They're turning his biopic into a tribute show. I really disliked him, you know? I miss him so much now. I need to ask you something."

Tia makes an elegant gesture.

"Would you like to be part of the new Unit?" asks Uzma.

"I don't know," says Tia. "Who else is in?"

"Well, me. Vir. Jason, Anima. Aman."

"Aman's in the new Unit? Does he know?"

"Not yet. Wu. That Guy. Jai, if we find him. We might get some more from the new lot. Or poach from the other teams."

"I'm not joining the Unit," says Tia. "I'm quite happy here, and I need some rest. And I have an island to run. There's a scientist on it that I've left unsupervised for too long, and he appears to be planning a dinosaur invasion."

"I'm sorry to hear that."

"I don't speak for all of us, though. You should ask one of the New York Tias. Now sit. Eat."

Another Tia arrives and sets down a tray in front of Uzma. Tia-from-the-door sits as well, curling up on the sofa, looking curiously at Uzma.

"You look great," says Tia.

"So do you," says Uzma. "Tell me what happened."

So Tia tells her how she found Aman. How Aman had sent her a message the moment he'd arrived at Norio's hideout. She'd been five minutes away. When she'd reached the building and broken her way in, she'd found Aman and Norio lying unconscious on the floor, with an old-fashioned computer burning between them.

"What did you do with Norio?" asks Uzma.

"I told him I would give him five minutes, and then I'd chase him. I told him to hide, and hide well, because I could really look everywhere. He ran."

"And you chased him?"

"No. But he doesn't know that."

"And Kalki?"

"I don't know," says Tia. "I'm still looking for him all over Tokyo. But I don't think I'll find him."

"So someone else might have him."

"It's possible. Maybe Aman can tell us more."

"So you got Aman out of there."

"Submarine. Mumbai. Pretty straightforward. He was out almost all the way through. Talking in his sleep."

"He hasn't been in touch with me at all. Does he still have his powers?"

"He said he does, but going online hurts. He took a pretty big hit back there. Whatever it was that Kalki did..."

Uzma stretches. "I'll take him back with me," she says.

"That's between the two of you. I'm staying right here until I leave."

"Back to the island. More secret super-scientists?"

"A few. I picked up Rowena too, by the way. I've decided to inject everyone in the world with her blood over the next few years."

Uzma struggles to process the scale of Tia's project, and fails.

"You're going to cure every disease," she manages finally.

"That's the plan," says Tia, and smiles. "Also, there are lots of bits of the world I haven't been to yet. I'm going to fix that."

"Did you find Sundar?"

"Found his lab. Guards said he'd taken off in some kind of giant mole machine."

"Good for him."

Movement on the stairs. Aman descends, dressed in not-very-heroic pyjamas, most of his hair standing straight up. Uzma considers running at him theatrically, but restrains herself. She's been forgetting, more and more frequently, that she was born and raised British.

"Get down here," says Tia. "We've been discussing our relationship, and how you've been taking us both for a ride with your smooth-talking ways."

Aman freezes on the steps, and remains frozen until Tia and Uzma both laugh. He walks nervously into the living room and finds a spot on the sofa as near the door as possible.

"So," says Uzma. "What happened?"

"Well, the world appears to not have ended. It is the next day, right?"

"Yeah."

"Well, then you tell me," says Aman. "Does everyone in the world have superpowers or not?"

"That's what Kalki did?" asks Uzma.

"Looks like," says Tia. "The short answer is yes and no, Aman."

"Try the long one."

"A few minutes after you told me where you were, the sky turned red," says Tia. "I saw a man fly out of a window. This kid on the street turned into a unicorn. I heard a lot of explosions. I didn't stop to ask questions. I came and got you. By the time we left the building, everything seemed normal, or as normal as it gets. We spent a lot of time underwater, Uzma flew over, and here we are."

"As far as we can tell, everyone got powers for a few minutes," says Uzma. "You'd blocked most newsfeeds, so we still don't really know. It's been crazy. We thought it was a Third Wave, actually – not just in the air, but on the ground. Of course the first thing everyone did after getting powers was post on the internet. But whatever it was, it faded after a while. These global magic events always do."

Aman sits and stares into space for a while.

"Everyone was a super for a few minutes," he says finally. "Isn't that something. I'm glad there are limits on Kalki's power. But he'll get stronger. Maybe he'll do this again one day."

"We answered your question," says Uzma. "Now tell us what happened to you or I'll Tell you to."

* * *

Aman swiftly tells them what he'd been through in Tokyo, about commanding Kalki to give everyone superpowers, about the world turning white, about the feeling of falling endlessly through space and time somewhere far above the earth. Kalki had appeared before him then, full-grown, a massive man-horse holding weapons he didn't have names for. Kalki had laughed, and told him many things he hadn't understood or didn't remember, drawn three lines of fire between them, turned, and vanished. Then Aman had seen things he couldn't describe, swirling galaxies that turned into cells, strange worlds growing and decaying in seconds, until it had all turned into a blur of colour and he'd faded away into utter darkness.

Uzma and Tia watch him in absolute silence, and say nothing even after he's stopped. Aman wonders if all this is still part of the dream, if he's still on that first flight to Delhi all those years ago.

But then Uzma walks over and holds him, and he's sure, though he's shaking, that this is no dream.

"So," says Tia. "What are you going to do now?"

"Eat," says Aman, looking at the tray with Uzma's lunch on it. "I'm starving."

"We're going to go back to New York and form another Unit," says Uzma. "Then we're going to fix the world, one problem at a time."

"Norio said we'd end up becoming super-tyrants," says Aman. "He said it was inevitable. Privileged few ruling the world, keeping everyone else down. Considering we've pretty much shut down the UN and are controlling world communications and we can be anywhere and make anyone do what Uzma wants, maybe we should worry a little."

"Yeah, well, Norio is an idiot," says Tia with feeling.

"Hang on," says Aman, and shuts his eyes. Another Tia comes in from the kitchen with more food.

"Japanese," she says. "It seemed right."

After a few minutes Aman opens his eyes and takes in the sight of Uzma and two Tias shovelling sushi into their mouths.

"Third Wave," he says. "The magicians say they've made a new dimension."

"Let me guess," says Tia. "It's invading us."

"What does it look like?" asks Uzma.

"Just mud, rock and water so far. No signs of life. They think it's habitable. They want terraformers, super-architects, game designers and general world-builders."

"And they want me to go in there because I'm super expendable," says Tia. "Not going to happen."

"We'll talk about it. Right now they have this girl who makes short-term fictional characters, and they're going to use them to test it."

He gives them a huge smile.

"We're going to colonise another dimension," he says.

"Nice," says Tia, and eats some more. "We don't have any sake. Will vodka do?"

"Always," says Uzma.

"They've also spotted what looks like a spaceship over Azerbaijan. Someone made aliens. I have no idea what that means. And what did they see in Iceland last night?"

"Dragon," says Tia.

"How did you guess?"

"I have branches in Iceland. But they think it was a hoax."

Aman leans back, his eyes glowing. "Sometimes I really like my job," he says. "Third Wave, people. Large numbers of supers believing in things make them exist. Get excited."

"Yay," says Uzma in a voice of doom. "Does this mean we're going to make more gods exist?"

"I said get excited," says Aman. "Don't make me panic."

"You know, a new episode of our animated adventures is out," says Tia. "You want to watch it?"

"No," says Uzma.

Tia nods and waves the TV on. They watch in silence, eating like wolves. In the episode, Jason and Anima have a fight because of a devious water-manipulator, and Uzma stops a corporate tycoon from privatising drinking water in Africa. It's not bad.

"Did you watch *He-Man* when you were a kid?" Aman asks Uzma as the credits roll.

"Haven't even heard of it," says Uzma. "What is it, wrestling?"

"I can't believe you haven't seen *He-Man*," says Aman. "It was the most important thing in my life back then. We had just two channels, though, so it had to be. Sundays. It was right after the *Ramayan*. Or before. Or maybe it was the *Mahabharat*. One of the big epics, anyway."

"I can see you remember it all very clearly," says Uzma. "But I grew up in a different country, remember? And I was never into cartoons. I had real-life friends."

"I can't believe I love a girl who doesn't know *He-Man*, but that's not the point I'm making here," says Aman. "After every episode, they'd have a bit where they sort of explained the moral of the show. Trust your friends, don't tell lies, that sort of thing. The thing is, that doesn't happen in real life."

"I'm glad that you've figured out the difference between real life and cartoons," says Uzma. "But if it has just happened, after, what twenty years? Bit worrying."

"Deal with it. What I'm trying to say is, it's perfectly okay if we don't have some kind of life-changing realisation every time we have an adventure. Especially given how often weird things happen to us. We'll do the best we can. It's our job. But maybe it's time we started actually enjoying what we do."

"I do," says Tia. "But then I have the best power of all."

"You can't actually enjoy your job, can you? Not if you're supposed to clean up the world every day," says Uzma. "Every movie star I've ever met has told me there are ups and downs and the only thing you can hope to do is survive and not go crazy. But they all reach a point where they hate it all. Because it's work. And they're just actors. I just wish the stakes weren't so high all the time. People dying because I should have done my job better. And it never gets better, you know? Every day is a new battle. It never ends, you never win, and it never gets easier. Look at us right now. We just saved the world, right? I think we did. And we already have fifteen more global crisis-type things to deal with."

"Fair enough," says Tia. "But that's just whining, isn't it? We're bloody superheroes. Think of it like you're the most talented person in the world at something. Then you just have to keep doing what you're good at, don't you? You don't really have a choice. Of course it's going to be horrible sometimes. But what else is there? You two – you just worry all the time. Of course you'll make mistakes. You'll fail. And you'll get up and do it all again. But do you ever sit down and think how amazing it is that you're getting to do this? I was blown away when the world changed from cassettes to CDs! Uzma, you got off that plane thinking you'd have a little adventure. Just look at everything you've done. Did you ever dream any of this was possible?"

"Obviously I didn't," says Uzma. "Though I was an idiot then. And I'd never failed at anything. I just assumed the rest of my life was going to be a series of great successes. And of course nothing turned out exactly the way I wanted. I suppose it's true for everyone. You think your life is going to be like a superhero story, and then it turns out your superhero story looks a lot like life. I just wish there was a break between sequels, you know? Where you loaf around, and people get excited because you're going to be back soon. All I've ever wanted these last few years is some rest."

"Then get some rest," says Aman. "You don't have to start running the world right away. We could all just go on holiday somewhere."

"Right," says Uzma. "Like that's possible."

"No, it isn't," says Aman. "But it's nice to think about it. I think we just have to decide to be happy, doing what we do. That's my *He-Man* moral for today. We decide to be happy because there's so much good work left to do. So much we don't know, and will find out. So many people we're making things better for. We can be pioneers and inventors and bandits and pirates. And we can build a new world. Obviously there's going to be a lot wrong with it, but maybe it'll be better than it was before, and when we die people won't be in a massive hurry to tear it apart immediately."

"So," says Tia. "What are you going to do now?"

"This," says Aman. He opens a holo-screen in front of his face.

"Who are you calling?" asks Uzma.

"Everyone," says Aman.

Every screen in the world lights up. On phones and TVs and floating screens, on space stations and deep-sea subs, Aman's face appears.

"My name is Aman Sen," he says. "I'm head of the new Unit."

Uzma raises her eyebrows.

"Co-head," says Aman quickly. "We're going to make the world better. The Third Wave just started. We've built a new world, and you can start a new life there. We've made mistakes with this one, and we're going to fix them. I know things look bad right now. Governments are falling everywhere – by the way, we can see you, China. It's not just governments. I know the Utopic board is watching – and I think I know where you live. Anyway, I'm digressing. I just want to say – don't worry. The world is in good hands. Our hands. So... yeah. Be nice."

He looks at Uzma and Tia trying not to giggle, and frowns, and realises the world is watching him, and stops. He tries to smile reassuringly at the world instead, sees his own grimace in the screen, and shudders. He thinks of a thousand other things to say, cannot remember a single word in any language, is silent for a few seconds, and blinks in despair. The screen disappears.

"So, public speaking course," says Tia.

"Was I terrible?" asks Aman.

"You were," says Uzma. "But I love you anyway."

"I don't know what I was thinking," says Aman. "I got it all wrong."

"Yes," says Uzma. "Deciding what you want to say helps."

Aman opens another screen.

"I'll try again," he says.

## ACKNOWLEDGEMENTS

The world of *Resistance* would not have survived without the dashing deeds of the following super-squadrons:

The Gootniter Squad: Super Sanghamitra and Josh the Bold.

Titans of Industry: Cathwoman, The Grand Sophie and The Green Gargantuan.

The Zeno Agency: Trusty John and Zesty John.

Home Base: Grasshopper Girl, Sister Sinister, Rocket Rehan and Fluffinder Singh Dhoni.

Assorted Toughs: Worker Sarkar, iBultu, Mr Thames, The Not-so-Old Brewer, Pu the Pugilist, Earthlight, Insidinus, Mega Minna and Team ARF.

# ABOUT THE AUTHOR

**Samit Basu** is one of India's most talented and prolific young writers. He is the author of *The Simoqin Prophecies*, *The Manticore's Secret* and *The Unwaba Revelations*, the three parts of The GameWorld Trilogy, published by Penguin Books India, and *Terror on the Titanic*, a YA novel published by Scholastic India. *Turbulence* was published in the UK to rave reviews and won *Wired*'s Goldenbot Award as one of the books of 2012.

Basu's work in comics ranges from historical romance to zombie comedy, and includes diverse collaborators, from X-Men/Felix Castor writer Mike Carey to Terry Gilliam and Duran Duran. His most recent GN, *Local Monsters*, was published in September 2013.

Samit was born in Calcutta, and currently divides his time between Delhi and Mumbai. He can be found on Twitter, @samitbasu, and at samitbasu.com.

# KOKO TAKES A HOLIDAY
*Kieran Shea*

Five hundred years from now, ex-corporate mercenary Koko Martstellar is swaggering through an early retirement as a brothel owner on The Sixty Islands, a manufactured tropical resort archipelago known for its sex and simulated violence. Surrounded by slang-drooling boywhores and synthetic komodo dragons, the most challenging part of Koko's day is deciding on her next drink. That is, until her old comrade Portia Delacompte sends a squad of security personnel to murder her.

"A vivid and brutal old-school (in the best sense) cyberpunk headkick." Richard Kadrey, *New York Times* bestselling author of *Devil Said Bang*

"A jet-powered, acid-fueled trip of pure, rocking insanity." Stephen Blackmoore

"*Altered Carbon* with a dash of Tank Girl attitude." *Library Journal*

# HOT LEAD, COLD IRON
*Ari Marmell*

Mick Oberon may look like just another 1930s private detective, but beneath the fedora and the overcoat, he's got pointy ears and he's packing a wand. Among the last in a line of aristocratic Fae, Mick turned his back on his kind and their Court a long time ago. But when he's hired to find a gangster's daughter sixteen years after she was replaced with a changeling, the trail leads Mick from Chicago's criminal underworld to the hidden Otherworld, where he'll have to wade through Fae politics and mob power struggles to find the kidnapper and solve the case.

"A potent mix of gangsters and magic… gripping, fantastical." *Publishers Weekly* (starred review)

"Thoroughly entertaining… Urban fantasy fans should be all over this one." *Booklist* (starred review)

# NO HERO
*Jonathan Wood*

What would Kurt Russell do? British police detective Arthur Wallace asks himself that question a lot. While he's a good cop, he prefers his action on the big screen. But when he sees tentacles sprouting from the neck of a fresh corpse, the secretive government agency MI37 comes to recruit Arthur in its struggle against a threat from another dimension known as the Progeny. But Arthur is NO HERO! Can an everyman stand against sanity-ripping cosmic horrors?

"A dark, funny, rip-roaring adventure." *Publishers Weekly*

"This hilarious and action-packed mix of Lovecraftian horror, mystery, and urban fantasy will appeal to fans of Harry Dresden and Charles Stross." *Library Journal*

"So funny I laughed out loud." Charlaine Harris, #1 *New York Times* bestselling author

For more fantastic fiction from Titan Books in the areas of sci-fi, fantasy, steampunk, alternate history, mystery and crime, as well as tie-ins to hit movies, TV shows and video games:

### VISIT OUR WEBSITE

# TITANBOOKS.COM

### FOLLOW US ON TWITTER

# @TITANBOOKS